LONG WAY
FROM HOME

ISBN - 13: 9780615905068
ISBN - 10: 0615905064

Printed in the United States
First Edition: 2013

LONG WAY FROM HOME

A NOVEL BY

LENNY SHULMAN

Dedicated to the memory of

Peter Eliseo

Who always knew the right thing to say

1

This wasn't how his first day on the reporting beat was supposed to go–
Ray Mercado, the New York Mets' star slugger, lying semi-conscious on
the locker room floor, blood from his busted nose splattered across Dan's
knuckles.

It wasn't Dan's style nor his intention. It wasn't even his sport coat; he'd
borrowed one to satisfy the dress code. Now there'd be dry cleaning involved.

The beat covering the Mets opened up after veteran Newark *Star-Ledger*
sportswriter Nestor Stipes fell out of the Shea Stadium press box and onto the
protective netting behind home plate during the fourth inning of a day game.
Substance abuse was suspected—actually, it was pretty well documented—and
Nestor, after being fished off the screen, was sent to dry out for what figured to
be an extended period. Dan inherited the plum job, not knowing it would spoil
after five hours.

The day had begun well enough. Carrying his portable typewriter and flashing
his credential, Dan was waved through the media entrance to Shea and found
his way upstairs to the press box. "Dan Henry" had been hand-written on a
piece of paper and taped to the counter in front of a seat toward the third-base
side. Soon, the veteran beat writers approached, busting his chops until they
settled on Dan's rookie hazing.

"First day?" asked the lady at the press box kitchen as Dan made his fifth trip
in 30 minutes to get lunch and drinks for the other writers.

"How'd you guess?"

"The food's not that good."

"Neither's the atmosphere."

5

"Don't worry, half those old farts will be asleep by the time the game starts."

The Mets were already playing down to their talent level. This 1984 edition wasn't predicted to contend for a pennant, and here in mid-May they were 20-25 and already six games in arrears of the Braves.

Dan watched intently from his press box perch as the home team fell behind early, managed to tie the score, and then proceeded to boot the game away 6-2 through a series of errors and lackadaisical play. Dan wrote most of his article as the game progressed, and at its conclusion, headed downstairs with the other newspaper writers to collect quotes to add to his story.

Ray Mercado had failed to win a contract extension before the season, and the supersized first baseman, infamous for his prickly personality, had now taken sullen to a new level. The regular reporters knew to tread lightly around him, and, after having gotten the usual "we have to play better" quotes from manager Lou Shelton, they loitered in the area of Mercado's locker, waiting for a signal that he was willing to share a few precious syllables with them.

Mercado had kicked a routine ground ball that led to the winning runs scoring, and also struck out with the bases loaded to end the game. He seemed to Dan a natural subject from whom to extract a quote, and anxious to get back upstairs and top off his piece, the rookie stepped into the breach.

"What happened on Stargell's grounder?" Dan asked, talking to Mercado's side while the player sat facing his locker, slowly removing his socks. Mercado swiveled his head slightly to shoot a dirty look at his inquisitor, silently shooing him away.

"Did it take a bad bounce?" Dan was actually trying to give him an out.

"Get out of my face," Mercado said, not bothering to look at Dan this time.

"I'm not *in* your face," Dan replied flatly, not noticing the other writers taking a step back in unison.

Mercado rose up to his 6-foot-6 height, muscles bulging out of his arms and popping through his shoulders and across his bare chest. He moved inside Dan's air space.

"Now you are."

Dan figured his position as a writer protected him, but he waited for the behemoth to sit back down.

"So, was that a fastball you struck out on?"

Mercado launched off his stool and threw a wild right hand that whipped by Dan's head as he lurched back away from it.

Dan had been surprised by the first punch, but he was flabbergasted that this bag of rocks was winding up for an encore. Danger buzzers deafening his brain, Dan dropped his pen and notebook, and calling on the judo lessons he hadn't wanted to take in junior high school, shot out his arm to intercept the wide right-handed haymaker coming toward his left eye. He detoured the punch around and behind him, throwing Mercado off-balance in the process.

Dan's survival instinct kicked in along with three years of frustration and rejection. He'd never before laid a menacing hand on anyone, but here he was with a millisecond to decide whether to break new ground. He launched his left fist toward Mercado's unprotected mug, landing flush on his nose and causing Mercado to trip back over his stool, his head smacking against the blue and gold colors of the Mets logo on the carpet.

Two team trainers arrived to administer to the prone slugger. Smelling salts appeared. Shelton ran out, saw which of his players was involved, and ushered Dan out of there.

One of the older writers called after him. "Beginner's luck."

2

Maybe with a little more experience Dan would have seen it coming. But at 22, and on the first job where he had to fill out tax forms, he'd actually expected his editor at the *Ledger* to have his back. He retained only snippets. "We support you 100%, but…" "Wedding notices." "Obituaries."

Now, on the train back to Manhattan, unemployed again for the first time in a week, Dan moved his eyes away from the newspaper being read by a guy on the opposite bench, avoiding the picture of Mercado and trying to forget his own participation. He stared at his hands as if they would provide clues to how it all went wrong so fast. Attached to his longer-than-normal arms that had gave him a distinctive whip motion and made him a pretty decent pitcher in high school upstate, they were clasped together between his shins, rocking with the motion of the train. He was tall and thin with curly dark hair and not particularly well-dressed. There was nothing about Dan that put him out of place on this late-morning train, well past the hour when the city's hot shots would have hurried toward their executive offices in the toney high rises. This train was for the job seekers and domestics and errand-runners; people with more time than money on their hands.

Perhaps "Blow me" wasn't the most measured response to the man that had hired him six days earlier. Dan hadn't the nuance to play ball with a guy who went in the tank as soon as the water was presented him. Especially someone entrusted with bringing news to people; making decisions that affected how well-informed his readers would be.

The train lumbered across the Harlem River. Dan watched one perfectly aligned street after another stretch out, bisected by rows of horrific brick tenements, some so close to the tracks he could make out the brand of milk left on the windowsills for refrigeration. Not a blade of grass in sight, not even on the pathetic patches of dirt over which hung lines draped with laundry.

Dan felt grateful for the open spaces of his childhood upstate in Watervliet. Then came the shiver of realizing he'd left that for this city, and besides some freelance work there was no visible means of support keeping him from the shady side of the street.

3

Sonny Catapano couldn't have found a more fitting location for his law practice. He was just off Times Square, the action center of the city, depending, of course, on your course of action. His office was halfway up a 20-story building with age on it, reached via a rickety elevator whose inspection sticker gave comfort to no one. What passed for a lobby once you got to Sonny's 'suite' were a couple of vinyl chairs that looked like reclamations from a dentist who had committed suicide, with a fake wood table between them on which lay seven-month-old magazines aimed at mechanics and hunters. The receptionist's desk held the day's mail; there was no receptionist, nor had there ever been one.

Dan entered the inner sanctum, traveling straight back in time, say, 30 years or so. Yellowed Venetian blinds blocked out some of the sun, except where they had bent or come off completely, letting shafts of light in to splash the pea green walls. The desk was heavy metal with rounded corners, and it took effort to pull out the drawers. Matching gray file cabinets lined the wall near the door. The only new piece in the room was a telescope mounted at the window, and judging by its downward angle, Sonny wasn't using it to study the constellations.

He looked up from a phone call as Dan entered, but didn't acknowledge him. Sonny was short but solid as a fire hydrant. He had liquid green eyes that never left his prey when engaged, light brown hair always on the borderline of greasy, and an ever-present Marlboro.

"Screw you…Oh, it's a conference call? Then screw the both of you."

Sonny hung up.

"Charming as always," Dan said.

"The guy owes me five grand. You want me to jerk him off in Macy's window?"

"I'm sure you'll be plunging those fees into new furniture," Dan said, glancing around the office.

"Oh, excuse me. You from *Ladies' Home Journal*?"

"Do you actually see clients up here?"

"Just the gym bags who insist on it. Which would be you."

"Hard to believe you wouldn't get more foot traffic in this part of town," Dan said, eyeing through a gash in the blinds the neon "Show World Topless" sign blinking from the nearest corner.

"Hey, don't knock it. Within a half-block there are hookers and decent deli. You can get sucked and served and be back at work in an hour. Easy."

Dan stepped away from the window, noticing now the three newspapers spread across Sonny's desk, all turned to the sports section and all sporting headlines about the Mets star slugger getting slugged.

"Shit," Dan said, passing the desk with no inclination to look any closer. He wiped off the chair in front of Sonny's desk before piling into it.

"What's sandpapering your ass? Your 15 minutes have arrived. Bleed 'em for all they're worth."

Dan tuned Sonny out whenever he tried to get serious, which wasn't often. Sonny was six years his elder and from an old-line Italian family that owned half of Utica—the good half, if you bought that Utica had one. He had been raised a straight-arrow Republican Scotch drinker until broadening his boundaries after moving to the city for college at NYU and law school at Columbia. Sonny possessed a brilliant legal mind that he added to a rapier wit and a streak of wildness bent on making up for lost time.

They'd met at a *New York* magazine Christmas party. Dan had penned a profile of the New York Jets head coach for the mag, and Sonny did legal work for the publication's parent company. Near the bar Sonny was raking several executives over the coals when the head man, Richard Ingersoll, joined the group.

"Hey, Dick, here's my card," Sonny said with way too much familiarity, producing one from his pocket as quiet engulfed the group.

"For what?" Ingersoll said, puzzled.

"I heard your wife wants a divorce."

Ingersoll relieved the awkward silence by laughing, then ripping up the card. "I'd never be that lucky," he retorted, drawing more laughter.

Sonny had balls that big. There was no woman he wouldn't make a play for. Rejection slid off him like an avalanche. Dan, a prisoner to his own thoughts of insecurity where women were concerned, admired Sonny for that spirit. He began zoning back in at the end of the lawyer's speech.

"…We can sue the Incredible Hulk, not to mention the team, for assault, discrimination, and a half-dozen things I haven't come up with yet. A hundred grand, we play our cards right."

"I don't want their money."

"Fifty without breaking a sweat."

"I don't want to be that guy, Sonny. 'He's the one punched the baseball player.' "

"You already *are* the guy who punched the baseball player. More importantly, you're living on my couch."

"I thought you enjoyed having me around."

"Yeah, as much as I can enjoy someone who has a dick and a hairy ass. Let's get the money, and at least you'll be *somebody*."

"You that desperate to get your name in the paper?"

"Chicks read the paper, right?"

"Not the ones hang out with you."

"This is a gift horse delivered to your door."

"It's your door, Sonny, not mine."

"With all due respect, you're an idiot."

"I knew you'd understand."

"You know I'm renting the place out while I'm in Italy. You got a plan?"

Dan had nothing.

"Great," continued Sonny, "There's a sidewalk vent on 11ᵗʰ Street. Hot and cold blowing steam 24 hours a day. You can meditate on your purity."

4

"Call me Ishmael." It was the last memory Dan had of normalcy. Mr. Rubin had just started reading from "Moby Dick," spraying his lispy enthusiasm on the front row of his 10th grade English class. There came a knock at the door, and then Rubin talking to someone in hushed tones.

"You need to go to the office," Rubin said, having walked straight over to Dan.

The knot in his stomach grew with each step; he could feel the shock welling up. Outside the office Mrs. Peters, the school secretary, was talking with the nurse, Miss Sims. They appeared to be waiting on Dan as he approached.

"Dan, Principal Colton will drive you home." The principal strode out of his office, quickly pulling on his jacket with his car keys in hand.

"If this is about that library book, I told her I'd replace it," Dan said, knowing it wasn't.

"Son," said Colton, "your father died."

Dan's hands reached out to the principal's coat sleeves, trying to shake different words out of him. His nails slid down the parka, searching for something to hold onto, a pole to survive this blizzard. All he found were pitying eyes and a silent ride home and a hug from his mother, who was busy making a dozen phone calls trying to stay busy before she lost it. Dan closed the door to his room but could still hear the worst details that had been kept from him. Gall bladder surgery. Found cancer. Inoperable. Suffering.

Dan's 15-year-old mind became haunted by a sickening stream of thoughts. He hadn't gotten to say good-bye. His belief system—everything he had known in life—was torn apart as he was ripped from the cocoon of childhood; in one moment the safety net that was his family shredded into loose ends.

Dan searched for a meaning in the ruins. He landed on: Time is short and precious. Don't settle. Impatiently he waited for the future, burning hot to escape toward something else out there, beyond his vision. When security is exposed as an illusion, the fear of the unknown disappears. Dan only feared what he could see.

How much longer could he afford his integrity, Dan thought as he strode down Lower Broadway, playing Sonny's words over in his head. He turned his collar to the spring rain beginning to fall and moved closer to the storefronts for protection. How long before he took the settlement and accepted himself as another pawn in the system, his life one big buyout? How much longer could he search for the irregular hole that fit his jagged peg?

This would be getting close to the finish line. Three years removed from dropping out of journalism school, Dan still burned to become something more than a short-order deadline chef, but reality and his grand game plan hadn't yet met.

His days as a star student with blue sky ahead had been replaced by a thunderclap of indifference once he landed in Manhattan. He'd had professors who'd confused his edginess with some form of genius, but on the streets his singular and unique point of view turned out to be very singular and too unique.

He spent six months making appointments with 'women's doctors' and writing a manuscript, but "The Sex Life of Gynecologists" came up dry at the publishing houses. His "Hallucinogens and Invisible Energy Patterns" turned out to be a bad trip, Ronald Reagan having replaced Carlos Castaneda as the country's favorite shaman. "Mafia Mother," about a fictionalized Ma Barker running a deadly crime family, was gunned down.

The three years in New York had produced a parade of form-letter rejections, unreturned phone calls, awkward meetings over drink (never plural), and the occasional freelance piece to support his subsistence lifestyle.

How much longer could he with a clean conscience rely on the helping hands of others, asking them to compromise when he refused to?

And what would that compromise look like? Covering city council and school board meetings? Writing ad campaigns for a better laundry detergent? A return back home upstate to do construction? He thought about boarding the Greyhound at Port Authority for his exit from the city, the destination sign on the bus reading 'Failure.' The chill bouncing through his body wasn't from the rain; it came from white fear of having to embrace the conventional. The bravado he fronted to Sonny was cracking, the yolk of uncertainty running over his head.

Things always look brightest before the dusk.

Crossing south of Houston Street, Dan knew he had thrown that punch the day before for a reason. It was out there somewhere over the horizon, like the west wind you hear before you feel.

5

Despite Sonny's carping, Dan didn't sue the Mets, but allowed his attorney to make a threatening call or two that resulted in $10,000 of "make this go away money" from the account of Ray Mercado. Dan gave Sonny four grand for rent and split the remainder between The Fresh Air Fund, which sent poor kids to summer camp, and the Humane Society.

But the peace of mind Dan convinced himself his good deeds would buy wasn't for sale. He sat at the small desk in Sonny's living room in front of the typer, but nothing flowed between his brain and fingers, not even the stuff of surefire rejection that was his hallmark. His thoughts ran scattershot, tripping wildly along unconnected lines. Like some sleep-deprived desperado thinking so much about sleep he could never get there, Dan tried to force himself into productivity. A nightmare.

One afternoon he penned some bad haiku just to see something on paper. Nothing rhymed with Watervliet.

Ritual intervention. Exorcism. Hypnotists. Dear Abby. He mulled over each far longer than a healthy person should.

Dan opened the glass door to Discount Records, a huge store that served as a clearinghouse for the downtown music scene that had produced bands like Talking Heads, Blondie, Lou Reed, and The Ramones. The store was managed by Dan's good friend from college Mitch Ryan, a music junkie waiting for a DJ job to open up at one of the city's FM rock stations. Dan had helped his buddy out working the past two Christmas rushes.

"You're kidding, right?" Mitch said after Dan explained how he'd like to start working at the store to try and take his mind off everything else. Dan's expression belied any trace of humor.

"You're not kidding," Mitch corrected himself. "OK. On one condition."

"What's that?"

"You can't slug anybody."

"I can't promise anything."

"That's good enough."

6

The store's frantic pace kept Dan busy and engaged. MTV had pumped new interest into the music business and the stream of NYU students parading through entertained him. Dan was well versed in most genres, his only hesitation coming in the classical section, a sprawling foreign world with a catalog system all its own. Dan was clearly in over his head when a customer sought a Rachmaninoff symphony cover of an Austrian original.

"You got anything by Ben Tovin?" this from an earnest, college-age black hipster one morning.

"What kind of music does he play?" Dan said, looking for a lead.

"Ben Tovin. Y'know."

Dan laughed hard on the inside, getting the name the second time around.

"Old dude? Wrote those long jams?" Dan asked.

"Yeah."

This was one of the few classical moves he could make. He led the guy to 'Ben Tovin,' better known as 'Beethoven.'

Dan dug the nightly invites to one of the lower eastside dives to hear a band that somebody around the store knew about or played in. Grabbing a quick knish or falafel for dinner, he enjoyed the energy in the dank clubs; felt the same alienation from society expressed by the musicians on the platforms that served as stages. He jotted down notes on a small pad, feeling this could be the backdrop for a project. Inspiration coming back.

After a long day at the record store and a night in the clubs, Dan returned home late to find Sonny hoovering lines of coke off the coffee table flanked by twin blondes on the sofa—Dan's bed. After flashing Sonny a quick 'Should I leave?' gesture, Dan was waved into the soiree by his roommate, and entered a scene that was right out of some swinging '60s Swedish stewardess fantasy. Why not, Dan figured; it's all grist. Dan passed on the powder, but attempted to get up to speed with a couple quick hits off the tequila bottle he kept nearby.

"So, you girls having a good time?" Dan asked, trying to get acquainted. He was answered by a string of giggles.

"They don't speak English," Sonny stated. "It's beautiful."

The girls giggled in agreement.

·"You're an animal," Dan said to him with a hint of admiration. "So how exactly do you communicate?"

"Universal language," Sonny replied, fingering his spoon.

"You going for both of them? And it's OK with me if you are."

"Share and share alike. What are friends for?" Sonny said, quoting an Abbott and Costello routine they were both familiar with. "That is, if you're man enough."

Typical Sonny, Dan thought. Truth was, he was ambiguous. Dan never possessed that 'pussy at any cost' attitude that most red-blooded American males convinced themselves they needed. Nothing against sex; Dan just wasn't going to compromise a whole lot to get it. There had to be some level of connection and comfort for him to make a play.

This situation though, he could spin either way. The blondes were pretty, and they certainly appeared willing.

"You know how old they are?" Dan asked, trying to slow down the action.

"You're kidding, right?" Sonny said dismissively.

"I'm just trying to figure out whether it's rape or statutory rape," Dan said, moving the conversation toward his friend's legal ballpark.

"No jury in the city would hold us culpable once they got a load of these two."

"What if they moved the venue to Connecticut?"

"We'd probably be looking at 3-to-5," Sonny said comically matter-of-factly.

"You gonna represent us?"

"Yeah, cost you nothing in legal fees. Now, you wanna pretend to be a man?"

"I'll take the one with the huge front porch."

"Yeah, right. You'll take Ingrid over here and like it."

Sonny grabbed the hand of his date and off they padded into the bedroom. Dan's girl was quite handy helping him fold out the bed and getting the sheets and blankets situated. They slipped into their love nest, her body warm and welcoming on his. He was about to lock lips.

"Your friend seems like an asshole," she said, "and we didn't want to have to talk to him while we were doing the blow. But you're all right."

Dan about convulsed with laughter. "I do like your style." And off they went.

The next morning Sonny handed out business cards to the blondes, his phone number underlined, and made gestures to mimic making a call.

"You gonna know it's them by the giggles on the other end of the line?" Dan asked.

"I don't want to hear it. You owe me."

Dan threw his arms up in the air, palms facing Sonny. "All right, all right, no shit for three days." He smiled widely as the girls left.

There was a little extra bounce to Dan's step as he pulled into the Korean grocery on the corner for a couple of buttered rolls and an orange juice before heading to work. But nobody there cared about his evening, and the city unwound another day, Dan restocking the bins while further uptown Sonny waited for his phone to ring.

7

Dan had just finished scribbling notes on the New York underground music scene when he ambled over and engaged a customer who held up a pair of albums by reggae performer Peter Tosh. Dan reeled off three or four other LPs that would be back in stock, and their song lists.

The woman, impressed, introduced herself as the label rep for Island Records, and the two of them hit if off for the better part of the morning. Dan had, for a college journalism project, done a soup-to-nuts profile on *Caribbean Beat*, a monthly mag that covered reggae music. His work pleased not only his professor but the magazine's editors, who encouraged him to stay in touch. The rep, Liz, was doing advance work for Tosh's upcoming concert in the city, and offered to arrange an interview if Dan could get the article into the magazine.

Two weeks later, on a Sunday morning, Dan and Mitch found themselves entering the Westbury Hotel, a nondescript joint in the 20s. When they were let into the room after announcing their business at the door, they found Tosh reclining on the bed, his back against the headboard, with a half-dozen fellow Jamaicans scattered about the place, and a manager attempting to keep some sort of order. Each of the Jamaicans was working on his own giant spliff—marijuana joints rolled in paper the size of a loose-leaf page.

As Dan tried to start the interview, Tosh took control. He tested Dan to judge whether he was worth the time. The first topic of discussion was the war in Nicaragua, currently being waged by proxies of the United States; then came U.S. politics; then economic issues; then the treatment of minorities and the poor. Jamaica was, away from the strips of tourist hotels along its beaches, an impoverished country, and reggae was the voice of the powerless. Tosh saw everything in his country and the world through a political prism, and although his music had carried him out of poverty, he was not cleansed of the pain as long as others suffered.

Dan was able to hold up his end of the conversation just fine. After 20 minutes Tosh asked, "You smoke on Sundays, mon?"

Dan knew Sunday had nothing to do with it. Tosh was asking if he smoked weed. Mitch beat him to the answer.

"Sundays, Mondays, Tuesdays…"

Tosh nodded at the man sitting closest to him, and the dreadlocked assistant got busy rolling one up for the white kids. The manager used the brief break to complain—to Dan.

"A half-hour and you don't even ask about the music?"

"Hey," Dan replied, his hands gesturing that it was Peter's agenda. He caught the spliff thrown his way, and Mitch and he joined the party while Peter began talking about music.

Dan was surprised at the amount of bad blood Tosh professed between himself and Bob Marley. The two of them, with Bunny Livingston, had grown up together in the shacks of a shantytown, and had formed the Wailers, which became the most famous reggae band on the island. When they became popular enough to be signed, the label exec wanted to market one man, not a faceless band, and chose Marley as the safest front person. Tosh felt betrayed by the label and worse, by Marley, who'd gone along with the arrangement.

"They tell me I can only have one or two songs on each LP," Tosh told Dan. "I have some things to say also, you know."

So the Wailers split up, and while Marley shaded his music toward a melodic populism, Tosh's work veered toward a hypnotic, harder-edged, and less forgiving beat. Marley would retain the Wailers name and go on to play arenas while Tosh performed in clubs. Here was a man who gave up sure success and celebrity to stay true to himself, knowing he had something to say and that nothing was more important than saying it. Without compromise. Dan, buoyed by the high that enveloped him, fixated on Tosh's honor.

After an hour Dan thanked his hosts, and along with Mitch and 3/4s of the spliff they could not finish, took his leave, satisfied he'd gotten a great interview and blown away with the power and inspiration Tosh threw off. He and Mitch first had to deal with being as high as they'd ever been on grass--in just three or four tokes each. Tosh had not stopped smoking the entire time.

"How the hell does he do that?" asked Mitch as they hit the street.

"I don't know," Dan said. "One more hit and I'd be laying in the hallway like a room service tray."

That night Mitch and Dan made Peter's show at Kidd's on First Avenue, running into Liz outside, who ushered them upstairs to the VIP room before the concert. It was the perfect spot to make another dent in the gift given them that morning.

Dan was pretty good at remaining unimpressed by celebrity—just ask Ray Mercado—a good attribute for a writer. But he couldn't help but feel a certain pride when Peter took the stage, lit in purple hues and wearing flowing robes and sunglasses. He began with his lighter material--some tunes he'd recently cut with Mick Jagger and Keith Richards backing him that had been getting decent airplay in America.

As the show progressed, the material became heavier, the songs longer, the grooves uncompromising. Late in the set he performed "Get Up, Stand Up," a tune he'd co-written with Marley, and a song both played during their shows. While Marley's performance of it was powerful, Tosh preached it; sermonized to his audience.

By evening's end Dan was wrung out from the music and the power of a man committed to his beliefs; who could not be bought; who made art for his people out of protest; who challenged power fearlessly. Dan still had the fear of failure and of reaching deep inside himself. Mitch and he slapped five on the great show as they hit the outside. Dan reminded himself to do better.

8

Dan was working the counter of the store a couple days after the Tosh show when a guy about his age strode in. The man, whose thinning hair made him look older, began fumbling his car keys, wallet, and a datebook around, two of the three dropping on the counter.

"Sorry. I was looking...I need an instrumental theme, music for a TV show I'm doing," the man said, failing to make eye contact as well as get himself organized. "Something with a groove."

Dan studied the man; was about to say something, but swallowed it. He led the way to the R&B aisle and pulled out an album with a green cover from the first bin.

"Nothing better than Booker T. and the M.G.s," Dan said, casually offering the LP to his customer. "'Time Is Tight.' Best groove out there."

The man looked the back cover over briefly.

"That's funny. I used to listen to this all the time."

"I know, Gregg. It's me. Dan."

"Holy shit," the man said, actually looking at Dan for the first time and then embracing him. "You've got to be kidding me."

Gregg Gold hadn't changed much. He was always an absent-minded sort, which Dan thought peculiar given how tightly wound he always was. They'd grown up on different ends of the same town, not going to school together until they'd reached junior high. But they knew each other well enough before that through Little League, which is where Dan's initial dislike of Gregg hatched. Gregg's father was always the league commissioner and a manager and always seemed to get the calls. Dan was never on their squad.

Come junior high, they found themselves teammates for the first time. Riding the game bus together and sharing jokes in the locker room, they started to thaw out and bond.

They ended up together at Syracuse sharing a house for two years before Gregg moved to Miami to stage-manage a talk show and Dan lost touch with him. They caught up over lunch at Gino's, a corner pizzeria close by the record store.

"The day they brought me up to interview at the local ABC affiliate here, two guys quit," Gregg was telling Dan as the cheese pie arrived at their table, crust thin with just the right amount of glistening grease caressing the cheese. "They hired me around the time I walked in."

Dan found his opening as Gregg stuffed the tip of the slice in his mouth. These guys built their friendship taking shots at each other. "Not bad for a C student who didn't know what the hell he was doing." Dan wasn't surprised by Gregg's quick ascension. He was totally focused when pushed in a certain direction; linear in a way that Dan's rambunctious thought process could never accommodate.

"So you're doing great, at the record store and all," Gregg shot back. "Is that where sportswriters go after knocking out first basemen?"

"I believe I blazed that particular path, thank you."

"You have to be a complete asshole to start a brawl in the locker room."

"I didn't start it. You really think I'd pick a fight with that cement-head?"

"Well, it looks like a great career move."

"You may have seen my work in various magazines, oh, wait, that would take someone who actually reads," Dan answered, knowing Gregg's literary commitment didn't get past *National Lampoon*.

"OK, you got me, I missed your articles. Probably the only person in the city," Gregg said. Dan was glad his friend was still a slob, watching him wipe tomato sauce off his cheek and chin.

"You missed a spot on top of your head. Oh, sorry, that's a hair."

"That's funny," Gregg said, not smiling. "Look, if you're tired of selling Neil

Diamond records to lonely girls from Brooklyn, you'd be perfect for this show I'm producing. For real money."

"Thanks for looking me up, by the way."

"I've been busy, I'm sorry. But running into you like this is beshert."

Dan loved it when people threw around Yiddish words. He had a great friend growing up whose parents would break into Yiddish when they argued and didn't want their kids to know what they were talking about. Dan wished he'd learned more of the language because of its resonance, the sound of the word often mirroring its meaning.

Beshert, loosely translated, means something that is meant to be, handed down from the Almighty Himself. Dan had to admit it was freaky running into Gregg like this.

Gregg continued the sell. "It's the last frontier. Sunday morning sports show. Virgin territory, we'll have it all to ourselves."

"That's because nobody's awake then."

Ignoring his friend, Gregg said, "We need someone to write us in and out of topics, do bumpers to commercials, some research."

"I don't know, Gregg. I haven't been too lucky in sports lately."

"Do not make me go get some stranger."

By the time they threw in the napkins, leaving two slices on the silver pie tray, Dan had agreed to come down to the studio the following day. Gregg reached for his wallet to leave a tip and couldn't find it anywhere.

"Must be in the car."

"Some things just do not change," Dan stated, picking a couple of singles out of his pocket and tossing them on the formica.

9

G regg walked Dan around the studio. The program, to be called "Sports Talk," was still two weeks away from shooting, and nothing on the set indicated it was even that close to air. Dan had to admit, to himself, of course, that Gregg had come up with a decent idea. Sunday mornings *were* the vast wasteland of television programming, yawning deserts where nothing grew, populated by wacky preachers and infantile cartoons, mostly indiscernible from one another.

It was where local TV stations dumped their allocation of 'community programming,' which they promised their local governments in return for a license. These shows were mostly a 3rd-string anchor talking to a block association spokesperson about bicycle lanes on a turnpike. The shows were unsellable to advertisers, thus becoming a dumping ground for government-funded, public-service ads about the dangers of the latest children's disease or warning landlords that housing discrimination was illegal.

The sports concept could bring viewers in and justify paid ads, creating a new revenue stream. People gambling on football games could get late-breaking news on injuries and weather reports. Fans of the local teams would see interviews with their favorite players. Insomniacs would get something to take their minds off the fact that they were still semi-awake.

Gregg walked Dan into a noisy, open room, a couple dozen people talking on phones or running around.

"Home, sweet home," Gregg said too enthusiastically.

"You kidding?" complained Dan. "I couldn't write here."

"Hey, Shakespeare, it's television," Gregg said, already wanting to move on. "C'mon, I want to introduce you to the talent."

Dan got a kick out of that 'talent' business. It was the industry term for whomever was in front of the camera, whether they actually possessed talent or not. Well, you couldn't just call them clowns, Dan thought, though it seemed more fitting. He followed Gregg over to a series of pre-fab walls that had been put up to act as small dressing areas for the talent of the show.

The first one they came to belonged to Leonard Terry, who had retired from linebacking duties with the New York Football Giants two years before after a solid career.

"Leonard, meet Dan Henry, your writer," Gregg said upon entering the enclosure.

Terry was a mountain of a man but friendly. Dan's hand got lost somewhere within the handshake and might have taken a search party to locate had Terry not eased back.

"You got to make me look good," Terry said to Dan.

"Well, I'll make you *sound* good," Dan responded. "I can't guarantee anything about your looks, man, that's up to you and your Creator."

Fortunately, Terry gave a deep belly-laugh to this.

"I heard that," he said.

"I loved that interception you made in the playoffs against Dallas," Dan said, showing off some sports chops, "but we got to work on your endurance. You looked like you were running underwater."

"That was me in peak form," Terry laughed.

Gregg ushered Dan down the studio a little way and knocked on the door that had "Buck Shyrock" written in the middle of a star.

"You boys lookin' for me?" came a voice from over their shoulders.

"Buck, this is Dan Henry, a writer for the show," said Gregg to the impossibly Middle America-looking Shyrock, who at age 40 still had a shock of white/blonde hair befitting a 12-year-old.

"Nice to meet you," Shyrock said mechanically, a greeting he'd likely repeated 10,000 times since arriving in New York from Oklahoma after being a first-round draft pick of the Mets 12 years before. Shyrock had enjoyed a solid career as an outfielder while never quite fulfilling the promise he'd shown in the bush leagues as a teenager. His once-blazing speed had been compromised by a series of injuries, and the power that once surged through his bat had devolved through the years from extra-base hits to singles. Upon retiring Shyrock did some announcing work for ABC in the post-season, and this gig came along as a byproduct of that.

"Don't make them words too big or I'll have trouble sayin' 'em," Shyrock was telling Dan with a laugh, though the writer correctly sensed he wasn't joking.

"Don't you worry. This isn't Shakespeare," Dan replied, sneaking a look at Gregg.

"Who?" asked Shyrock.

"Floyd Shakespeare. Used to pitch for the Cubs," Dan said.

"Never faced him," Shyrock said. "Good to see ya."

"Don't say it," warned Gregg after Buck left.

"Say what?" Dan protested.

"Whatever's rattling around up there."

"He had a helluva curveball," Dan said.

"Who, Shyrock? He was an outfielder."

"Floyd Shakespeare."

"See, that's exactly the wiseass stuff I mean," said Gregg.

"What?" Dan said, professing an innocence that didn't fit.

"Come on, I want you to meet Mike Hopper," said Gregg. "And try to behave yourself."

"You want me to put on a tux?"

Mike Hopper was known, or at least his writing was, to everyone in the city. He'd had a column in the New York *Daily News* since before electricity, and his sources were legendary, always feeding him leads that put him out front of other reporters. His "Short Hops" column every Sunday, with the latest rumors and gossip, was must reading. Now a graying lion, Hopper had increasingly pushed politics into his writing, which turned a lot of readers, like Dan, completely off, since Hopper's politics steered hard to the Neanderthal Era. Gregg's nerves were not without cause.

Hopper was a short man too old for the crew cut he sported, wore a cheap sport coat, and held a non-filter cigarette. He was intently reading pages of his own copy when they approached.

"Mike, I want you to meet Dan Henry, who's going to be writing for the show," Gregg began.

Neither Hopper nor Dan offered a hand to the other. Hopper barely cast an eye over the top of the paper.

"The jocks need a writer; not me," he offered by way of greeting.

"This is television, Mike. The show needs a writer," Gregg tried again.

"Henry...you the guy that busted up the Mets locker room?"

"One and the same."

"That gorilla had it coming to him."

Dan wasn't going to touch the racial reference by acknowledging Hopper's support.

"It was an unfortunate incident," Dan allowed.

"Those people think everybody owes them something. You did the right thing."

Refusing again to accept the backing, Dan looked at Gregg and moved away from Hopper.

"'Those people'?" Dan said to Gregg when they were out of earshot. "I could have knocked the crew cut right off his head."

"Not so fast, slugger, I think he used to be a Marine," Gregg offered.

"I doubt it. His type are usually drugstore cowboys. All hat, no cattle."

"Come on, there's one other person..."

"Haven't we done enough?"

"Don't make me rip up the contract I haven't offered you yet. Let's go meet the boss, the station manager."

Gregg led Dan out of the studio and into another hallway where the doors came less and less frequently, marking the high-rent district. Gregg greeted a secretary.

"Hey, Joan, is he here?"

"If he's not, someone's doing a heck of an impersonation of him. Go on in."

Dan smiled at Joan as they passed her desk on toward the inner sanctum. Always treat the secretary kindly, Dan had learned. They held the power; the key to the gate. And they could always use a quick joke, an agreeable word, an understanding brother-in-arms.

A middle-age man, thinning dark hair, was ending a phone call when they entered.

"The pasta was overcooked and under-heated last time, just so you know… Yeah, well, we'll see when it gets here."

Jerry Romano hung up and turned his attention to Gregg and Dan.

"Bastards think they can live on reputation forever. Gregg, whattaya got here?"

"Jerry, this is Dan Henry, pen-for-hire. Dan, Jerry Romano."

Romano rose up to his modest height and extended a hand across the desk, which Dan happily took.

"Gregg's said a lot of good things about you. But since I don't trust him, I've read your stuff myself. Very good."

"Thanks," Dan said, certain that Romano had never seen a word he'd written. "We have something in common."

"What's that?"

"I don't trust Gregg, either. But I love the concept of the show."

"Good, because you're going to be working your ass off on it, and I expect results immediately."

"As well you should."

"People run around this town calling themselves writers. Where I come from, you better prove it. Talk don't mean shit."

"Where's that?"

"Where's what?"

"Where you're from?"

"Right here in the city. What, you don't pick up accents?"

"Loud and clear."

"Anyway, if Gregg says you're good…well, he hasn't screwed me too badly yet, right, Gregg?"

"I think we've done pretty OK for ourselves."

"Damn right, we have, and we're going to do even better. Dan, it's good to have you onboard."

"Thank you, sir."

"Jerry."

"Jerry."

"Now get out. Here's lunch."

Gregg and Dan passed a harried delivery guy juggling several white bags from Padrino's, a red sauce joint around the corner. They left the building through a side door out into the sunshine of New York.

"Therapist's dream in there," offered Dan. "Quite a collection."

"Someday you can write about it."

"If I'm around long enough."

"I'll see you tomorrow. We can start throwing around topics."

"I got one--your penis envy."

"Screw yourself."

"I love you, too."

"Who is this clown Sonny Catapano?" demanded Gregg into the earpiece of Dan's phone the following morning, getting Dan's attention off his raisin bran.

"Good morning," Dan answered in mock cheerfulness. "How are you today?"

"Does this guy actually represent you? He's a complete dick."

"He's a narrowly respected, high-octane attorney," Dan replied calmly.

"Yeah, well that certainly disqualifies him from being a dick." Gregg was on edge. "He's an inch away from screwing the whole deal."

"What did he ask for, two weeks' vacation?"

"He asked for double the salary we talked about. You need to take care of this."

"I'll see you in a coupla hours. My cereal's getting too soft in the milk. I hate that."

Dan dialed Sonny's office number. Even through the phone, Sonny's voice could be intimidating, or at least very disturbing. "You hump, I told you not to talk to them until I was finished."

"I didn't want to be finished before I got started," Dan replied.

"You're tying my hands here."

"Since when do you mind being tied up? Speaking of which, ever hear back from the flying twins?"

"Yeah, they called and wanted your number. Seems they'd never seen a dick that small."

"Just get it done."

"You've got to let me make this deal."

"Sonny, Gregg is a friend of mine. I don't care about the money."

"Did you come here on a fuckin' turnip truck? Do you know anything?"

"Yeah, I know you're a royal pain in the ass, and apparently you've found a field where that comes in handy. Congratulations, not everyone can make social retardedness work for them."

"I should be charging you double for this phone call."

"Put it on my tab. And let me know if you find triplets."

10

D
an and Gregg began hanging out after work at Rudy's, a bar and grill catering to the sporting set in midtown. With his wife, Audrey, in Florida tending to her parents, Gregg much preferred spending the evening hours out in company.

Dan hadn't much thought about how quickly his environs had changed, at least until the night a week before the opening show when he invited Mitch to join them.

"How many transfers is it gonna take?" Mitch had asked in jest, but from Lower Manhattan to midtown, all of about five miles' distance, the universe changed. Avante garde at Rudy's wasn't the latest punk rock band; it was ordering the sea bass instead of the steak. These were lawyers, agents, accountants, and media types that were getting ahead, taking the fast track to prosperity. They had neither the time nor inclination to struggle or ponder alternatives.

"So, when's it air?" Mitch said halfway through his first Absolut screwdriver.

"Sunday," Gregg replied.

"How's it going?"

"Not good. I got a writer whose hand I gotta hold."

Dan piped in, "What you got is a pair of ex-jocks who need cue cards to say 'Hello,' and a hard-ass prima donna who doesn't want to listen to anyone no matter how much help he needs."

"Sounds promising," Mitch said.

"He's a genius," Dan said, nodding toward Gregg. "If it works, he takes all the credit. If not…"

"Then the show's all about him," Gregg said.

The joint began filling up after 7 p.m., as the late workers poured through the double doors ready to talk themselves up and see who could further their careers and love lives. Gregg and Dan tore into some New York strips; Mitch was a vegetarian, but was holding his own while attacking a mountain of lettuce and beefsteak tomatoes. He was talking up a band that was making their debut down at the 22 Club on Lower Broadway, the event of the week around SoHo.

The talk continued through a round of after-dinner drinks before Mitch checked his watch and swiveled off the high bar chair heading south. Dan took a pass on going downtown to check it out.

"Really good guy," Gregg said as Dan watched Mitch hit the doors to the street.

"Yeah, he is." Dan was relieved whenever mutual friends of his got along, a situation that was about to be severely tested.

"Hey, dick wad." The voice was unmistakable to Dan, who knew Sonny would be in his line of sight as soon as he turned around.

"Nice work, ass wipe," Dan said, faking hostility toward his friend. "Only an hour late."

"The lights were against me. Besides, didn't this place get shut down by the health department? The cook was jerking off in the steak sauce."

Dan figured he'd change gears, though he knew whatever relief he bought would be preciously temporary. "Sonny Catapano, Gregg Gold."

"Always nice to put a face to the nasty phone calls," Sonny said, shaking Gregg's hand.

"Geez, you're kinda short for a shark, aren't you," Gregg responded.

"How about a drink?" Dan tried.

"Make it a double, if the big TV exec is buying," said Sonny. "Jonathan Walker, Black."

"Am I going to get a signed contract someday, like tomorrow?" Gregg asked, addressing Sonny. "It's not like anyone else is beating down his door."

"You gonna let him talk to you like that?" Sonny asked Dan.

"He was talking to you," Dan corrected his attorney. "And he's right."

"Shut up, you hump. When I ask a rhetorical question, do not answer it."

"I can't cut him a check until I get the contract back," Gregg said.

"Get him the contract," Dan said, piling on.

"Didn't I just tell you not to speak? Who's side are you on?"

"Mine."

"That's the first thing you've said that makes sense," Sonny said before turning his attention back to Gregg. "We'll get you the contract. But don't expect the renegotiation to go this easily."

"Something to look forward to," Gregg countered. "Ah, the drinks."

Sonny immediately did his best to catch up for time lost, draining his double and motioning for another before turning to survey the crowded and noisy room.

"Nice that you guys hang at a gay bar," he started in. "Look at this place; where's the tail?"

"They probably heard you were coming," Dan offered.

"There are more women than this in the Jets' locker room."

"What were you doing in the Jets locker room?" chimed in Gregg.

"Checking on your sister. She said it was the air conditioning blew her dress off."

"You know, you're wrong, Dan. I kind of like this guy," said Gregg.

"He grows on you," Dan said. "Too bad for him, he doesn't grow."

"You guys are fascinating," Sonny said with ample sarcasm, "but I'm going to see what I can do with those girls over there."

"Which ones?" Dan said.

"It's not real hard; they're the only ones in here," Sonny said, swiping the glass of Scotch off the bar as he made his move to the far corner.

"OK, now it's my turn—don't say it," Dan offered to Gregg.

"Don't say what? He's charming. If you like rattlesnakes."

"He may be spoiled potato salad, but he's on my side of the paper plate."

"Grab your drink. There's somebody over there I want you to meet."

Dan followed Gregg toward a couple of suits standing around a small table yukking it up.

"Vic…"

"Gregg, what's going on?" After the two shook hands, introductions of the seconds were made, as Dan shook hands with agent Vic Murray and aspiring agent Brian Brown.

"We'll kick off and defend the south goal," Dan said, imitating a team captain at the coin toss of a football game. It was a bit that never failed to get a laugh.

"You should be a writer," Vic noted.

"He is," answered Gregg. "Unfortunately, for me."

"You're working 'Sports Talk?' " Vic asked, clearly up on his sports media.

"Yeah, if you call that work," Dan said.

"Having to work Mike Hopper? That's work. No, that's punishment, cruel and unusual," Vic said with conviction.

"I see I'm not his only fan," Dan said to Gregg.

"Hopper's screwed more people than a hooker at the Bunny Ranch," Vic intervened. "He's got no enemies—only his friends hate him."

"Vic's sore because Hopper's written some not-so-nice things about clients of his," Gregg explained. "These agents have memories like elephants."

"You don't need a good memory to hate that guy," Vic said.

"All right, can we change the topic?" Gregg tried.

"No," shot Vic right back. "Let me tell you about that cocksucker, Dan. I used to handle Vance Rossi, remember him?"

"Second baseman for the Phils for a few years," said Dan. "Had some pop in his bat."

"Yeah, he could play a little. Not the brightest bulb in the circuit, and a crazy man out on the town every night. He's slowing down, fighting a bunch of injuries. His career, if it's not over, you can see the end from where he is. So I get him a great gig as a color man for the Phils home games on their cable channel.

"Turns out two years before he flipped Hopper the bird when he's trying to interview him. So now Hopper calls me, says he's got a story about Vance screwing four hookers and a dog one night, and he's printing it unless he turns down the job. All right, I'm kidding about the dog, but that's how vindictive this son of a bitch is.

"So I'm on the horn with him, asking him to give the guy a break. I massage his nuts for about 20 minutes mending fences that ain't even broken, and by the end of it, he says he's calmed down, and I figure that's the end of it. The cocksucker prints the story two days later, Vance loses the job before he's said word one into a microphone, and now he's driving a limo in D.C. moving Iranians around to discos. Nice, huh?"

"But he looks good in the driver's cap," tried Gregg unsuccessfully.

"I will harass that S.O.B. to the grave, and beyond," Vic said, spitting the words out. "He's a ruthless, reactionary, mean-spirited, miserable piece of shit, and those are his good points."

"Well, clearly you're running out of derogatory adjectives, so this game's going to have to end soon," Gregg said. "You find anything out about the Nets moving to Brooklyn?"

"There's a little smoke, but no fire yet," Vic said. "I don't think it's happening. Too many palms outstretched, and not enough grease to go around."

"Hey Vic, you jerkoff." Dan and Gregg lashed their necks around to find Sonny insinuating himself into the middle of things.

"Who the hell let you out at night?" Vic said. "Somebody call a cop."

"You two know each other?" Dan and Gregg said simultaneously.

"He handled my divorce. Both of them," Vic said with pride. "Got me out completely unscathed. He's a genius."

"I feel sick," Gregg said.

"I told you—the steak sauce," Sonny said before ordering another round of drinks. "Let's keep this party rolling, since nobody's getting laid."

11

The premiere of "Sports Talk" was just days away and Dan spent long hours in the newsroom working on the ins and outs of an ever-changing lineup of topics the hosts would be tackling Sunday morning. The universe seemed to be cooperating with the show's launch. A huge betting scandal involving NBA referees had just broken, and Dan had lined up a retired ref to appear. Then came the news an NFL star was busted running a cockfighting ring—you couldn't make this stuff up. Plus an international ping pong tourney was taking place in the city, and you couldn't go wrong with that, unless Hopper decided to break out a pejorative term for the reigning champ--who was of Chinese descent--a 50-50 proposition.

It was all ready past 6:30 when Gregg strode up to Dan's fort.

"What the hell are you still doing here?"

"Bucking for overtime."

"Forget it. Rudy's?"

"Nah, I got plans."

"Date?"

Gregg took Dan's silence as an affirmative.

"All right, give. What's her name?"

"*That's* important information."

"Name."

"Linda."

"And...?"

"And what?"

"C'mon, don't make me beg."

"I ran into her at the market last week."

"So you knew her all ready?"

"No, I literally ran into her."

A New York story. Dozens of women each day caught Dan's eye. He tried to visualize their life history in a matter of seconds based on their look, a mannerism, an article of clothing, the way their hair lifted in the breeze as they passed on the street. They could be crazy or famous, wealthy or innocent, from France or Kansas, or any combination therein.

Dan, as always, had stopped at the grocery on the corner for an orange juice and buttered roll on his way into work, and he was tearing into the latter when he bumped into a woman in the doorway, the butter overage that oozed from the roll rubbing against her chic-looking trench coat.

"I'm sorry," Dan said, producing a napkin and trying to wipe the offending grease off the fabric.

"It's OK," she managed, but stood still for him anyway. Dan was making slight headway, and in his final flourish, his hand rubbed hard enough to catch a fleeting feel of her breast.

"Sorry again, I'm usually not this clumsy so early in the morning."

"You mean it gets worse?" she asked playfully.

"You know, since I'm down two faux pas already, I'm gonna just let it all hang out," Dan said. "Can I buy you a drink sometime?"

"Do you think you can keep from spilling it on me?"

"I'll do my damndest."

Dan situated their meeting at The Dugout, a tavern in midtown. As the name implies, you enter by walking down several steps to an unpretentious drinking hole, a local joint in the middle of the biggest city in the world.

Dan rushed the few blocks from the studio, leaving Gregg in his dust. He didn't want to be late and add "unreliable" to Linda's first impression of him as a bumbling fool. He took the stairs in one jump and made a too-quick entrance through the doors, relieved after an eyeball inventory that Linda hadn't yet arrived.

Across a narrow aisle from the bar he found a table that looked onto 49th Street, and waited, the nervous internal back-and-forth raging. Could she have agreed to meet him just to get rid of him that morning? Sure. But she had looked directly into his eyes, and he had sensed some level of engagement there. But now he had challenged her with this out-of-the-way blue-collar joint. Had that tipped her over the edge? She likely wouldn't show. Yes she will. Have a little confidence in yourself. Why? There were tons of guys more accomplished who would take her to the Plaza or some happening celebrity hangout. What would she want with him? Those guys were all assholes. You're real. She would have picked up on that instantly. You're kidding yourself.

On he went with this silent tennis match for several minutes. He was shocked out of his self-inflicted torture by Linda's voice as she stood over the table.

"This seat taken?"

"Hey, you made it," he said, instantly regretting the implication of doubt.

"Didn't I say I would?"

"Well, you know how flighty some people can be, especially in a high-society atmosphere like this."

"I love this place. My dad has brought me here."

"Well, I'm crazy about your dad. He's obviously a man of taste, and wonderful genes."

"Aren't you the smooth talker for being such a klutz."

Linda had lost the trench, and Dan, badly wanting not to show it, was aching to sneak a look down from her face to see what shapes he could make out. On the periphery, there was everything to like about the long-haired brunette with the crystal green eyes staring back at him.

"Yes, I am a man of words, but hopefully not too many of them. I don't want to bore you with my brilliance."

"That's probably not going to happen."

"But enough about me. How did you get to be so witty and beautiful?"

"If you'd like to keep your promise and buy me a drink, I'll try to explain."

Dan was glad Linda allowed him to escort her home in a cab down to the East 20s, and happier still when she asked him in for coffee, an invite he accepted even though he never touched the stuff. Linda repped toy companies and was doing quite well at it, but Dan was a bit surprised at apparently how well, given the brownstone whose steps they were ascending after he paid off the cabbie.

This was a gorgeous part of Manhattan, the three-story buildings rich in history yet kept up immaculately, one in concert with the next. Fifty years ago Dan could imagine armies of kids blasting Spaldeens—rubber balls—off the stoops playing makeshift games of baseball while their mothers cradled young ones in their arms or gently swayed them in baby carriages lined up along the street. Today, with the playgrounds shifted to school gyms or organized sports, the streets were much quieter and dignified, with the dog walkers making sure to clean up every piece of evidence.

Dan's surprise didn't end at the home's exterior. Inside, they were greeted by a nanny, and by Linda's 5-year-old son, Sam, who was as delighted to see his mother as she was him. Introductions were made.

"I'm Sam," the boy declared to Dan.

"And I'm Dan. We almost rhyme."

"Almost. Do you like my Mom?"

"Why, sure. Who wouldn't?"

"She's very nice."

"And it's way past your bedtime," interrupted Mom herself. "Now you get on into bed and I'll be right there to tuck you in."

"OK. See ya."

"Good night," Dan called after him before turning to Linda. "Very shy."

"He likes you. Shall I put on some coffee?"

"Not for me, thanks, but I'll take some milk and cookies, if you can scare that up."

"Just what I need, another child. Make yourself at home. I'll be right back."

As Linda brewed a cup for herself, Dan asked about the building. Her father, Linda explained, was a successful partner in a legal consulting firm that handled major corporations, including several sports teams. During the last recession he had cash to invest and bought several brownstones at the right price, keeping a couple for the family and dealing off the rest at sizable profits once the economy recovered. Money does tend to follow money, after all, Dan thought.

Linda had balked, unlike her brothers, at taking up law and joining the family business, and so had forged her own way, with great determination so as to prove herself, and had succeeded both in work and at raising Sam, the two projects she threw herself into. Yet, she didn't appear driven, at least not outwardly in that crazy way that many people do, all Type A and on the muscle.

"Will Oreos do?" she sang from the kitchen.

"Original or Double Stuff?"

"Original, of course," she said, appearing with a tray carrying cookies and milk for him, and coffee for herself. "You don't look like a Double Stuff guy, although there was a lot of butter on your roll, as I recall."

"The best butter I ever ate," Dan tried, "because it brought me to you."

"Nice try. You work out?"

"Run every morning. Gets the juices going. You?"

"There's a gym here in the neighborhood where I sweat out the day's aggravation."

"So, Sam…were you married? I mean, I'm sorry, I don't mean to pry."

"No, it's all right. More like a one-night stand. Guy turned out to be a jerk. I almost cut his nuts off."

"Well, I guess I should be going," Dan said, rising from the couch with comic timing.

"Was it something I said? C'mon, finish your cookies. And for God's sake, stop being so polite and start dunking them."

"You truly are the woman of my dreams," Dan said, sinking an Oreo deep into his milk until it was falling-apart soft before dropping it into his mouth. "Oh, look, I got some on your shirt. I need to clean it off."

"You've already used that line."

12

"*Sports Talk* is the best thing to hit Sundays since brunch. This 30-minute jock fest is quick and breezy, treating sports as they should be—as fun, not rocket science."

Dan put down the issue of the *Daily News* from which he'd been reading to Gregg, and picked up the *Times*. "Considerably more informative than your standard daily sports report, *Sports Talk* utilizes the talents of the likable former athletes Leonard Terry and Buck Shyrock, who are joined by veteran New York scribe Mike Hopper over a very watchable half-hour of topics sprinkled with opinions…"

"Here's the *Post*," said Gregg, handing the paper to Dan.

"What are you, illiterate?"

"Superstitious. You're two-for-two. Why break up a good thing?"

"While I hate to admit that I played hookey from church, alright, I don't hate to admit it since I haven't gone in 13 years, *Sports Talk* makes for a great excuse for those who'd rather hear about baseball than the bible. With an easy-going likeability and a sense of humor that doesn't always spare himself, Leonard Terry could be a breakout star on the small screen…"

Dan looked up. "I think we done good."

Another copy of the *Post* came flying down on the desk between Dan and Gregg. "What an asshole." The speaker was Mike Hopper.

"Mike, we got great reviews," offered Gregg.

"I guess you haven't gotten to the part where he says I have a face made for radio and a voice made for newspapers."

Dan couldn't stymie a snort of laughter, drawing looks from the other two.

"C'mon, Mike, the guy writes for the *Post*. You expect him to say something nice about someone from the *News*?" Gregg said.

"There's nothing wrong with my goddamn voice."

"It's certainly loud enough," offered Dan, drawing another look from his friend.

"He's probably a fuckin' Commie."

"I heard he has sex with his toy Poodle," Dan said.

"You got a source on that?" Mike was interested.

"Mike, relax, the show was great and everyone loved it," Gregg tried. "We have to go to a meeting."

Gregg shoved Dan ahead of him and away from further conversation with Hopper.

"Can't we stay and talk some more?" Dan said over his shoulder.

"Do you have to try and piss him off every chance you get?"

"How can't you? He has the disposition of a prison guard."

"A 5.3 rating. We absolutely crushed them." Jerry Romano had invited Gregg and Dan to dinner that evening at a midtown steakhouse a couple of blocks from the station. Romano was so excited he was chewing and talking simultaneously, the result of which was juice from his filet mignon flying indiscriminately around the table. Dan had already dabbed at a spot on his shirt sleeve and was pretty sure part of the ratings numbers just landed on his cheek.

"There hasn't been a Sunday morning rating like this since the Pope died, and how often can you count on that?"

"I don't know, they tend to be pretty old," Dan offered, but Romano was running roughshod over any potential interruption.

"Nobody else did more than a 1.1. Complete domination. You guys did an unbelievable job." Romano had to pause here to throw back a healthy portion of his second Manhattan, allowing Dan to concentrate on his New York Strip for a heavenly moment.

"You know what this means, don't you," continued the station manager, hacking into his filet with passion.

"Raises all around?" asked Dan. Romano allowed the line to curl around the table for a moment.

"Hah. It means the competition is gonna come after us. Hard. You know that line about imitation being the sincerest form of flattery? Bullshit. They're gonna try to steal what we've got."

"Maybe we can convince them to take Hopper," Dan offered.

"It means we've got to be twice as good. We've got to have fresh ideas and new segments and stay two steps ahead of the bastards." The steak juice was really flying now, and Dan subtly backed his chair away from the table and to his right, toward Gregg, to try and get out of the line of fire. "We cannot rest on our laurels, no matter how good they are."

"Does this mean we're being picked up for a second week?" Dan said, emboldened by his suddenly strong position.

"A second week," repeated Romano, looking toward Gregg. "Where'd you find this guy? A second week. We're going to be here for years." As this thought began swirling around Dan's brain, Romano's attention quickly turned. "Waiter, more rolls."

"Did you ever get the feeling your boss is, I don't know, a psychopath?" Dan and Gregg were walking the short distance from the steakhouse to Rudy's for a drink or two to revel in their success.

"So he's a little weird. Who isn't?"

"Well, when you put it that way, I guess he's not so bad…if you wear a lobster bib and football helmet to dinner. The guy sprays fluids like an exterminator."

"Must you always find fault?"

"You're kidding, right? You concentrate on what magnificent human beings people are?"

"Would that be so bad?"

"No, Mother Theresa. And good luck with it."

"OK, Sunshine." They entered the bar, which was buzzing for a Monday night. "How about you be a great human and buy me a drink…for a change."

"That won't be necessary." Brian Brown appeared in front of them, and the young agent-in-training apparently had sway with the company expense account. "I've got this round. Vic's back at the table."

Dan and Gregg nodded their thanks and headed across the room. All the faces looked friendly, as though they recognized the glow of success around this pair of hit-makers. Dan imagined everyone was buzzing about *Sports Talk*, although he knew that was just a fleeting fantasy and he laughed at himself and his briefly raging ego. He had barely tamped down his flight of fancy when Vic Murray rose from his table to greet them like triumphant returning gladiators.

"Here they are, the biggest things to hit sports since Instant Replay. Great show, guys. Great show."

"Don't forget the ratings," Gregg said.

"You think it could be a great show without the ratings? What planet are you from? But artistic success plus ratings? You guys are the tits."

"I've got a sawbuck says you didn't watch it," challenged Gregg.

"I didn't, but everyone's been talking about it," Vic said without a hint of guilt. "You know how I know it's good?"

"I can't wait to hear," Gregg said without emotion.

"CBS is already planning a knock-off."

"That didn't take long."

"One whole day."

"What are they paying their writers?" Dan asked.

"Nice loyalty," said Gregg.

"Yeah, like if the show tanked your boy Romano wouldn't be looking at the fine print trying to can me tomorrow."

Brian joined the party with pairs of drinks in each hand and distributed them.

"To the future," intoned Vic by way of a toast.

"To the present—it's all we got," Dan said, taking down half the double Bourbon in one swoop.

"How would you guys like Dick Webster for the show?" Vic asked, referring to the head coach of the New York Football Giants.

"Before or after he gets fired?" Dan answered too glibly considering Webster was a client of Vic's.

"No one gets fired before training camp, and no one gets fired with the kind of big season the Giants are sitting on. He could use the pub."

Dan deferred to Gregg.

"I think he'd be good," Gregg said, "but this isn't softball. He'd have to answer some questions."

"He'll answer whatever boy genius here can come up with," Vic said, nodding toward Dan. "Just stay away from the ex-marriage to the centerfold."

"Oh, sure, who'd want to hear anything about that…except every single viewer we have," said Dan.

"I knew I could count on you."

13

Dan and Linda were getting together a couple of nights a week and Dan looked forward to each one. Linda was different than the girls he'd known. She possessed a steely inner strength, and Dan felt himself wanting to peel back her layers and get to know more. She was clearly his equal, or superior, in looks, intellect, wit, spirit, money, or whatever else served as a benchmark. Which led him to ask her, as they left the theater one night after seeing a 'chick flick' starring Meryl Streep, "Why do you like me?"

"What do you mean?" she asked, buying time.

"Straightforward question," he replied.

"Isn't the woman supposed to be the one asking stuff like that?"

"I'm getting in touch with my female side."

"You would actually make a very attractive girl."

"And you're avoiding the question."

It was a pleasant autumn evening as they walked up Lexington Avenue, but the silence was now making both of them uncomfortable.

"You're a sloppy eater, which I find very sexy," Linda finally said, but Dan wasn't much interested in either of them cracking wise at the moment. He was trying to understand his feelings about her, through her.

"Not even a smile?" she tried, again to no effect. "You know, I talk about stuff like this with my shrink and it's not that much fun."

Dan felt disappointment welling up in him. He wasn't used to wanting to open up like this to a woman.

"So you'd rather talk to your shrink than to me?"

"She charges good money. I feel compelled to talk to her."

"Y'know, I know all about using humor to deflect what you don't want to deal with. I wrote the book on it."

"I read it. Outstanding." They reached a storefront Carvel's ice cream shop. "C'mon, I'll buy you a flying saucer, or something messier."

There was a short line in front of them. Both looked up at the menu hanging behind the counter, though each knew it by heart. "I really, really like you," Linda said, breaking the awkward silence. "I guess I'd rather not talk about it right now. Okay?"

Dan said nothing.

"Did you hear me?"

"Oh, you don't like the silent treatment?" Dan delivered the line with a playful push of his arm against her shoulder. "Don't like being hung out to dry?"

She pushed back at him.

"What can I get you two?" asked the ice cream attendant.

"Something to shove in his mouth," she said.

Linda that night made a rather unusual request of Dan: that he get together with her father for lunch. Not the three of them; just the two guys. Dan feared that the meeting would be one of those "Your intentions with my daughter better be good" things. But sitting down across from Lawrence Sandler proved much more complicated than that.

Dan had little choice but to agree to the first get-together. He suggested a pizza joint on the corner of Madison and 38th. Sandler ignored that proposal. He had a terrific propensity for pushing past comments and ideas he found unworthy, putting them in his personal missile launcher and sending them out of the galaxy never to be heard from again. Thus the initial, and each subsequent sit-down came in a room tucked away on the second floor of what seemed to Dan a private club on Madison at 53rd downstairs from Sandler's office.

Dan warned Sandler on the phone he didn't own a suit or a sport coat, and wasn't likely to go out and purchase one. Sandler, undaunted, said one would be provided and sure enough when his girlfriend's father strode to the table,

Dan was seated wearing a gold-patterned sport coat three sizes too large.

"That jacket looks ridiculous," Sandler said matter-of-factly upon sitting.

"I couldn't agree more," Dan responded. "As I mentioned on the phone, I don't…"

"I know all about the Bohemian front, the rebellious higher moral ground until the first person waves a couple of bucks in front of you." Sandler was throwing this out there like flicking an insect off his sleeve.

"I assure you my morality is as low as yours. I just don't own a sport coat." Dan refused to be intimidated, and his directness caused Sandler to look at him briefly and grant a moment of respect.

From what Dan could gather, Sandler and his wife had raised three children before their divorce, the two boys becoming successful attorneys entrenched in beautiful homes out on Long Island. Ten years after the divorce, as he sat across from Dan, it was tough to tell whether Sandler spent his evenings fine dining the most eligible society dames in the world, or in his underwear at home with a fine cigar and a Johnnie Walker Gold, or whatever the hell the top color was. Nor could you tell by spending time with him whether it mattered to Sandler one way or the other.

Sandler was a very smart man, both intuitively and through experience; a guy so powerful his job defied description. He knew the world in which Dan was working; knew the players within each organization, at the TV networks, major advertising houses, the team owners, and had full knowledge of each one's skeleton closet. He impressed Dan with his description of Jerry Romano as "a three-bit lowlife." Sandler spent his work hours extinguishing fires behind the scenes as businesses and lives hung in the balance. But he displayed nothing but a calm casualness. Pulling the perpetrators of malfeasance back from the brink, where possible, and designating the launch of the indefensible off the ledge had no perceptible affect on him whatsoever.

That same lack of emotion carried over when the topic turned to his daughter. He seemed as at ease as Dan was awkward in discussing Linda.

"She's more like me than my sons are," Sandler told Dan. "Good poker face, even keel, paints the picture but lets you draw the conclusion. That's why she's so good in business. She's quick with the jab, but a helluva counter-puncher too."

Dan wasn't embracing the boxing metaphor, picturing himself the cut-up opponent with one eye already closed and the other swelling. That story ends with blood in the spit bucket and diminished brain capacity.

"Be careful about pressing her for too many answers," Sandler was saying as their King Crab legs were presented by the ghostly silent wait crew. "She doesn't like fighting from against the ropes."

Dan looked thoughtfully at the crab before him, which he began prying from its shell, but his mind wasn't on the late crustacean. He was using the temporary silence to try to remember his exact words when quizzing Linda the other night about what she thought of him. And he was even harder at it trying to determine how much of that conversation was now in the well of the man sitting across from him. He didn't need to think about it too long.

"Accept that she likes you enough to bring you into her life," Sandler said, not missing a beat as he dipped a forkful of crab into warm butter sauce. "Anything more than that, who cares why it happens. You'll never figure it out anyway. Be thankful what you have. Once you start questioning why, you're only going to screw it up."

Dan would have liked to counter the advice, but for once was speechless. Sandler had yet to say anything he strongly disagreed with, but the style of the delivery was so off-putting the message was tough to absorb. And what trumped all that was his wonderment that Linda was downloading their personal conversations not only to her shrink, but to her father. Dan couldn't remember sharing anything more than a girlfriend's name and hair color with his mother.

After the crab had been vaporized, the warm napkins had taken on the grease of the food, the cognac sipped (by Sandler), and the set-to about to end, Dan figured he'd make a daughter/father team game of it.

"So, sir, what do you think of me?"

Sandler didn't hesitate pushing his chair back from the table while answering. "I don't judge anyone by what they say."

14

Leonard Terry was, in fact, becoming the breakout star of "Sports Talk." The former gridiron hero proved the perfect complement to the abrasive Mike Hopper and the aw-shucks Buck Shyrock. He was the most conversational and relaxed in front of the cameras, telling stories of life in the locker room with breezy humor and a touch of self-deprecation. Viewer feedback was strong behind him, which led to a brief pow-wow among Jerry Romano, Gregg, and Dan in Romano's office.

Romano, holding a couple of sheets of paper whose contents were already familiar to him, said, "Make sure you have plenty for the colored guy to do. People like him."

"The colored guy?" Dan asked with an edge, drawing a quick look of suppression from Gregg.

"Leonard Terry," Gregg said by way of prompting Romano.

"There's only one on the show, right? We all know who we're talking about here." Patience was not Romano's long suit. "His Q ratings are through the roof."

The intercom buzzed. "Mr. Romano, your 10 o'clock is here."

"Ah, the Jap tailor. He only comes through once a year. Takes measurements, and three months later these great shirts and suits show up, 30 cents on the dollar what you'd pay here. Keep up the good work, boys." Then, into the intercom, "Send him in."

It wasn't just Terry's easy-going personality that had fueled his popularity on the show. He had a lot of friends still playing football around the NFL, and access to information. A recent show was running short and the boys needed to fill two minutes at the end, so Hopper casually asked if anyone had any picks for that day's games. Terry tabbed the Green Bay Packers as a prime home underdog, and the Pack ended up not only covering the four-point spread, but winning the game outright.

Dan immediately picked up on the potential of making picks a weekly staple of the show. He was taking on more responsibilities and making decisions, freeing Gregg up to produce other programming. Dan was now booking guests, pulling clips, and running rehearsals, becoming not just the writer but the de facto producer of the program. When Gregg resisted using gambling as a tent pole, Dan insisted.

"I don't want the show dependent on guys picking winners," Gregg said. "What if they go in the tank for a month? We're going to be a laughingstock. We'll lose credibility."

"The newspapers are full of guys picking games and horses," Dan countered. "Look at their bankrolls—80% of them are losing, but people still read them day after day to see who they like."

"This isn't a handicapping show."

"No, but three out of four of our viewers are making bets on games, and they like this stuff. You think we should give them what they want, or stuff down their throats only what you like?"

"Why are you such an asshole?"

"I'm only an asshole when I'm right."

Dan did take Gregg's warning under consideration, though. Picking games wasn't the only way for Terry to make a name for himself. Dan remembered back to a conversation he had earlier in the week with Vic Murray at Rudy's. Murray was telling him that Hap Richards, a hard-throwing right-hander who'd been spinning his wheels trying to get people out in the hitters' paradise that was Coors Field in Denver, was about to get dealt to the Mets.

Dan sought out Leonard Terry in his dressing room before the next taping. "What's up, my man?" Terry stood up to greet him. "You keep making me sound good, understand?"

"That's what I'm here for."

Dan watched the program tape from his vantage point in the control room, where he could look over the shoulders of the techs and see exactly what the cameras were seeing. Toward the show's end, Hopper hit his mark perfectly, causing Dan to almost have a warm thought for him.

"Before we go, what can we look for this week?" Hopper asked his co-stars.

"I'll be down in Miami opening a restaurant and looking for a girlfriend," Buck Shyrock said with a winning smile. "Anyone interested, come on over to the Lobster Trap on the beach."

"Leonard?"

"Mike, look for the Mets to get busy this week. My sources tell me they're very, very close to locking up a quality arm from a Western Division team, and are willing to deal one of their middle infielders to get their man. This one could happen very soon."

"Any names?"

"Well, I wouldn't be surprised if Hap Richards is gettin' the old Samsonite out of the attic."

Hopper signed off and Dan cruised out of the control room, very happy with the show. He became happier still two days later when the Mets called a news conference to announce they had acquired Richards for shortstop Juan Crespo and a pair of minor leaguers. The timing couldn't have been better. The New York *Times* was running a feature story on Leonard Terry that week, and the writer included this latest bit of prognostication in the piece, elevating Terry to near seer status. The publicity was great for Terry, and for the show. Almost everyone was happy.

"What the hell do you mean you didn't know? Do you still work in the front office?" Hopper was screaming into his dressing-room phone before the next taping, the victim being his source in the Mets organization. The explanation coming back at him was lengthy but not particularly satisfying.

"I know you don't make the trades. Unlike you, apparently, I understand how a front office works. But how in hell could you not know anything about it? I got a goddamn ex-jock here kicking my ass on this scoop while my supposed sources either don't know a damn thing or worse, are holding out on me.

"You'll get the next one? You better get the next one or you'll be buried under so much bad press you'll need a fucking backhoe to get out."

As Hopper slammed down the phone, Dan entered, having heard enough to be cheered. "Hey, Mike, having a nice day?"

"What do you want?"

"I'm good. Thanks for asking. Listen, the predictions segment is getting so popular, we're going to expand it. Each of you will come up with a pick or a prediction each week, OK? With your great network of sources, this should be right up your alley."

Dan departed, leaving Hopper muttering out loud about his Mets source. Dan smiled broadly as he returned to his desk, where Gregg was awaiting him.

"I don't like it when you look so happy," Gregg said off Dan's smile. "Something evil is going on."

"That really hurts."

"Yeah, I could tell."

"Did you come here to bring me down?"

"No, I have a box for the Breeders' Cup at Belmont Saturday. You and your clan interested?

"Gregg, we're on a roll. Let's certainly go play the ponies."

15

Dan's head was in its usual tug of war when it came to opening up to Linda. She seemed unlike any woman he'd known. Airy and breezy when it came to feelings, she didn't seem to need to know where she stood with him. That made Dan antsy. Linda's reticence and the words of Lawrence Sandler ringing in his head: leave well enough alone and don't push. His internal dialogue see-sawed off that. He realized he was vulnerable to a woman for the first time, and it scared the crap out of him.

He, Linda, and Sam were cavorting around Central Park on a beautiful autumn morning, enjoying a magical mix of the aroma of dead leaves, the visual of live, colorful ones, and the feel of the brisk fall breeze that played around them. Sam and Dan threw a hard foam football back and forth, Sam doing most of the running and Dan leading him skillfully on long passes across the park's Great Lawn.

"Nice arm," Linda noted. "Did you play?"

"Not organized. But we had neighborhood games, one part of town against another. I threw a pretty good spiral."

"Quarterback in football. Pitcher in baseball. You have a need to be in control, don't you?"

"Apparently not, since I'm with you. All right Sam, go down and cut outside toward that big tree."

Dan led Sam with a beautiful spiral that the child hauled in with delight and began a run up the field against imaginary defenders.

"Go, Sam. Go." Dan braced for the line he knew was coming.

"You think I'm in control of our relationship?"

"That surprises you?"

"Well, yes."

"The person who doesn't express their true feelings, that's the person in control."

"It's 14-0," Sam said, approaching with the ball. "I'll go deep and you kick off." He flipped Dan the ball and went running on in front of them.

"I wouldn't be with you, I wouldn't have my son here, unless…"

Dan looked at her, prompting her with a circular motion of his hand to continue on with her thought.

"…I trusted you completely."

"You *trust* me? You trust your plumber."

"OK Dan. Kick it off."

Dan took a few steps forward and swung his leg through the ball, sending it in a majestic arc across the lawn. Sam tripped himself trying to get under it, and the ball bounced away from him, engendering a chase to reel it in.

Dan and Linda both knew what he wanted to hear, but those words would have already come if they were going to.

"Linda, when I talked to your father, I got the impression he has heard our conversations."

Sam had found several boys his age anxious to run around and play some two-on-two, leaving Dan out of the mix. Linda wasn't in a hurry to answer the implied question put to her.

"He's smart, and he knows me."

"Do you talk to him about us?"

"He's like my best friend."

"So the word you're looking for is 'yes?' It's a little creepy to me, Linda, I gotta tell you."

"I don't know why."

"Because you don't feel the need to communicate your feelings to your… whatever I am to you…but you toss them out for public consumption to your father?"

"Maybe it's a little unusual."

"Ya think?"

"Dan, I'm not going to apologize for being close with my father. I'd be foolish not to use him as a resource."

"This isn't a business deal, Linda."

"Look, Dan, we're good. I'm sorry I can't just toss around the 'L' word like throwing a football. It's not that easy for me. You're going to have to be patient."

"So it's a time question?"

"I don't know what it is. But if you feel about me like I do about you…"

Dan knew there would be no answers on this day and so called off the inquiry. The autumn around them still held its beauty, which might be worth embracing for the moment, the alternative being the lurking cold of a harsher future.

Dan collected Sam and they bid good-bye to Linda, who was due at a bridal shower up in Westchester.

The boys arrived at Belmont Park and the Breeders' Cup, a sort of World Series of Thoroughbred racing where the best horses in various divisions ran in a year-end competition.

Joining Gregg in the network's box were Dan, Sam, and the irrepressible Sonny, who arrived on the scene with a dog-eared copy of the *Daily Racing Form* marked up with his proposed winners.

"You mutts ready to make some money today?"

"Christ, there goes our good luck," Gregg said, only half in jest.

"Sonny, this is Sam. Sam, this is Sonny. Sam, you don't have to talk to him if you don't want," Dan said.

"What are you doing hanging out with these losers, kid? Stick with me, and by tonight we'll be bangin', uh, having fun."

"Nice," Dan said to Sonny, then nudged Sam. "Here they come."

The horses for the Breeders' Cup Sprint race were walking out onto the track in front of them, a grand parade of horse flesh set off by the colorful silks worn by the jockeys aboard them. As the track announcer introduced each participant, Sam was transfixed by the lineup of horses striding past them.

The thing about horse racing is, to become a fan, you almost had to go to the track as a child, taken there by a father that felt there was something in the competition or the gambling or the beauty of the horses that was worth passing along. Dan had loved it from the first trip with his father and uncle to Saratoga, just 20 minutes from his home. He started filling out index cards with horses' names and their finishes, and combed the daily newspaper for the race entries, waiting for the familiar names to run back so he could follow their progress. Looking now at Sam, Dan felt he was doing something good for the next generation.

The horses finished their post parade and now broke off into jogs as they loosened up in preparation for the three-quarters- of-a-mile Sprint. Dan and Sam walked up from the boxes and inside to the betting windows to make their wagers, although Dan would have to do the actual money exchange with the clerk.

When they returned to the seats, Sonny was holding court for Gregg and perfect strangers on why Sauce Wagon, starting from the inside post position, couldn't lose. Dan chuckled to himself, knowing full well they all could lose, and all but one would, the daunting mathematics that made this game so difficult for its owners, trainers, jockeys, and gamblers. But he knew better than to interrupt Sonny's pontificating, so he waited for it to end before commenting.

"Not a chance, and certainly not worth the odds at 3-1," he said matter-of-factly when Sonny came up for air.

"What are you talking about? The horse has been in front in every race he's run, and he's going to have position going into the turn."

"There's too many other speed horses right outside him, and they're going to be breathing down his throat the whole way around there."

"What do you know?"

"Not a thing."

"The horses have now reached the starting gate," blared the track announcer over the public-address system.

The crowd stood as one on cue, many applying binoculars to their eyes, others craning their necks trying to see the loading process going on across Belmont's huge infield.

"You feeling good?" Dan asked Sam, who gave a confident nod as he held his mutuel ticket in a tight squeeze between his thumb and forefinger.

"And they're off," intoned the announcer. "Sauce Wagon begins quickly from the inside, with Lost Banner breaking alertly and now joined from the far outside by Jokerman. These three go very fast early."

"Stay right there," screamed Sonny. "There's nothing to this game."

The horses finished their backstretch run and were racing through the turn before coming down the stretch in front of the grandstand.

"Jokerman has a desperate nose in front. Sauce Wagon is being hard ridden down at the rail. My Parfait splits those two and looms a danger with an eighth of a mile to run, and now here is Rapid River getting loose on the outside and hitting his best stride. Jokerman trying to hang on, but Rapid River coming at him down the middle of the track..."

Sam had climbed up on his seat to get a better view, and was on his tiptoes, held by Dan.

"C'mon, Rapid River, c'mon boy," screamed Sam as the horses now flashed in front of them nearing the wire. "C'mon."

"And at the line it's Rapid River to win the Breeders' Cup Sprint by a length and a half. Jokerman gamely holds second, with My Parfait third. Sauce Wagon finished fourth."

"Yes," screamed Sam, who now had the attention of the entire section.

"Way to go, kid," a guy in the next box said. Dan exchanged a big high-five with Sam, having gone along with Sam's choice himself.

"How much did I win?" Sam asked him.

"At 6-1, about 30 bucks," Dan told him.

"Yes."

"I guess he *could* lose, after all," Dan said to Sonny, who in deference to Sam was cursing more quietly than he'd have liked.

"Yeah, great, you're a genius," Sonny said.

"Smart enough to know about beginner's luck," Dan said, nodding toward Sam.

"All right, kid," Sonny said to Sam. "How'd you come up with that horse?"

"Easy. He took a dump when they were walking by us. I figured that'd lighten him up for the race."

"Oh, Christ, I'm just gonna shoot myself."

"Why take the fun away from somebody else?" asked Dan.

And so it went for the remainder of the day. Dan made enough to treat the crew to a steak dinner in midtown, minus Sonny, who was literally sick to his stomach by day's end, and had to hurry home to recover before a date with a porn star in training.

"Dan, this is the best hamburger I've ever tasted," Sam gushed as he navigated through the huge chunk of chopped sirloin in front of him. Sam was thrilled with his day at the track, and was still on the adrenaline high of seeing the horses and winning money and being out with the 'guys' for probably the first time in his life. Dan was thrilled for him, too, recognizing the specialness of the occasion and feeling, as much as he could, what fatherhood must be like, the joy that came with showing a piece of the world to an impressionable boy.

"The winner goes to dinner," Dan imparted to Sam with a playful tussling of the boy's hair.

Gregg felt the moment too. "Any chance you'll come back to the races with us again, Sam? We could sure use your help picking winners."

"Sure," said the boy, blessedly innocent of parental permission or anything else that could possibly get in the way of his enjoying life. Dan looked at him with admiration, remembering to when he felt the same pure high of a life surrounded by love and love alone.

The joy was still with Sam when he and Dan arrived back at Linda's later that evening. Sam rushed to his mom and the words tumbled from him quicker than she could absorb them. The horses and the gambling and the money and the hamburger and the characters and the people cheering for him. Once the crash came, Sam fell hard asleep, and as Linda emerged from tucking him in, Dan took her in—t-shirt, tight jeans, heeled slippers.

"Thanks for showing Sam such a good time," Linda said, sitting close to Dan on the sofa. But Sam wasn't what was on either of their minds at that moment. They seized one another in a hug that vacuumed all the air out from between them, and kissed hard, both needy and hungry. They made love with abandon on the sofa, pausing ever so briefly to push up the volume of the stereo to cut down their own noise should Sam wake up. Fortunately, he didn't, because the music was ill-equipped for the task.

"Dan, I want to explain about earlier," Linda said after they'd laid quietly catching their breath for a couple of minutes. "I know it's hard on you, but I have a really tough time trying to…"

"You know what, Linda? I don't feel like talking," Dan said gently.

"But…"

Dan lifted her up in one fell swoop and carried her into the bedroom, showing great agility in closing the door with his leg before depositing the both of them onto the satin sheets of her king-size bed. He, too, was feeling the rush of the day, and looking at the beautiful woman inches away, was sure he'd never loved another as much. At first she giggled as he started in on her again, but in no time she was joining him in another fit of passion, and they made love once more, this time gentler, smoother, and longer. After an hour, they were every bit as exhausted, and every bit as dead asleep as was Sam across the hall.

Dan was up early the next morning, a Sunday, to get home and clean up before heading in to tape the show. He was surprised to hear the phone ringing as he stepped out of the shower.

"You have a good time babysitting last night?" It was Sonny.

"It's 7 o'clock. Your porn-star-in-training untie herself and go home already?"

"I had her in more positions than you see in those books they sell on 14th Street. She was hanging upside down like a bat."

"Even money she gave you rabies."

"She was very clean; insisted on taking a bath first."

"Great, sounds like a girl you could take home to Mom, if Mom was blind and senile."

"Well, I'm sure we didn't have as much fun as you—did you have a nice, long talk about your feelings?"

"Sonny, I gotta get to work, so if you're gonna brag about this one, hurry up and finish."

"They sent a contract proposal for next year. Five percent raise. I'm gonna stuff it up Morono's ass."

"Romano."

"I'll stand by my pronunciation. Just wanted to let you know. I'm out to cruise the newsstands looking for lonely broads buying the Sunday *Times*."

"Chicks buying the *Daily News* would be more your speed. A lot less smart."

"Let me remind you of two key words here. Porn actress."

"When I get my lobotomy, Sonny, you're going to be my hero."

16

Thanksgiving was fast approaching. Mid-November marked one of the few breaks in the sports calendar, the best time for "Sports Talk" to take a hiatus for six weeks.

The crew busied for the last show before the break. Gregg was heading down to Florida to scoop up his wife, Audrey, and bring her up north, while Dan looked forward to the weeks leading up to Christmas in a festive New York City in which he'd have nothing much to do except enjoy the holiday atmosphere.

Even Hopper had seemed in a good mood as he arrived for the taping of the season finale. He was heading for the baseball winter meetings in Hawaii—a paid vacation if ever there was one. Dan was with Gregg going over the lineup of topics for the show when a shout came from over near the set.

"Somebody call 911!"

An assistant director leaned in over a motionless figure on the floor. Dan rushed over to see Hopper prone. "All right, let's give him some air," Dan said. "Have we called an ambulance?"

"Yes. They're on the way," said a cameraman. Dan took off his jacket and placed it under Hopper's head, propping it up. He began pumping on Hopper's chest and performing mouth-to-mouth resuscitation, which he'd learned in a first-aid course his mother insisted he take back when he was a kid.

"Do you know what you're doing?" Gregg asked.

"I'm not going to hurt anything; time can be everything here." Dan continued working on Hopper, and confirmed that he had a pulse. In what seemed a lot longer but was just five minutes, a team of paramedics burst onto the studio floor and got to work, proceeding to continue what Dan had just been doing. Dan receded into the background, catching his own breath. Gregg came over to check on him.

"Don't worry," Dan said. "He's too mean to go this young."

"Who's in charge?" asked one of the paramedics. Gregg stepped forward. "He's stabilized. We're going to take him to St. Vincent's."

They loaded Hopper on a gurney and rolled him to the ambulance. Back inside, an eerie silence cut through the festivities.

"Keep the talent calm," Gregg said to an assistant. "We'll push back shooting an hour." He motioned for Dan to join him on the march to Romano's office.

"How the hell could he have a heart attack right before the last show?" asked Romano.

"He said he was sorry he couldn't have saved it for a more convenient time," Dan said, not even sure his sarcasm would slow the station manager.

"Did he say if he was coming back?"

"Uh, Jerry, we should probably plan to go on without him today," said Gregg.

"Who's going to host the show? Can we get one of our sports anchors?"

"We've got less than an hour, and we're going to have to go live as it is," Gregg said.

Dan broke the silence. "I'll do it." Then, more silence.

"Maybe I can get Bob Woolf," offered Romano.

"He's 85," said Gregg.

"Did anyone hear me? I said I can do it," repeated Dan firmly. "Nobody knows the show better than I do. I'll get us through this."

Greeted by another deafening silence, Dan left the office to prepare for the taping. Gregg caught up with him five minutes later on the set.

"I don't give a shit if he's OK with it or not," Dan said. "The show's got to go on, and I'm doing it."

"He said it was all right," Gregg told him.

Dan battled some nerves as he sat on the set under the hot lights. There was a Teleprompter—how tough could it be, he told himself, taking a deep breath and trying to keep himself from sweating profusely.

"You OK?" Gregg said, telling Dan more than asking.

"Yeah."

"Just relax and don't fuck it up."

Dan did a solid job steering the show. Everyone was shaken, and Leonard Terry had some tough moments trying to concentrate on the topics at hand. Buck Shyrock, unflappable as usual, was actually a very solid presence. It went smoothly enough.

Romano called Gregg and Dan into his office after the taping.

"Very professional. I'm proud of you guys. You came up big when the going got tough."

"Thanks, coach," Dan said with fake sincerity.

"We've got a lot of challenges going forward," Romano said. "The colored guy's agent just called. He's taking a job with CBS."

It had been a hallmark of Dan's life, starting early, that whenever he looked to be on easy street, trouble was just around the corner. When he was convinced he had his algebra or geometry mastered, here came a 70 on the next test. But the opposite was also true. When things appeared bleak, somehow there was a turnaround in the offing. A tangible tingle running through him told Dan this was one of those moments where the ship starts listing in a new direction.

Dan walked all the way from midtown to Washington Square in the Village. Superstitiously, he walked under the arch to enter the park, as always, and past the early afternoon chess players and skateboarders. Mitch had invited him to come down and check out a band he was managing. It was a second job for Mitch, a chance to grab for the golden ring. Dan thought it a great move and wanted to be supportive. The group, called Plus Minus, was playing an outdoor gig in the park, and Dan found Mitch feverishly at work helping set up the equipment.

"You a manager or a roadie?" Dan asked Mitch from behind.

"Hey," Mitch said, turning to see his friend. "Is there a difference? The equipment guy got sick or something. Part of the territory."

Dan rolled up his sleeves and jumped in, helping Mitch carry a large amp and stack it on another. They worked in tandem to get the gear in place, Dan nodding to the guys in the band as they connected it all up.

"How was the show?" Mitch asked.

"Pretty weird. Mike Hopper had a heart attack just before taping. I sat in and hosted."

"Really? How'd that go?"

"Pretty OK. I mean, I didn't have any Ralph Kramden 'Chef of the Future' moments. Tell you the truth, I kinda enjoyed it."

Dan had always thought of himself as a guy very comfortable behind the scenes; writing in a room by himself. He'd never thought about taking it public. But he *had* enjoyed doing the show, and the pressure of having to perform when the light went on. It wasn't much different than writing on deadline, staring at the blank white page knowing he had to fill it up with words that made sense together, and fast. It was a skill not many people possessed. Until someone actually stared into that abyss of having to make something out of nothing, they didn't realize how hard it could be.

Dan was now forced to confront the possibility that there was a hidden ham inside him looking to come out.

"Hey, man, caught you on the tube before." This was the drummer, nonchalantly commenting before leaning in to set up his kit.

"What'ya think?" Dan heard himself say before thinking.

"I was kinda on the run. Had to get down here. But it was cool."

Mitch laughed. "The people have spoken."

Dan and Mitch were both sweated through by the time the band began tuning their instruments. They retired to a bench, where Mitch produced a couple of iced beers from a Playmate ice chest.

"To the journey," Mitch said, and they clicked bottles before guzzling.

The band sounded really good, Dan thought. It was five guys from Queens, and clearly they'd been inspired by another group of guys from there who gained fame as The Ramones. Midway through the first tune a crowd began materializing as if by magic, assembling at the center of the park from all directions, and Dan marveled at the gravitational pull of music. Take music, shake hard, and wham, instant party. There had to be 400 people listening by the second song.

Mitch tore into a box and pulled out a pile of t-shirts with the band's logo, plus and minus symbols, on them. Dan gestured for some, and the two were soon working the crowd hawking shirts for 10 bucks apiece. They moved 50 of them during the hour set. Three people told Dan they had seen him on TV earlier. He was amazed how many people are watching any random channel at any time. It was a monstrous medium, that box. When the music stopped and the crowd had evaporated, Mitch and Dan pumped up the band over what a great show they'd done. Mitch gave each of them a hundred bucks from the shirt sales.

Dan walked home through the failing afternoon light, his thoughts returning to the limbo of his life. He was a mid-level, if skilled, operative in a minor endeavor that happened to be disseminated out on the popular medium of the day. What did it ultimately mean, though, and where was he heading with it? When the novelty wears off thoughts of the big picture—troubling thoughts—push their way back in. Getting there might be half the fun, but what was the other half?

17

Gregg returned from Florida with Audrey, whom Dan had known since the couple first met in college. She and Gregg were the longest-lived couple he could think of from his generation, and there was plenty to be said for longevity and love, given most people's failure at both.

Their place was in the lower 50s on the Eastside, a mostly nondescript but pleasant enough neighborhood near the carpet district. Manhattan was broken down into all sorts of districts defined by the preponderance of certain businesses within an area of a block or two. The diamond district. The theater district. Here, companies mailed out millions of carpet samples to the well-to-do around the world, and eventually covered the floors and deadened the noise of the rich and famous everywhere.

The movers had delivered far too many things to fit into even this good-sized apartment, and the Golds were having to make a lot of decisions about what stayed and what went into storage. Dan helped move things around until a room or two were settled, but when Audrey took a phone call from her father, he was happy to have some one-on-one with Gregg.

"We have to talk," Dan said.

"Uh-oh."

"Why uh-oh?"

"Because when you get all serious like this, it's trouble."

"I resent that. You being right, that is."

"You need money?"

"Much worse than that. I'm not gonna do the show anymore..."

"What?"

"Hear me out. I'm not gonna do it unless I host."

From Gregg's silence Dan surmised his ultimatum, though delivered as softly as possible, had gone over like a fart in church. Gregg looked at him like he'd just soiled the brand new sofa and then poured grape juice all over the cushions to clean it up.

"Dan, you're not a name..."

"And I don't have the experience, and I'm rough around the edges, and I don't look like a television host. Should I go on? I know all the reasons to say 'no.' Here it is, though: I can be very good at this. Better than just about anybody you'll be able to bring in. Gregg, look, I'm grateful for what you've done for me. I really am. I've enjoyed the work and it's been fun hanging out with you. I just don't want to spin my wheels doing the same thing forever."

"It's been one season."

"I know, but if not now, it's going to be season after season, and we both know the time's never going to be right."

"You could eventually move on to something else."

"I *like* this show. We've got something here. We've made it something."

"You got one thing going for you. Hopper called; he may need surgery and he's not coming back."

"Have they found his heart yet to work on it?"

"They're bringing in a search and rescue team. Look, I'll talk to Romano."

"Gregg, talking about it isn't good enough. I need you to advocate for it. We both know Romano isn't going to go for this without a push."

"That would be my suspicion."

"Listen, I don't want to put you in a jackpot here. Think about it. If you don't believe I can do it, or I wouldn't bring something unique, then forget it. I'm not asking you to do something you don't believe in. If it's no good in your mind, then that's it. No hard feelings."

"Really?"

"Maybe one or two."

"I'll think about it, all right?"

Audrey entered the room. "I didn't get to tell you, Dan, how cool it is that you and Gregg are working together."

"Yeah, well, I'm trying to teach him a few things," Dan said.

The season offered a sprinkling of sensory delight, it being Christmas time with the large department store windows dressed in scenes of gaiety to attract shoppers. Santa driving a train around one; reindeer climbing faux mountains in another; and snow falling over a small village looking like a Currier & Ives scene around the block. It was a time to pause and enjoy the moment, and there was nothing like a child to put it in perspective.

Dan showed Sam around these grandiose displays and loved watching his reaction to the animation. It not only reminded him of his own childhood and those feelings of uninhibited wonderment, but interacting with Sam gave him a glimmer of hope that he might just be good at fatherhood if and when the time came.

Linda, Sam, and Dan made the rounds. For the first time, Dan went ice skating at Rockefeller Center in the heart of Manhattan. The trio held hands and made a chain around the ice, Sam working hardest to keep up, and enjoying it most when his mother tumbled and he got to help pick her back up amid the laughter. Dan flashed his skating prowess, learned on the frozen upstate ponds of his winter youth, breaking away and swirling speedily down the sheet of ice and into the corners, his outside arm swinging while the inside one was tucked in for cornering and quickness. He swerved in and out around the other skaters, one step ahead of their movements to avoid any collisions, all the while looking to impress his company.

"How did you learn to skate like that?" Linda asked when they were settled off the ice surface, enjoying the requisite hot chocolate with Sam also managing a candy apple.

"There wasn't much else to do in Watervliet in the winter," he said. "I wasn't into ice fishing."

Dan tripped back in time, remembering those weekend mornings getting to the pond with a dozen friends to play hockey. The hysterical laughter when Glen Simon fell into the water chasing a puck to the one spot at the pond's edge that remained unfrozen, his pants so stiff after the water froze on them that he couldn't bend his knees.

Those were the good times Dan figured would go on forever.

The day after Rockefeller Center, Dan headed upstate to visit his mom, always a bittersweet trip. He wanted so much to make her life better. Though young, she never ventured out socially after his father died. Dan's older sister likewise retreated into a shell, expelling any feelings or need to understand, living on the surface from then on.

Once the Greyhound reached Albany, Dan could feel his stomach doing gymnastics. The tinted windows could not conceal that upstate New York in winter is 17 shades of gray. All of the small Victorian houses looked in need of repair, the porches piled high with snow or ice. Even the snow was gray, or darker, depending on how much slush passing traffic had piled up on the banks. The stand-alone ice cream signs outside the corner markets, rusted from the moisture, croaked as their springs took up the wind.

The air itself felt liquid, so wet that it cut right through clothing with a damp chill even when there was no precipitation falling from the gloomy sky. Nobody walked these streets by choice. At a gas station every breath of a man filling his car was visible, and it had nothing to do with the cigarette he was surreptitiously pulling on against common sense.

Dan had the driver let him out just before reaching downtown Watervliet, on the southwest side of town across the road from the pond. He carried his travel bag to the small parking lot where he and his friends would put down and tie on their skates. Greeting him was a new sign that announced the prohibition of fishing, swimming, skating, or any other activity that made life bearable. By order of the City of Watervliet. Dan was hardly trying to go home again, but this sign would have ruined any delusions he may have entertained.

He was about to start the two-mile walk to his mother's place when he heard a familiar thudding sound repeating every few seconds. Walking around past the sign closer to the pond, he saw a solitary boy, maybe 15, smacking pucks toward a makeshift net he'd set up along the pond's edge, a wooden board lining the bottom to guard against the pucks finding the numerous holes in the webbing. The kid had nice form and a pretty good slapshot, and Dan waited for him to complete shooting the line of a dozen pucks before making his presence known.

"Hey."

"Hi." The kid was tentative, not knowing the nature of Dan's visit.

"What's with the sign? I used to skate here all the time."

"Last year a kid fell in. Dumb fuck, anyone could tell it had started to melt. Almost drowned. The family sued the city."

"Lowest common denominator."

"Sorry?"

"Laws are always made to protect the dumbest assholes at the expense of people who have brains."

"Pretty much."

"So, do the cops hassle you?"

"Nah. They can't see here from the road, and none of them's too anxious to get out of the car when it's this cold."

"No games, though?"

"Nah. We get ice time at a rink in Schenectady. Friday nights around one. Not a bad league."

"You killin' 'em with that slapper?"

"Doin' OK."

"Keep going with it. It's a great game." Dan turned to leave, but the kid wasn't finished.

"Where you live now?"

"Manhattan."

"Cool."

"See all the world you can."

Dan began the trek to his childhood home, which he'd last visited two years before. It startled him whenever he returned, how small it all seemed—the town, the home, the rooms, even by the cramped Manhattan standards he was now used to. It was like entering an elementary school and trying to sit at the desks or drink from the water fountains.

It was mid-afternoon, what little light the day provided starting already to fail. Dan stopped at the market closest to the house for a soda, and knowing nobody in there, continued on quickly.

His mother, like the house, seemed to be shrinking with each visit. She looked well enough, but it was her lack of spirit that most concerned him. Dan's life was the result of his internal rage against just that, his self-promise to push on toward something, anything, but the status quo. His mother gushed over his new job, and Dan got a 'maybe' from her when he offered to bring her down for a taping. Just a few minutes after his arrival, Dan was surprised by the doorbell, which his mom cheerfully chased down.

She greeted a stranger to Dan, introducing him as a reporter from the Watervliet *Press*.

"We don't get many celebrities here," the man, Steve, told Dan by way of explanation. "Your mom called and said you work in TV in New York."

"I'm hardly a celebrity."

"But you work in TV in New York."

Dan could see he was not getting out of giving an interview to the local weekly newspaper. Shooting his mom a quick shake of the head, he settled in. Maybe it would be fun to see how this local fellow would handle the inquisition. It constituted action around here and Dan was a good sport about it, telling a couple of safe anecdotes and giving Steve more than enough to mount a perfectly fine feature story, if he was up to the task.

The three days weren't all bad. The food was good, everyone was healthy enough, and he got to see his sister and her family, though that didn't qualify as a thrill. Not surprisingly, she had married as uninspired a man as she was a woman, and they'd conceived a pair of equally uninspired children. Unlike Sam, who was bubbling with the excitement of youth, Dan's niece and nephew were like movable window dressing, and after dinner he ceased trying to pull any sort of conversation out of them.

On Christmas Eve, Dan slipped away to the neighborhood tavern. For such a family holiday, the Anchorage was packed, indicating plenty of folks in these parts were living outside a nuclear unit. The joint hadn't changed in the least since Dan used to come in with his baseball buddies—all underage—and drink away afternoons putting in cheap tap beer. The ropes and barrels of the nautical theme were right where he'd left them, along with the sign above the register: "Ve Get Too Soon Olde, Und Too Late Shmart."

The bartenders and cocktail waitresses all wore Santa hats and Alvin and the Chipmunks' Christmas album played on the stereo. Dan pushed through to the bar and ordered a draft for old times' sake from a barkeep who looked vaguely familiar. When the man spun around with the glass and reached for a napkin, it hit Dan.

"Russell?" He thought of the baseball team's shortstop, Russ Carlisle, with whom he had shared plenty of times right here.

"Yeah."

"Dan."

The man looked closer at him now. "Henry?"

"Yeah."

"Holy shit. How's it goin', man?"

Russell was at least 75 pounds north of where Dan remembered him. He was always big for a shortstop, but powerful, and a good natural ballplayer. But the man in front of him would have had a tough time keeping up in a keg softball league.

"Can't complain."

"You look good. Where you livin'?"

"I moved to the city."

"Albany?"

"New York."

"No shit. You'd never catch me down there."

Dan held his thought about the relative merits of the town where they stood.

"Hey, Sintar was in last week," Russell continued. "His mom died, and he's back living at home. Taking over his old man's quarry business."

"The Rocks," said Dan involuntarily. Then, off Russell's look, he added, "Our Little League team that his old man sponsored. Remember? We were The Rocks."

"Yeah, that's right. Even back then you couldn't hit."

"Please, what are you, going senile? You full-time here?"

"Nah, I'm a fireman."

"They got a pole strong enough to support you?"

"Blow me."

Russell got called to the other side of the bar. They enjoyed a couple of stories in between Russell lumbering around filling orders. Dan observed the room full of strangers trying to get merry against the odds. Familiar melancholy filled him. He finished a third beer, zipped up, and headed back into the freezing night.

18

Back in the city just before New Year's, Dan had not been optimistic ever since late morning, when Gregg called and asked to meet him at Rudy's that evening. He knew the players enough to realize if Jerry Romano had been the least bit agreeable to the idea of Dan hosting "Sports Talk," he would have had him into the big office for a 30-second pep talk before his attention limped off toward lunch. People who sensed their meetings could go badly set them up for public places to minimize the possibility of screaming or violence.

All afternoon Dan had to push thoughts into and out of his head of what he'd do if the show disappeared from his life, and couldn't come up with any remotely attractive alternatives. He turned "Stop Making Sense" up loud on the stereo and waited out the time, wondering how a short day in December could go on so long.

"How was upstate?" Dan wasn't much in the mood for small talk, but remained civil for the moment answering Gregg's opening salvo.

"Cold and depressing—and that was just my family."

"I'm sure they felt you were a ray of sunshine."

"What happened with Romano?" Dan asked, putting an end to the sparring. Gregg paused for effect, looked around.

"Right to the point. I like it. I got you four."

"Four what?"

"Shows. If he's OK with you after four, he'll sign you for the season. Believe me, I had to fight like a maniac to get that. He wasn't exactly jumping up and down with joy."

"No pressure, huh?"

"Hey, you're getting a shot."

"You're right. Thanks for going to bat for me."

"I actually think you could be good. Make me a genius."

"Four episodes? What are you, a moron?" Sonny had agreed to take precious minutes at an uptown 'Gentleman's Club' he favored to advise Dan. "I told you never to make a move without me."

"It was the best we could do. I got no leverage."

"That's because, as I think I've told you on multiple occasions when you've acted like a complete dipshit, you don't know how to negotiate, and you don't know how to sell."

A burly gentleman made his way over to them. "Sonny, you drink with me tonight. Thanks for the smokes; saved me a fortune."

"All right, Sal, and don't worry about my friend here. He can't handle more than a coupla white Russians."

As Sal moved off, Dan fixed Sonny with a look until Sonny broke the silence. "What?"

"You're running unstamped cigarettes around town?"

"Keep your voice down. Just here. The guy's done me a lot of solids and I happen to know some people."

"You're a fucking officer of the court."

"This look like court to you?"

"What's the matter, you need help from the boss picking up strippers? That's pretty much what they're here for."

"The disease-free ones are a little trickier. I can't help you on a four-episode deal there, killer. You'd better pray they like you, and fast. Then we'll hammer them. And if you make another deal without me, I'll have you hung by your nut sack."

Dan stood up to leave but had one more scab to pick. "By the way, I could handle about 30 of these watered-down…"

"Hi, Sonny," chirped a buxom blond who sidled up to the bar. "I get off in an hour."

"Then I'll get off in an hour and a half." Giggling, she returned to work. Shaking his head, Dan headed for the night, wondering if the entire solar system was insane.

It was a different atmosphere preparing for the second season of "Sports Talk." There were two knock-off shows now in direct competition, one hosted by an obnoxious sports radio personality and the other, on the local CBS affiliate, having lured Buck Shyrock over with a contract that far exceeded his value. Dan was actually happy to be starting the season with a clean slate. He would have been happier still if he'd been given some say in who might be part of his line-up.

"Would you stop already?" Gregg said to him as they watched the show's new set being built. "Every single day it's the same thing."

"That's because we're 10 days out and we don't know who's on the show, and you won't even let me make a suggestion."

"You can suggest whomever you want, but it won't mean shit. It's who we can get."

"'Afford,' you mean. We made money all last year, and now we're being nickel and dimed to death."

"Bullshit. Look at that set. Those chairs--Ethan Allen."

"Who's going to be sitting in them?"

"Will you stop it?"

"How am I supposed to prepare a show when I don't know who I'm talking to? Maybe we can just have Howdy Doody and Lamb Chop on stage. I'll do it with puppets."

"Great idea. It'll make it easier to string you up when you keep annoying me. We're expecting to announce something soon, maybe later today."

"Any hints?"

"No comment until the time limit is up."

Dan had to laugh at that one, something Gregg was counting on. He was quoting an episode of the old "Superman" TV series, which they both watched religiously as kids. Superman had set a dummy up with a tape recording that kept repeating that one line while the crime fighter flew about bringing a criminal to justice. Gregg motioned Dan to follow him away from the set.

"Look," Gregg said, "I know this isn't the optimal situation. But you can't have staffers walking around listening to you bitch—about anything. You're the quarterback here now."

"You're right. Apparently, there's a first time for everything."

Three days later Dan found himself sitting on a dais at Gallagher's Steak House in midtown at a luncheon to introduce the season's "Sports Talk" cast. The big name was Earl "Duke" Robinson, a hero in New York after leading the Knicks to their first championship in 24 years back in the early '70s. Robinson had always been known as a guy around town—fast with his clothes, cars, and women. He was already doing analyst work on the Knicks radio broadcasts, where he neither distinguished nor embarrassed himself.

It definitely could be worse, Dan was thinking as he listened to Robinson answer questions from a respectable number of local media. Robinson was definitely a 'name' that would bring attention to the show. It would be up to Dan to squeeze whatever he could out of him. But New Yorkers liked this guy, and Dan knew that goodwill would be worth whatever time it took to get him comfortable on the program.

Next to Robinson sat Marv Wallace, another easily recognizable New Yorker. Wallace had been a star running back for the New York Giants in the early '60s and eventually coached them for a couple of nondescript seasons at the end of that decade. He was a no-nonsense guy, which included his drinking, and a strong enough personality where he might just make a nice counterweight to Robinson's cool persona.

But Dan was most proud of the presence of the man just to his right—New York *Post* cartoonist Sammy Carpill. Universally known as 'Carp,' which is how he signed his work, he had been part of New York since Willie Mays was playing stickball on the streets of Harlem. He constantly was introducing characters in his daily, single-box cartoon on the sports page who became mainstays in the life of the city. A small man with a high-pitched voice and thick eyeglasses, Carp was a character, and it was Dan's idea to go after him for "Sports Talk." On each show Carp agreed to sketch out a drawing that would then go to the lucky viewer who answered a trivia question correctly. When he finished poking at his dessert of mediocre New York cheesecake, Dan looked down the row of faces on the dais and was satisfied. He had his roster in place. It was time to go win.

"Thanks to our great crew here in front of, and behind the camera, and join us next week for another edition of 'Sports Talk.' Bye, bye, everybody."

With the stage manager's "And we're clear," the season's first episode of "Sports Talk" was in the can. Dan got up to shake hands with his fellow on-air performers. The show had gone extremely well, he thought, the segments moving at a strong tempo and flowing into one another. He was particularly pleased with Marv Wallace, the tough-talking football guy who displayed a welcome sense of humor in his banter with Dan and Duke Robinson. When Duke went on about athletes always being concerned with giving their best, Marv countered that some guys were much better on certain days than on others, due to factors as disparate as marital relations and how many times they had broken curfew that week. His riff led to Carp drawing a picture of a football player with his helmet on backwards, which ultimately was won by Mike in Jackson Heights, Queens.

Gregg hopped up on the set as Dan finished rallying the troops.

"I hate to say this, but that was damn good," Gregg offered.

"Whoa, you sure you want to go on record with that?" Dan said, hiding his relief.

"I liked it."

"Do you have to sound so friggin' surprised?"

"That was really good, Dan." This was Sam, rushing up to hug Dan, with Linda a few paces behind.

"Ah, see there?" said Dan.

"So, Sam," Gregg said, "you liked the show?"

"Dan was great. I don't know about the other guys."

"The others were fine also, Mr. TV critic." This was Linda, whom Dan had taken to Gregg and Audrey's for dinner a few days before. He hadn't previously introduced her to them, and vice versa, and felt it was well past time he did so. Everyone said afterwards what a lovely time they had and how nice it was to meet one another, but Dan was looking for clues at the scene that would cut through that usual malarkey.

His sleuthing had found nothing out of the ordinary. The women paired off, with Linda giving Audrey a verbal tour of some must-see destinations for shopping and culture that a newcomer to the city shouldn't miss. Gregg and Dan amused them with war stories from their childhood, including tales from the baseball locker room, where they had first heard about this wondrous thing known as sex.

"Why doesn't that surprise me, that you learned about girls in a locker room?" Audrey said to her husband.

"Where did you think I learned to do tricks with my bat like that?" Gregg retorted.

"You're gross," his wife protested. "And in front of company."

"Well, I'm thankful Dan learned what he did, no matter where he learned it," Linda offered.

"That's the right attitude," Gregg said.

"I suppose we're very lucky girls," Audrey said with over-the-top sincerity.

Dan was glad Linda had come to the taping for the first time. It was, to him at least, indicative of a slowly growing commitment on her part, no small thing in his mind. Here he was ready to go deep with a woman, and she's the one hitting the brakes. What would you expect, he told himself, that things would go smoothly? He'd figured he was not going to be lucky in love. Bad family experience. Early awkwardness around girls. Locker room mentality. Now he wanted that luck.

"Can we go get an egg cream?" Sam was great at bringing it all back to basics.

"So early?" Dan said.

"Oh, Mom already made me eat breakfast before we came here."

There was a place, Radio, that had opened a few blocks away, and was set up like the candy store that all New Yorkers lived close to when they were growing up. They had the silver tumblers that were filled with malt, milk, and ice cream, and attached to the green blenders that mixed the concoction into a thick, creamy taste treat. There was a smell about those old-time places—the malt mixed with the wood floors and candy counter and soda fountain that was unique.

"If it's O.K. with your mom. Let me collect some things. Gregg?"

"Sounds darn good, but I gotta make sure the show gets up. You kids run along. Dan—10 o'clock tomorrow with Jerry."

"I wouldn't miss it, except for a few hundred things I could think of."

"Don't think. Just be there."

20

"We got a 4.3. PIX did a 2.8. CBS 1.5." Romano was reading the overnight ratings to Gregg and Dan in the corner office Monday morning. "Not bad. But we've got to get it higher."

"How about getting the marketing department more involved? I haven't seen any spots on the station, and I've been asked to do exactly one interview in the past week." Dan was taking an assertive tact with his boss.

"You think I don't know how to market? Where do you think that 4.3 came from? Your good looks?"

"Probably would have been higher based on that," Dan said, rubbing his face. "I'm just saying, I could do more interviews…"

"Don't worry about the marketing. Just put a good show out there."

"What did you think of yesterday's?"

"I thought it was a 4.3 I want it to be a 5."

"Maybe if I had a contract, it would help me focus better," Dan said, earning equally dirty looks from Gregg and Romano.

"Don't get cocky," Romano warned. "We have a lot of work to do."

"I'm sorry. I'll try harder to have the best-rated sports talk show in New York City. Oh, wait, we already are."

"Gregg, get your boy out of here before he ruins my breakfast."

As Dan and Gregg made their way to the door, Joan, Romano's secretary, entered with a full-on meal—eggs, hash browns, bacon, rolls, coffee. Dan lifted a strip of bacon off the plate and ate it, saying loudly enough for Romano to hear, "Hmmm. Good bacon," before exiting.

"You have to agitate him like that?" Gregg was shaking his head, trying his best to scold Dan.

"Can he say, 'Good job. We're number one in the ratings. Well done. Way to go?' There really is something wrong with him."

"That's how these guys are. They're always looking for something more. Trying to find the next big thing. Stay one move ahead."

"You have to pay attention to what's in front of you. Be here now. Live in the moment."

"Yeah, well, I don't think Romano is a big fan of Ram Dass, or whoever the hell you're reading for enlightenment these days, O.K.?"

"Well, it would do him some good. '4.3.' I'll shove that 4.3 up his…"

"Shut up and put your energy into the next show. Do us all a favor."

"Only because I like you."

Less than an hour later, the phone on Dan's desk rang. The caller ran right over Dan's "Hello."

"You weren't bad on the show." It was a male voice, but Dan was having trouble placing it.

"Thanks."

"It's possible I could help you. Lunch Wednesday. Noon."

The click in Dan's ear represented the end of the conversation, the weirdness of the non-exchange bringing into focus that he had been listening briefly to Lawrence Sandler. The fact he had offered to help, or at least implied it was possible that he might help, gave Dan both a slice of pride and a feeling of dread.

Dan accomplished at least one goal during the course of the next day. After shopping a couple of hours, he found a smart-fitting sport coat to wear at lunch across from Sandler. Dan was feeling rather rakish, sitting at 'their' table in Sandler's club, stylishly downing a Coke while waiting for his host. He kept his head up, hoping to be noticed now that he was part of the great world of show business, but none of the dour patrons threw him a bone. Dan had to be content with his well-fitting attire.

"Goddamn politicians can't keep their dicks out of the wringer," Sandler said by way of a greeting. He had come up from behind Dan, indicating he had descended from the elevator behind the table. Who knows what lives were made and destroyed on the floors over this sanctuary for the rich and entitled.

"Do you want to wash your hands?" Dan decided he would keep trying until he made this man laugh. Or smile. Or move some facial muscle.

"Hands? You need to go through a car wash when you're finished dealing with these people."

The waiter placed a drink in front of Sandler. It was impossible to know its ingredients, as no mixing straw adorned it. "The usual, sir?"

"Yes, please." The waiter turned to Dan. "And for you, sir?"

"The usual, of course." As the waiter departed, Dan added for Sandler's benefit, "Whatever it is."

Sandler seemed preoccupied, so Dan carried the early conversation. "So, you watched the show…"

"Linda asked me to." The clear implication was there was no way in hell Sandler would have lowered himself to such programming otherwise.

"By the way, how are Linda and I doing?" Dan decided to fight attitude with attitude, considering it had long been building up in him.

"You don't know?"

"Well, you seem to know her so much better than I do."

"Sam likes you. That's very important…to me."

"Secretaries and kids," Dan said, mostly to himself.

"What's that?" Sandler asked.

"Just my philosophy of life."

"I'm sure it's fascinating," Sandler said while bowls of Manhattan clam chowder were placed in front of them. His silence for a minute indicated a changing of subject.

"The Yankees are making big changes next week," Sandler said in a low but urgent voice after his third spoonful of soup.

"They finished third last year. I'd expect them to move some pieces around on the field."

"This isn't on the field. Think front office, and dugout."

The current manager of the Yankees was Cookie Viallo, an institution who had been their catcher during all the championship years of the '50s and '60s. Everyone loved Cookie for his great stories and friendly demeanor, and he wasn't expected to be in job trouble regardless of the team's failure to make the postseason. Brian "Dirt" Mason seemed likewise ensconced in his position as general manager. He had put together the two championship teams of the '70s and was thus thought to have built up a career full of good will. In short, this was a blockbuster, if true.

"Let me get this straight. Cookie and Dirt?" Dan asked in a whisper.

Sandler never acknowledged the question. "I thought you might like to know. If you don't go with it Sunday, you miss it."

Dan swallowed hard, and it had nothing to do with the soup. He instantly knew what this meant—sticking his neck out on the chopping block to either have it cut off or to become a seer, all based on this impossible-to-figure weird son of a bitch sitting across from him in this anachronistic old boys' club in the middle of New York City.

"I guess it wouldn't get me anywhere to ask if you were absolutely sure."

"Ah, the shrimp oregano," Sandler said, showing enthusiasm for the first time as he prepared to attack the main course.

It wasn't until Dan stepped off the set after taping the next "Sports Talk" that the butterflies began flying around his mid-section. Right at the end of the show, during the 'predictions' segment, he let go with Sandler's scoop—stating the Yankees manager and general manager would be fired. The basketball guy and the football guy sitting with him on the set had no discernible reaction, but Carp the cartoonist shot him a meaningful glance, somewhere in between 'are you serious?' and 'why didn't you give me time to draw something on this?'

Gregg met Dan two steps from the set. "Do you know what you just said?"

"No, I had an invisible fainting spell." Dueling with his friend somehow made this more palatable.

"Where the hell did you get that?"

"No can do. Sorry."

"Look, I can take it out before I put the show up for airing."

"Gregg, would I have said it if I didn't mean to? It's a scoop. We've got it. Go with it."

"But is it true?"

"I sure fucking hope so."

Romano wasn't reading the Sunday ratings when he summoned Gregg and Dan to his office Monday morning, although they were still strong and better than the competition's. Instead, he had four New York daily newspapers spread out in front of him, and he was reading each of them quoting Dan about the Yankee upheaval. It was the top story in each sports section, and had led virtually every radio and TV sports report for the past 24 hours.

"I've had every goddamn Yankees employee from the president to the clubhouse boy call me this morning," Romano said. "And none of them are wishing me a happy Valentine's Day."

"That's too bad. Happy Valentine's Day," Dan said. This sparring would also help his nerves, which were plenty raw wondering if he'd committed journalistic suicide in the second week of a four-week contract.

"Where did this come from?" demanded Romano.

"I just made it up," Dan answered. "So we're going to have to sit tight this week and see if it actually happens."

"Do you know what credibility is? Do you realize we're finished, we're a laughing stock, if this so-called story is no good?"

"I know. I'm not a moron."

"That remains to be seen. Now get out of here."

Dan hadn't been able to concentrate on anything for the next couple of days, sitting at his desk like a zombie, and being treated like a leper by everyone from Romano to the lowliest intern. Even Gregg seemed to be avoiding him. Dan hadn't felt like going out to Rudy's, either, and with Linda out of town on business, he'd been heading straight home and staying away from any form of media except throwing music on the stereo hoping to escape. He had thought a hundred times about calling Sandler for any shred of information; an update; an affirmation of any sort, but was proud of himself that he didn't. Plus, of course, he knew it would do absolutely no good.

Now he thought about how many boxes it would take to clean out his desk. Not that many. It had been less than a year, and probably one load stacked on a hand truck would get him cleanly away from the place for good. That was comforting. Travel light. Sleep didn't come for long, nor was it deep.

The newsroom buzzed around Dan with its daily activities. It was mid-afternoon Wednesday and the evening news shows were being prepared. Equipment was being moved around, copy delivered here and there, and the humming wire machine rat-a-tatted in choppy waves as news came in and the cursor moved over the roll of paper that could be torn off and used by the anchors. Dan was so intent on his circumstances he didn't notice the bells sounding on the Associated Press ticker indicating a breaking news story of significance, or the young news writer who approached his desk holding the wire report.

"Here it is—Yankees fire Viallo," the kid said.

Dan took a moment to come around. "Let me see that," he said, grabbing the piece of paper and reading. It was just a headline and two sentences, with the bulk of the report to follow. But it was enough. Viallo was gone, and general manager Mason was right behind him. Dan was never so happy to see two guys lose their jobs.

Jerry Romano's attitude had undergone an amazing transformation by the time he welcomed the assembled press to his own news conference at noon the following day. Even a late-arriving meal wouldn't have knocked the smile off his face. He was launching into a lengthy monologue about "Sports Talk" breaking this huge story and the quality work done by everyone involved to bring New Yorkers the news they needed to know first and fearlessly. None of the media were paying attention to Romano. They were waiting for their shot at Dan, who sat on the makeshift dais disengaged as Romano droned on.

He barely noticed when Romano threw open the proceedings for questions, and the first one came right at him, wanting to know how he uncovered the story.

"Just good, solid reporting, good sources, and having faith," Dan answered.

In 10 different ways, 10 reporters asked who the source was, and 10 times, Dan answered with slight variations. If he revealed his sources, "even the guys at PIX and CBS would be able to break stories." If he revealed his sources, "they wouldn't be much of a source anymore." And on it went, with Dan reveling in the spotlight, brought back from the precipice of being booted out the door.

The media blitz didn't end for two days. Now, Romano finally took Dan's advice and was marketing the show for all it was worth. Everyone with a notebook and a camera came onto the "Sports Talk" set for a 'behind the scenes' look at where the magic happens. Dan gave the nickel verbal tour of his life and career so many times he was getting good at it. The weekend editions of the newspapers and every TV sports report did the feature story on the show that broke the huge Yankee shake-up.

Dan made one call in the midst of the blitzkrieg. It was time for Sonny to seal his deal with Jerry Romano.

The following Monday, "Sports Talk" ratings hit an unbelievable 7.1, drowning the competition. What previously was a black hole for ad revenue—Sunday mornings—had now turned into hundreds of thousands of dollars for the station, and, by extension, hero status for Romano as far as his ABC bosses went. He was the genius who green-lighted this bold new venture and, unlike most, it had turned into an astounding success, both critically and financially.

As far as the trickle-down effect, it didn't hurt Dan either. Sonny made sure he got in Romano's door the same day those ratings hit the street. His position couldn't have been stronger. Romano had no choice but to extend and enhance the contract of the show's writer and star, and Dan had insisted that Sonny get a bump for Gregg as well.

That night, Dan was more than happy to head to Rudy's for a major celebration. Sonny had already alienated their cocktail waitress as Dan strode in to join him. Sonny spied him over the rim of his glass, the contents of which were quickly being poured down his hatch.

"I told the bimbo the drinks are on you tonight, sport," Sonny said before Dan had hit his seat.

"Oh yeah, for the lousy 90 grand you got me? I told you nothing less than six figures."

"You'd be making six figures with two of them on the wrong of the decimal point without me," Sonny said, already chasing down the server with his eyes.

Ninety thousand was a ridiculously large sum of money to Dan. Nobody who went into writing did so for the cash. There were much easier and surer ways to get paid. Dan was being rewarded for believing in himself. He had no idea what he'd do with this kind of money, although Sonny was helping him out with that, sending the waitress back for more as soon as she arrived with drinks.

"To the Cadillac of sharks," Dan said, clinking glasses with Sonny before putting in his first shot of the evening.

"To the best—me," Sonny answered as they immediately beat back another round.

"Looks like I'm late," Gregg said on approach.

"It's the luckiest man on the face of the Earth," Sonny said. "He gets my services without having to pay for them."

"Some luck," Gregg said. "Romano reamed my ass out for being forced to give me a raise. Said he'd be watching me like a hawk and I'd better earn it, or else."

"Or else what, the cheap prick," Sonny said.

Gregg grabbed one of the several shot glasses gracing the table and lifted it toward Dan. "Anyway, here's to a real mensch, a true friend, and a big-time TV talent." They all drank up before Sonny spoke.

"By the way, how *is* your TV show? I've never seen it."

They were still laughing when agents Vic Murray and Brian Brown joined the festivities.

"What'd ya get him, Sonny, a million a year?" Murray asked with a straight face.

"You're lucky your ex-wife's not getting that," shot back the lawyer.

"Congratulations, Dan, I was worried for a while there."

"Oh, you mean when they put the noose around my neck and sprang the trap door? No problem."

"So where'd ya get the story? I didn't hear a thing."

Sonny jumped in to protect Dan. "Who said you know what the fuck is going on? 'I didn't hear a thing.' You don't hear a lot of things. Like when your wife was banging that cop outside the mayor's office."

"You know, Sonny, I hate when you get a head start on me. Waitress, a bottle of whatever these low-lifes are drinking."

Dan was feeling no pain as he lurched out of his cab outside Linda's place. Oddly, he wasn't flat-out drunk despite the amount of booze he'd ingested. The adrenaline from the past week overrode the alcohol. He knocked gently, it being near midnight. He hadn't seen Linda in a week, and wanted to hold her. She opened the door, her face noncommittal upon seeing him, and quickly moved off, allowing Dan to let himself in. It wasn't what Dan had in mind.

"You alright?" he asked.

"I just got home, the trip was a disaster, and Sam's got a cold," she said. "I'm doing great."

She moved about the apartment, putting things away and cleaning up while he leaned on the breakfast nook, watching.

"I thought we might catch up."

"Dan, I honestly don't feel like entertaining right now. You said on the phone it was important. That's the only reason…you smell like a distillery."

"I've been drinking. That's what men do."

"Is that what men do?"

"Yes, and they sign contracts for $90,000. And they have TV shows that hundreds of thousands of people watch, and…"

"Can we do this another time?" Linda was still occupied by many things, none of them Dan.

"It's been a week since we've seen each other and I've got great news."

"Look, Dan, not right now, O.K.?"

"When?"

"Keep your voice down. Sam just went to sleep."

"O.K., Linda, I'll give you more time to miss me. Try real hard."

Dan let himself out, having never touched his girlfriend. He began the half-hour walk home, wondering if ever there'd be a time when his writing and his job and his love would all be in a place where he could enjoy them. When he could for a moment let out one long exhale, take in the wholeness of life, and be satisfied--for a day, a night, a moment, before the next shit storm gathered. He decided he wouldn't bet his new salary on it.

21

Dan's next meeting with Linda went better. They took Sam to Chelsea Piers, a recreational development downtown on the West Side overlooking the Hudson River. You could drive golf balls out toward the ocean, go rock climbing or ice skating, or take swings in a baseball batting cage, the latter of which Sam was doing while Dan fed quarters to keep the pitching machine hurling.

"Let the ball come to you, Sam. Don't reach for it." Dan knew he would have been a helluva Little League coach if he'd had the patience, and a kid, for it. There was no nuance in the game of baseball that was too small for him to study. He obsessed over tiny facets of each play on which the tide of a game might turn. "Keep your swing nice and level. That's it."

"How come you didn't become a ballplayer?" Linda asked.

"You think it's easy?"

"You seem to know so much about it."

"Knowing it is one thing. Believe me, it was my dream. I just didn't think I was good enough. I definitely wasn't good enough. Maybe if I lifted weights and found a professional coach…but we just didn't do those things. You played the games, and then you either began working construction or went to college. So now I just yell at the TV screen."

"Far less lucrative."

"Yeah, well, I don't have to wear those funny uniforms. Choke up a little, Sam. Move your hands up on the bat."

"I'm sorry about the other night. It was a really bad time."

"Nobody needs a drunk on their doorstep. I just wish you could show a little emotion along the lines of being glad to see me. But I guess you weren't, so…"

"Hey, love the show." This from a passerby. "Who the Yanks gonna get to manage?"

"Hopefully me," Dan answered glibly.

"I could think of worse."

"Yeah, probably including the guy they hire."

"Yeah. Keep up the good work."

"Thanks."

"Wow," said Linda. "Pretty soon you won't be able to go out in public."

"We need more quarters," demanded Sam, and Dan fed the machine before coming back to Linda.

"Know that I do enjoy seeing you, Dan."

"Hey," said a guy who just set his kid up in the cage next to Sam's, "You look familiar. You on the radio?"

"I *look* familiar?" Dan was about to crack wise when he got a small kick from Linda and brought it back down. "No, no, I'm not on the radio. Sorry."

Dan and Linda shared a good laugh as the guy turned his attention to his kid.

"A mind is a terrible thing to waste," Dan said.

"These are your people."

"Can we get a pretzel now?" Sam and his bat had appeared on the scene.

"I think we can do that," Linda said.

"How did it feel, slugger?"

"Pretty good. I'd say I hit about .380 with two home runs."

"It gets a little tougher when there are fielders out there."

"Oh, I counted them. I still hit .380."

Sam was such a good kid and Dan marveled at him. No crying, always an up attitude. And Dan also realized, as they walked to the concession stand, that he and Linda had their best times together when Sam was with them. While Dan adored the child, he figured this wasn't an altogether good sign. Linda obviously wasn't as comfortable with him—probably with anybody—one on one. She was a beautiful woman with a great child, and he wondered how many others had tried to unlock her emotions.

She would have already been paired up if it were easy, Dan told himself. And then he figured she wasn't much different from him. Could they actually make it together? The stars so rarely align for anyone. Not like how you read about in the 'happily ever after' stories. Not like when you're a kid like Sam and life is one big party of pretzels and baseball and running through the park and having people around all the time who love you.

They sat on seats around a plastic table. Sam tore into his food, while Dan wiped most of the salt off his own pretzel, ripped open a packet with his mouth, and squirted mustard all over it.

"So," said Linda, "does my father have any other big tips for you?"

They don't really align for anyone, those damn stars.

22

L inda had been right about one thing, although she'd been kidding when she said it. People began recognizing Dan on the street. On the way to the corner deli in the morning to get his roll and juice, he could feel heads swivel in quick double-takes; people said 'hi' to him with a familiarity they couldn't put their fingers on. There were probably 50 channels now on cable television in Manhattan, and yet, when you asked someone if they saw a five-minute snippet of something, the answer was oftentimes 'yes.' People were travelling in parallel lines—going separately in the same direction.

The recognition didn't stop with random looks from strangers. Dan could sense a difference in how people at the station treated him. "Sports Talk" was a bona fide hit, or as big a hit as one could have nine hours before prime time. The show's ratings had settled in the upper 5s, meaning more than 400,000 New Yorkers were tuning in weekly, a huge number for Sunday mornings, which told Dan that an awful lot of people used sports as their religion. Assistants new to the station would start out calling him Mr. Henry, which he immediately corrected. The show began getting mentioned in p.r. material sent out by the local network, and promo spots for the show appeared on sports programming and throughout the day Saturdays.

Fortunately, Gregg was always around to keep things real.

"Nice pick on the Knicks game yesterday," Gregg greeted Dan on Monday morning, referring to Dan predicting they'd lose to the lowly Hawks.

"Hey, I let Marv make the right call. What are we gonna do, agree all the time? That makes for a lively show."

"My grandmother could have picked that game. And she died two years ago."

"I'm sure her love of the Knicks eased her transition to the afterlife."

"Romano wants to see us."

"I hate those five words."

"I know."

"Then why do you keep saying them?"

"I love seeing you miserable."

They marched off toward the executive offices. Outside Romano's chamber, Dan, without breaking stride, barked to Joan, "Hold my calls." Getting the laugh he was looking for, Dan followed Gregg into Romano's lair. To the surprise of nobody, Romano was balling up the wrappers from his breakfast. Tossing them into his garbage can about two feet away, Romano let out a Marv Albert-style "Yes!"

"Brilliant shot, sir," Dan said.

"The short ones can be the trickiest. You got a tuxedo?"

"You want to take this one?" Dan said to Gregg.

"You, you," Romano said to Dan.

"Let me think for a minute. No," Dan said in two seconds.

"Get one."

"Your concern for my wardrobe is tremendously gratifying, don't get me wrong," Dan said. "But maybe I should start out with a suit, and work my way…"

"We've been nominated for a Big Apple Media Award. It's a black tie dinner, and I don't want you embarrassing yourself…or me."

"In that case, I'm going to need etiquette lessons. Do you use the little spoon for coffee, or cocaine?"

"What category are we up for?" interceded Gregg, trying to change the conversation's gears.

"Best sports show."

"Is your bargain basement tailor due back this week?" Dan piped up.

"Out of here. Now," Romano barked, shuffling papers, any papers, around on his desk.

Vic Murray called just as Dan had returned to his desk, and insisted they meet for lunch in midtown, strange since they normally saw each other multiple times a week at Rudy's. This was a first. And Murray blew off Dan's suggestion they try a new Mexican joint that opened to decent reviews in the upper 30s, insisting they dine instead at a linen tablecloth chophouse called Matty's. He also nixed Dan's suggestion of having Gregg join them.

The maitre d', after briefly surveying Dan's casual clothes disapprovingly, led him to a rounded corner booth where Vic was already working diligently on his first Manhattan of the day.

"There he is," Vic said a bit too enthusiastically. "What'aya have?"

"Coke. Ice." The maitre d', even more thrilled with Dan, departed to pass the drink order off to a busboy.

"What are you, a Boy Scout?" Vic chided Dan.

"I just don't want my head tied in knots," Dan answered with a practiced smile. He knew there had to be a very specific reason for this lunch, and he was going to let Vic set the tempo.

"How's the show going?"

"Great. You really should watch it sometime."

"Sunday is usually when I have the kids. On the go, keeping them entertained. Spending money. Alleviating guilt."

"Sounds like a busy day."

Dan's Coke was brought to the table. Like a kid, he tore the end of the wrapper off the straw and thought about shooting the remainder at Vic, but merely pulled it off and took a sip of soda.

"You got kids?"

"None that I know of."

"Mine both look like my ex-wife. I have trouble getting over that, them reminding me of that...bitch."

"That's genetics for you. Those crazy X and Y chromosomes, and so forth."

"Dan, I'd like you to do a favor for me."

Dan suppressed any words that might be construed as an affirmative reply, and instead stared at Vic, silently telling him to proceed.

"I'd like you to mention Tom Reardon as someone the Yankees are looking at for manager."

Reardon was a career minor league catcher, which actually made him a viable candidate for a manager's job. Catchers, who call the game's pitches, ultimately filled more managerial posts than any other position player. Reardon had enjoyed some success managing AA and AAA minor league teams in the Cubs' organization.

"Is he?"

"Is he what?"

"Someone the Yankees are looking at."

"That's hard to say."

"He either is or he isn't. You're a smart guy."

"We've made it known to them he's interested. But I don't know what their thinking is."

"How does my mentioning him help?"

"It makes him more legit. So even if he doesn't get the Yankee job, it lifts his profile for, say, Pittsburgh or Cleveland, who are also in the market right now."

"The problem, Vic, is if I mention him and they aren't considering him, I look like an asshole to everyone in the Yankee organization."

"There's so much backbiting going on there, everyone will assume the guy in the next office has been talking to Reardon."

"Jesus, Vic."

"Are you gentlemen ready to order?" inquired the waiter.

"No," Vic said brusquely, blowing him off.

"I rep a helluva lot of players in this town," Vic continued, staring hard at Dan. "I know that."

"I can be very helpful--hell, I've all ready been helpful-- dropping a dime and telling you where they're going."

Dan figured something like this was the purpose of the meal, but it didn't make him enjoy it any much more. This is exactly what happens when people start recognizing you on the street. There's always a Vic on the scene, looking to cut off a slice for himself.

"You're not in kindergarten anymore, kid," Vic said, reading Dan's mind. "You got some juice. You got to know how to use it."

"I'm not promising you anything, Vic. I'll see what I can do."

"That's all I'm asking." Vic motioned the waiter over. "Another Manhattan here, and a Coke for my nephew."

23

Dan found himself spending less time preparing his show and more promoting it. He proved quite adept at yakking it up with whatever host or hostess was interviewing him. His quickness with a quip proved to be gold in such venues. Throw in an anecdote here and there, a little behind-the-scenes stuff, remember to spread the credit around, and voila! Instant guest.

He'd never admit it, but Dan was quite enjoying these appearances. Of course, they were good for promoting "Sports Talk," but he felt it didn't do any harm to be putting his name and face out in the public eye, either. It's not like he could trust Romano to take care of him indefinitely. Anything but. He knew Romano would throw him out with his Styrofoam lunch cartons if the ratings pointed the wrong way. Nor was Dan without an ego. After a life spent behind the scenes and too often fielding rejection slips, he liked the attention, if not all that came with it.

Two weeks after his lunch with Vic Murray, Dan did a show segment on the Yankees' managerial situation. He was compelled to tackle it, not because of

Vic, but because he broke the original story and it was still the number-one hot stove topic in town. Duke Robinson and Marv Wallace gave out their choices, and were able to inject humor, as the question was planned well in advance. So Wallace got a big laugh when he threw his own hat into the ring, arguing that baseball can't be that much different to coach than football.

"You know it's 'managing,' not 'coaching,' right?" chided Dan.

"Same thing. You're a genius when you win, and a moron when you lose," countered Wallace, as everyone broke up.

Carp drew an illustration of his choice to take the job, longtime Yankee third base coach Birdie Rosselli. Dan knew that would never happen; Rosselli was a classic second banana and the team was famous for going for a big splash. Which is why Vic Murray's boy, Tom Reardon, had no shot. Dan's own announced choice was Randy Hudson, second baseman for the team's World Series wins in the '70s and its bench coach the past two years. It was an inspired choice and progressive, since Hudson was black, and Dan knew he was stirring the pot, since the organization wasn't likely ready to make that leap of faith. It was just the type of cause Dan was comfortable championing.

Before ending the discussion, Dan threw in this carefully worded line: "Other candidates possibly under consideration include Stan Brubaker, Joe Hesse, Roger Leone, Tom Reardon, Link Dugan, Billy Graves, and yours truly." Not only did he carefully craft the sentence to water it down as much as possible, Dan added the laugh line to further lighten things.

"How fast would you take that job if they offered it?" asked a laughing Robinson.

"Very tough decision, leaving you three guys," replied Dan. "About two seconds."

It was a masterpiece of composition by Dan, fulfilling Vic's request without peddling his soul. He was quite happy as the taping came to an end and nobody questioned any of the names on his list.

Dan's growing celebrity had absolutely zero effect on Linda, which certainly didn't shock him. She seemed amused at his increasing vanity, and the presence of a tuxedo, of all things, when he showed up one evening to get her feedback on how to wear it and which accessories were appropriate.

"Is it Halloween again already?" Sam said innocently after completing his homework and spying Dan in the penguin suit.

"Actually, I'm going to a very important awards dinner where I might win something," Dan said, speaking to Sam but wanting Linda to know as well. "And you have to wear one of these."

"I don't understand why you want to get all dressed up for a dinner where you can spill food on your fancy clothes," Sam shrugged, heading to the kitchen for a snack.

"Do I need to wear the cumberland?" Dan asked Linda, removing the sash from the box.

"Of course, it's part of the outfit," Linda laughed. "And by the way, it's a cummerbund."

"It is? Really?"

Linda helped him on with it, wrapping it around his midsection.

"There. You know, you clean up pretty well."

"I hate to get dressed up alone. Will you come with me to this thing?"

"I don't know, Dan. It's your night. I'll just be a distraction…"

"Linda, I would really love for you to be there. Please."

"Well, I suppose to see you all formal and out in public would be worth it."

"Great. Should I rent you something? What do women wear to these things?"

Linda laughed, shaking her head. "You really have lived a…sheltered life."

"Nobody dressed like this where I'm from. Not even at funerals."

"No, I don't imagine so. To answer your question, usually something black and sexy."

"That sounds pretty good. You got something like that?"

Linda, fixing the bow tie on Dan's neck, squeezed it too tight in response. He gave her a meaningful kiss, pulling her in close.

"You're going to wrinkle your tux."

"I don't care."

"Yecch," Sam said upon seeing the clutching duo, and made his way back to his room.

The Big Apple Awards took place in a nondescript ballroom off the lobby of the Marriott Marquis Hotel in the heart of midtown. There was tension around the table as the pedestrian dinner—choice of mystery meat or fish—dishes were cleared and the awards portion of the program commenced. With Dan, Linda, Gregg, and Audrey were Romano (unaccompanied), a couple of other suits from the television station, and Dag Drenemann, owner of Sleep City, the mattress chain that was the main sponsor of "Sports Talk." Drenemann hailed from Denmark, where he learned to produce a better bed without springs, and brought his invention to the States to make his fortune, which he was very much in the process of doing. He seemed a nice enough man, particularly for a sponsor.

"Sports Talk" had competition in the Best Sports Show category from "Thoroughbred Live," a longtime horse racing program that had all ready won two of these awards; "Madison Square Garden Presents," also a past winner; "Coaches Corner," a show hosted by New York Giants head coach Al Senna;

and "Prep Beat," which looked at area high school athletes. Dan busied himself doing origami with his napkin.

When legendary late-night talk-show host Joe Franklin opened the envelope and announced the winner, it was indeed "Sports Talk." It seemed a popular choice, with a generous amount of applause greeting it. Romano let out a loud "Yeah" while Dan snuck a kiss on Linda before standing and heading to the podium with Romano and Gregg. Romano grabbed the trophy and the microphone and commenced thanking a series of suits and sponsors that killed the buzz. Gregg deferred to Dan, who chose to recognize the workers, including most everyone who played a part in staging the show, and his panel.

The following morning the set was buzzing, and Dan made a point of congratulating each person, no matter if they were intern gophers or technical whizzes. When someone asked where the trophy was, Dan set off to find the answer. He discovered it on the way to Romano's office. It was sitting on Joan's desk. Dan grabbed it.

"Tell him I took it, if he asks," Dan told her.

Dan returned to the stage, and a dozen workers passed the spoils around like they were a winning hockey team carrying the Stanley Cup. Each took a turn walking it around the studio before handing it off to the next as co-workers cheered for one another. They had just finished the ritual and placed it on the table on the "Sports Talk" set when Romano marched into the studio in full aggressive mode.

"Henry, where is my trophy?"

Dan moved directly to him while the others scurried for cover.

"*Who's* trophy?" Dan said.

"The trophy we won last night, goddamnit."

"The people who earned it are enjoying it," Dan said, meeting Romano's intensity stride for stride. "Would you like to congratulate them?"

"Well done, everybody," Romano managed with no emotion as he spied the cup on the table and went to grab it back. "But we have corporate visitors coming today, and it needs to be displayed where it will do us some good."

And with that, the station head completed his visit to the set and headed back to the corporate corridor clutching his prize.

"There you go, everybody, Politics 101," Dan announced. "Might makes right, power rules, and the big shots get the toys. So anybody planning to do something creative, wanting to be an artist or live outside the power grid, be advised. Somewhere, somehow, somebody will suck your blood dry."

"Yeah, but they won't have this." The set designer was carrying an even bigger cup, and placed it on the same table the other trophy was removed from. "We got it over at the props department, sprayed some gold paint on it, and bingo…"

"I love it," Dan said, and cheers went up from everybody before they got to work on the next show.

24

Tuesdays were Dan's day off, and on this March morning, the season still stuck on winter and Dan bundled up in his parka, he found himself walking past the bookend stone lions that guarded the New York Public Library in midtown. He paused to gaze at the majestic Kings of the Jungle that bordered the steps of one of New York's great buildings.

After a few moments, his focus shifted. While still looking toward the granite lions, Dan was now seeing the black-and-white photographs his mother kept in a drawer in her living room. The pictures were from a trip she had taken to Manhattan with three friends around 1950—they had to be in their late teens or maybe 20. They were posed right here, in front of the lions, petting them, reacting to them, but not brave enough to climb on top of them. The girls were laughing and having a good time and Dan could remember, going back to his childhood, how difficult it was imagining his mother that young and happy. It was as though the lions had eaten the girl in the photos. He saw ghosts of his mother and her friends right there, where they had stood 35 years earlier, and tried to rekindle their joy in the cold air, the people passing by failing to distract him.

It wasn't because of his mother that Dan was at the library. It was Linda. He'd been out to dinner with her the previous Saturday at an Italian place—Lentini's—on the eastside in the '80s. It was a family-style joint in a neighborhood where the families had plenty of cash. The kitchen nailed the campagnola—chunks of chicken, sausage, and potato mixed with peppers and onions. The conversation between them was fairly boilerplate, and Dan's attention wandered to a nearby table where three generations of a family were enjoying their meals.

"You've never mentioned your mother," he said matter-of-factly. So evenly, in fact, that Linda ignored it.

"Is she alive?" he tried again.

"Yes. As far as I know."

"That's an unusual answer," Dan said. "Most people would speak to that with some certainty."

"Do we have to get into this?"

"Get into what? It's an innocent question."

"She and Dad divorced when we were young and she didn't want anything to do with the family, so…that was about it," Linda said, hoping to close the category while opening up multiple new avenues.

"So she never wanted to see her children again?" he asked incredulously.

"I guess not," she said, again hoping to lock the door.

"Didn't your father ever explain it? Something must have happened."

"No, he didn't."

"Somehow, that's not a complete shock. And you never asked?"

"No. You about ready?"

That signaled the end of the topic as far as she was concerned. Dan stored it away, taking Lawrence's advice not to box Linda into a corner where they'd have to duel. Entering the library he headed for the archives where the microfilm of The *New York Times* was kept on file. Set up at a machine by a lovely librarian right out of small-town America, Dan began at war's end in 1945 searching each Sunday's marriage announcements.

He'd been there nearly two hours spooling the film, each containing three months worth of newspapers, onto the reels and methodically going through every Sunday edition, when he saw the heading from a 1949 paper a ¼ way down the page: Sandler-Goodman. There, pictured, was a young Lawrence Sandler posed with his bride-to-be, Roberta Goodman of Spring Valley, a lovely suburb just north of the city. They hadn't made the top of the page due to nuptials in the Harriman family, that being a longtime politically important clan in New York history whose money spanned back several generations longer than the relative nouveau wealth of the Sandlers. Still, second-position was strong in the *Times*.

Dan guessed that the former Mrs. Sandler, if the break was in fact so clean that she never bothered to keep up with her children, likely had reverted to her maiden name after leaving the clutches of Lawrence. If she hadn't remarried, Dan might have a line on finding the matriarch of this damaged branch of the family tree.

Upon returning the microfilm, Dan asked to see a phonebook. Anxiously flipping pages, his index finger eventually ran along five listings for 'Roberta Goodman.' Two were part of 'Mr. and Mrs.' listings and a third was a salon business. Dan honed in on the remaining pair. One had a downtown address on Court Street and the other was in the 70s on Central Park West. Both were good neighborhoods although different in character—new hip vs. established money.

Dan scrawled both numbers onto a piece of paper and returned the book. He made sure to rub one of the lions for luck before descending the grand stairs to the street. Back at the office, he was grateful nobody from "Sports Talk" was around. Dan wasn't in a shop-talk kind of mood. He plopped down at his desk and brought out the wrinkled paper from his pants pocket, staring at the numbers as if from their very being he could pick up a vibe. Ultimately, he went for Central Park West. This wasn't a family of hipsters, and if the divorce settlement was as large as Dan imagined, a place with a view of the park wasn't out of the question.

"Ms. Goodman?" Dan asked, being sure to use the non-committal female title. "This is Dan Henry, I'm the host of 'Sports Talk' on Channel 7."

"I'm afraid I'm not much of a sports fan," the voice over the phone replied.

"Actually, I identified myself because I didn't want you to think it was some wacko calling," Dan said. "I'm dating your daughter, Linda, that is, if I have the correct Ms. Goodman."

"Well, good for you, dear. How's that going?"

"Would you have time to talk?"

25

Roberta Goodman's place certainly wasn't a disappointment. Dan wouldn't have gotten past the lobby desk had he not been expected and his name left with the guards. There was a doorman and an elevator operator, and for all he knew, room service too. Ms. Goodman ("Call me Roberta, dear") was a charming and handsome woman full of confidence and comfortable in her lair. She graciously showed Dan around the place, although he got off the tour to gawk at the incredible view of the park from her living room glass doors and terrace. The décor was modern without crossing the line of ostentatious, and Roberta asked Dan to sit with her on a cream-colored wrap-around leather sofa. The woman who had been cleaning during the tour now brought a tray with a pot of tea, mugs emblazoned with 'Lincoln Center,' and a variety of inviting pastry, which Dan eyeballed.

"Dig in. They're from Zabar's, quite delicious, and you'll be saving me from devouring them all myself," Roberta said. She didn't have to ask him twice.

"We seem to have a problem communicating," Dan said after the formalities were finished, the pastries broken into, and the tea sipped. "Linda is very hesitant to cross a certain line. More like a barrier."

Roberta stared at him, emotionless.

"I'm sorry, was it a mistake for me to come and talk to you?"

"No, dear, not at all. I admire your gumption. After all, I'm sure she didn't give you my number. Have you met Linda's father?"

"Yes, several times. And each occasion is kind of bizarre."

"I understand."

"Ms. Goodman…"

"Roberta."

"Roberta--I don't want to rifle you for information, forgive me if I'm prying…"

"Well, I'm not sure you've come to the right place, Dan. I haven't seen my daughter in 10 years. My sons bring their families here; I go see them at their homes. But Linda…"

The phone rang, with Roberta quickly excusing herself and announcing she'd get it. A conversation ensued about a fundraiser for the Philharmonic the following week. Roberta was obviously very active in the arts, with mementos from the symphony, opera, ballet, and various other cultural organizations splayed about the living room. She ended the phone conversation while Dan was processing that Linda had lied to him about her brothers not seeing their mother.

"Has she talked about Susan?" asked Roberta, sitting back near Dan.

"Susan? No, not to my recollection."

Dan stared at Roberta, wondering into what family drama he had placed himself.

"Lawrence was very dashing when we met. We both came from good families, and by 'good,' I do mean wealthy. It was a whirlwind romance between two kids. We did all the things we were supposed to—bought a beautiful home; Lawrence started his employment in the penthouse and went up from there; we raised a full family. I came to realize Lawrence had a bit of a dark side, but I didn't know how dark it was, not until it was too late.

"The girls—Linda and Susan--were twins and very close, as you'd expect. I didn't dress them like doubles or any of that; that seemed so, I don't know, too cute by half. But they did everything together. They were very smart, much more serious than their older brothers, more determined, you might say.

"They were 13. I remember because it was the year they were going to all the Bar and Bat Mitzvahs—I don't know how much you know of Jewish tradition. I was walking Linda to a party a few blocks away. Susan hadn't been feeling well and remained at home. I stayed at the party for a bit—I was friends with the parents of the girl having the get-together. Linda was getting sick as well and we left early and returned home.

"I was going to put Linda to bed, and when we opened the door, there was Lawrence. And Susan. It seemed like an eternity. The four of us, frozen in place like some sick, twisted snapshot, a picture I've tried ever since to get out of my mind. Linda, and I'm going to play psychiatrist here, likely suppressed what she saw.

"The next year or two were God awful. I begged Lawrence to go get counseling, kept telling him he was sick, and he just got angrier. I tried to help the girls all I could. Lawrence absolutely forbade me to take them for help; he was more worried about his reputation than the girls' well-being.

"Susan was never the same. She withdrew and grew distant, even from Linda. Certainly from us. I never touched Lawrence again, never allowed him near me. It was a loveless marriage. When they turned 15, I sent Susan to boarding school in New England. I thought the change might help. I was naïve about that. Linda hated it that I split them up. I was just trying to save Susan. She'd become a stranger in her own home.

"Two months into it, Susan took a roommate's prescription pills and ate them all. Linda blamed me for Susan's death. After what her father did, she blamed me. I began divorce proceedings against Lawrence the day after the funeral. It was going to be messy with a lot of ugly charges, unfortunately, none of which I could prove. He bought my silence with an insane amount of money.

"I beat myself up over not fighting for Susan's sake, not punishing the man who did that to her. But ultimately he would have crushed it. He would have bought the judicial process, and the principle would have ended up buried along with her. So I took the money and I've tried to do the best I could with it. Bring joy to people through the arts, and establish an endowment for abused children that has raised more than $10 million the past 10 years.

"It's not a very pretty story, is it? All the wealth one could want and happy, healthy children, and then this…"

Dan had trouble catching his breath, extraordinary since he'd barely moved in 30 minutes. He danced around Linda's closeness with Lawrence, but Roberta couldn't answer the question one way or the other that hung, unasked, over the room. He thanked Roberta for her time, declined the offer of a pastry doggy bag, and retraced his steps down out of the world of the filthy rich and back onto the street, where he desperately needed the air and the time it would take him to walk downtown.

26

The weather had turned still colder in the late afternoon, and with it the city. Dan sneered at the chill, disgusted by all the sickness of the human condition and the thousands of terrible ways it could manifest. The ticking time bombs that click off second by second inside these anonymous bodies walking around. The explosions both overt and subtle. Criminal behavior, evil, the inability to love or communicate. Jails and psychiatric offices full of them, and so too the streets and offices and homes. He felt the shadows where nothing was as it seemed. The false advertising with which each of us presents ourselves to the world. For every Peter Tosh there were thousands who traded in the currencies of greed and lust and self-interest and purely sick cravings and sadness. Dan noticed now the sunken glaze of so many eyes passing by, the darkness that circled them, dirt brought to faces like a powerful magnet.

Dan's heart was filling with the failure of a relationship that hadn't ended. He'd thought enough times—warning signs flashing-- that it would get here. But through the suppression we all use he clung to the hope that makes life bearable. His grip now could only last for so long.

With night closing in, Dan didn't feel like going home. As if following some pre-programmed route, he found himself back at the base of those mountainous steps leading up to the library. Slowly he climbed past the strength of the lions and back into the womb of knowledge, afraid to confirm what he strongly suspected to be the truth.

Roberta Goodman had certainly seemed stable, but considering the family he was dealing with Dan wasn't in the mood to take anybody's word for anything. Back to the microfilm room he went, aided this time by a specific timeline to research. It was not lost on him that he now searched not the wedding announcements, but the death notices. It took 10 minutes to find the news of Susan Sandler's demise. The circumstances were appropriately vague, but there was nothing in the general dates and studied lack of description that even slightly contradicted Roberta's account.

Linda's inability to get inside arms-length with him, to be truly intimate, clear to him now, Dan began rolling different scenarios over in his head. All ended up at the same destination. The story hadn't changed since Adam and Eve. Somewhere Dan's mind played a trick, having him believe that just perhaps, after he laid all the cards on the table, Linda would finally find her knight in shining armor, the man who understood where her pain came from, and through that they could go on, grow, and discover the missing pieces that up to now had lain beyond their grasp. What choice did he have?

Dan's apartment seemed darker and danker than usual when he walked in, the only light coming from the blinking red diode of his phone message machine. Dan dropped his mail on the coffee table, turned on a lamp and turned up the heat, and peeled off his jacket. He retrieved his phone message, the voice of Lawrence Sandler knocking the wind out of him.

"Noon Friday."

Dan's initial anger was directed at the man behind that voice whose full sickness he had just come to realize. A man who would do the unspeakable to his own flesh and blood, driving an innocent child to an early grave, and be more concerned with saving face than seeking help. The man who had ruined Dan's relationship with Linda before he had even met her. He had disliked Lawrence from the first moment, then tolerated him for his own personal gain. And that pushed Dan's anger inward. How was he different from any other whore who was bought off for money or fame or the promise of something out there unduly gained? He allowed himself to be used, to be treated like an inferior by this man who operated at large only because he was able to treat everyone that way.

The TV show, the ratings, the scoops all of a sudden didn't amount to much as Dan stared across his room, seeing only rage where the walls and windows were.

27

Linda was in an unusually good mood when they met for lunch that Thursday at the Carnegie Deli in the theater district on Broadway. Dan's morning had been busy with a bunch of bureaucratic paperwork including evaluations of staffers and expense reports and budget meetings—a bunch of crap that had nothing to do with creating a quality TV show. They had also kept him from cementing a strategy for his meeting with Linda. He wanted to proceed slowly, cautiously, but he wasn't sure how calm he could remain, or figure out how to get inside an unapproachable topic. In lieu of a plan, he remained quiet but smiling while she carried the discussion over a series of mundane topics.

"Did I tell you Sam got almost straight A's in school?"

"That's great."

"The only 'B' was in gym. You might have to work harder with him on his ball playing."

Dan knew right then no strategy was going to save this. The right moment would never come.

"I know about Susan," he said quietly. Linda gave him a quizzical look, either not understanding or not wanting to, leaving the heavy lifting to him.

"Your sister. I know…everything."

"How…why in the world would you…"

"Linda, it isn't working between you and me. I'm like a familiar stranger in your life, but I can't get inside. I didn't know why. I tried to find out."

"Did my father…"

"No."

"How? I want to know how."

"Look, Linda, every day for the past year and a half I've been trying to find some way to connect with you. How to really connect. You wouldn't…look, I don't blame you for not opening up. Maybe I'm just not that important to you. Maybe you can't trust anyone. But you *are* that important to me."

"It was her, wasn't it? She pulled my sister and me apart, and now you. Right?"

Dan had picked the Carnegie because the ambient noise would drown out most individual conversations, but Linda's voice had now risen to a level that attracted glances from surrounding tables, people stopping in mid-bite of their sour pickles.

"You're not listening to me."

"She's a liar and you believe her."

"Linda, please…"

Linda grabbed her coat and rushed out of the restaurant as their food was being delivered. Dan got up, bumped into the waiter, pulled a twenty out of his wallet and dropped it on the table, and raced out after her just in time to see Linda close the door of a taxi that sped away before he could get to the curb. Damn cabs are never around when you need one, Dan thought, and when you don't want one, boom. He knew it was quite possible that arm yanking the car door closed would be the last he'd see of Linda Sandler.

88

Dan began walking simply to do something. He made a note to himself that he needed better shoes if he was going to continue doing all this thinking on the sidewalks. The meet with Linda went about how he figured and feared. The defense systems we carry around with us are all but impenetrable. Everything is everybody else's fault. Why try to understand our own shortcomings when we can rage at somebody else?

As he got downtown an hour later, Dan realized he truly was hungry now, having left the sandwich at the Carnegie untouched. He ducked into a pizzeria and ordered a slice, realizing all at once it was Gino's, the place he and Gregg had eaten the day they met at the record store. The slice was greasy and good; at least some things you could count on. Ten minutes later he entered the small vestibule of an older building on Lower Broadway. Dan took the ancient elevator up to the office space of Mitch's new business, CVC, a weekly magazine covering the exploding world of music videos.

It was the perfect business endeavor for Mitch, who had an endless amount of nervous energy that would be absorbed in creating and raising a magazine from scratch. A couple of enthusiastic employees scurried about the small space, creating cover art, watching videos, working the phones. Mitch's small office was piled high with VCR tapes and record company promotional posters and gadgets. Mitch was connected to some major dudes in the music world thanks to his days in college radio. It all felt right.

"Welcome to the wacky world of media," Dan said, settling into the folding chair in Mitch's office as his friend got off a phone call. "How's it going?"

"Great. We've signed up 200 subscribers in two weeks. And the right people too, at the major labels and the hot indies. I think we're gonna kick ass."

"I'm a little concerned about Plus/Minus. What happened to those guys?" Dan said, referring to the band from Washington Square Park.

"That's funny; Felix, the bass player, called today. One of them joined the Navy; one of them's in rehab; and one took a job selling insurance with his father's firm. I don't think they're gonna miss me."

"Rock 'n' roll. It's so goddamn reliable."

"So what's going on with you? How's the girl? You know, forgive me for saying so, but she seems a little too good for you. Classy, beautiful, sharp, funny…"

"We just broke up."

"Aah, you're better off."

At the worst of times, Mitch could somehow get a big laugh out of Dan, who filled his friend in on the details, not realizing what a fascinating story it made for when you weren't in the middle of it.

"Wow, the father sounds like a real dirtbag," Mitch said at the conclusion.

"Yeah, so am I for doing business with him," Dan noted. "You know, I've got agents using me to help clients; staffers using me to get ahead; ex-jocks using me to find better jobs, Sandler manipulating my relationship…I'm tired of all of it."

"C'mon, man, you could still be at the record store."

"Don't laugh. At least it was honest."

"No gain, no pain."

28

Dan purposely left his sport coat at home for his Friday meeting with Lawrence Sandler. Arriving first, he was helped on with the usual house garment by the maitre d', who was by now familiar with Dan and almost tolerant of him. The jacket fit as poorly this day as it had months earlier, and Dan sat down at Sandler's table. He hadn't prepared anything to say. Sandler presented himself five minutes late, as usual, and took the seat across from Dan. Their waiter was on them instantly.

"We won't be eating today," Sandler said.

"I'll have the two-pound lobster. Wrap it up to go," Dan deadpanned to the server.

"Nothing today," Sandler said firmly when the waiter looked at him for confirmation of Dan's order.

"I really feel like seafood," Dan said, trying to get under Sandler's skin any way he could.

"You've upset Linda. Very much," said Sandler. "Irreparably as far as you're concerned."

"I guess I just don't know the right buttons to push, like you do," Dan replied, keeping it low-key.

"You once asked me if I liked you. The truth is, I actually did a little bit. When I thought you were smarter than you apparently are."

"That makes me feel really, really good."

"You shouldn't believe what certain people tell you. You're a reporter, you should know that."

"Now that we're not eating and have all this time to kill, go right ahead and tell me your side of the story."

"There is nothing you need to know."

"Start with your daughter Susan. Tell me all about her."

Dan ignored Sandler's stare that silently screamed 'Shut up or I'll kill you.'

"Tell me about how a happy, healthy young girl suddenly became dark and depressed and withdrawn, even from her twin sister with whom she'd been inseparable."

Sandler continued to fix Dan with coal black eyes.

"Tell me why she killed herself."

"It's sad when people think they know something that they actually know nothing about."

"Alright, we'll start with Linda then. I know something about her. She has this very weird relationship with her father, a dependency that goes against everything else in her personality. And she has this impenetrable fear of intimacy with other people in her life, almost like, I don't know, something happened early on that made her distrustful. There, want to chat about that?"

"You know, I originally asked you here today to give you a major piece of news."

"Well, my loss."

"Now I only have this--Linda doesn't want to see you."

"Good thing I'm sitting. And thank you so much for being her errand boy. You know how messy these things can get in person."

"You were wrong, trying to bring this up to her."

"When were you wrong, Larry? When you had sex with your own daughter? Or did you actually screw both of them?"

"I, too, have had quite enough of you."

Sandler began getting out of his seat but Dan pushed the table forward, knocking Sandler back into the chair and pinning him against the wall.

"You listen to me, asshole," Dan said. "I don't want any part of you or your dysfunctional family. And if you're too rich and too powerful to get what's coming to you in this life, I pray you get paid back in the next one."

By now the other patrons were staring at the two of them, though their voices hadn't been raised. Dan got up, shed his sport coat, and threw it at Sandler, landing it over his head as he left the club.

29

Dan was finding it increasingly difficult to concentrate on work. Despite his brave words to Lawrence, he thought about Linda constantly, the excitement of that first day meeting her and how alive it had made him feel. The mind is an amazing piece of gear, rewinding to the good parts without all those annoying little details that spoil the fun. He knew it was over, at least 99.9% sure, but he had to hear it from her. A daily phone call had gone unreturned for three days, but Dan wondered if his absence would have had some effect on her. Not likely.

Then, of course, there was Lawrence. Dan needed to watch his back and not give anyone any reason to think he was slipping. As it was, rumors were flying around the station about changes up and down the organization. Something was in the air, and it wasn't the sweet scent of good and inevitable change. It was the unwanted smell of a pile of dog crap sitting on the living room carpet just out of sight behind the sofa.

"You feel alright?" Gregg said as Dan sat at his desk, staring a hole through his blotter.

"Yeah, why?" Dan lied.

"The meeting this morning with Romano, you didn't make one wisecrack. It was a first."

"Just off my game today."

"Linda?"

"Yeah, I guess."

"Don't worry, you'll get laid again. It might take four or five years."

"Thanks for the pep talk."

"Hey, that's what friends are for. How do you want to handle the hot dog segment on Sunday?"

"What?"

"The hot dog-eating contest. Remember?"

"Shit, that's this week?"

They had booked the defending champion of Nathan's hot dog eating contest on the show, and of course Dan would have to challenge him on the air.

"Can't we tape that one afternoon so I don't barf?" Dan asked hopefully.

"No shot. The guy's booked full. We've got him for the taping only."

"Make it three minutes. I can't get too sick in just three minutes."

"How about four? This is dynamite TV."

"What are you, nuts? You can't show me tossing on the air."

"No, but we can get right up to it. Four minutes it is."

Gregg walked away happy as could be. Dan thought about dialing Linda's number again, but held back. If only he could accept that things never work out, it would be so much easier.

You can't turn the page until you get to the very end of it, Dan told himself as he settled down onto the concrete steps of Linda's brownstone. He needed to hear it while looking into her eyes. It was 3 o'clock, a good half-hour before Linda would be bringing Sam home from school if they were running on their normal schedule, and so Dan pulled the afternoon edition of the New York *Post* out of his jacket pocket and commenced scanning the sports section.

It was a sunny spring day in New York, the kind you wished you could package up and trot out the rest of the year when the humidity of summer and the chill of winter set in. One week into the baseball season and the Yankees were struggling. The *Post* was screaming for the head of manager Dick Howard as general manager Mike DeJean preached patience, an attribute not in the DNA of the city's tabloids. Dan shook his head at the insanity of judging someone by the first eight games of a 162-game season, then remembered a snippet from his recent lunch with Lawrence Sandler—'I asked you here today to give you a major piece of news.' Holy shit, they really could be canning the manager already, Dan mumbled to himself. He'd need to check with every source he could muster.

"Hey Dan…" Sam's voice interrupted Dan's musing, but by the time he looked up, the youngster, remembering something Linda must have told him, had clammed up and uncharacteristically fallen in a step behind her.

"How ya doin' there, big guy?" Dan said, valiantly sounding upbeat.

Linda subtly pulled her son around her to the front, giving him the signal that it was O.K. to talk.

"Good. Can we play some more ball?"

"Well, I'd like that very much."

"Sam, go on up and tell Maria to fix you your snack. I'll be right there."

"O.K. See ya, Dan."

"See ya, big guy," Dan said, feeling guilty. He hated skirting the truth with the kid. When did the innocence end? When Santa Claus and the Easter Bunny were exposed as frauds? When a family member dies? When your first girlfriend breaks up with you? It's just a matter of time, and when they start coming at you, all the lies about security and safety and mythical creatures and the super-natural greatness of your parents, and love, they come in a torrent, drowning the beliefs that once made sleep so easy and waking so joyful. Sam deserved more; all kids did.

Linda and Dan watched Sam enter the house. Her expression offered Dan nothing.

"How are you?" he started.

"Alright. What are you doing here?"

There wouldn't be a lot of small talk.

"We haven't had a chance to speak. I just wanted to make sure of where things stood. Whether you think there's something worth saving here."

Silence.

"I miss you, Linda, I thought maybe you might miss me a little."

"Of course I miss you."

Dan knew right then he could fold up his newspaper and be on his way, but he somberly listened.

"If you need to make this about me, that's fine," she said. "I can handle it. I can handle anything."

"I'm not asking you to handle it, I'm asking if you have any feelings for me."

"Let's leave it be, Dan. We gave it a good shot and I don't regret anything."

"Don't you regret it didn't work out?"

"We have no control over that."

"How can you be so fatalistic? This is your life."

"I have a son I didn't plan to have. I had a sister who I certainly didn't plan doing what she did. Every day things happen that are out of our control and all we can do is react to them. I tried, Dan. The best I could. I've got to go."

Linda pushed on past the step on which Dan was sitting, walking up toward her home and out of his life.

The anguish and the emptiness and the anguish over the emptiness came rushing back over Dan the next few days, and would pull up a chair and make themselves at home for the foreseeable future. Relationship failure was certainly cause for panic; each time it seemed as though the best chance had passed, and now he would spend his days wandering alone in the desert, tortured by every song on the radio and each couple he encountered looking so happy together.

Dan sat in the darkness of the apartment trying to pinpoint what exactly it was that was wrong with him. He'd tried to commit. So what was it now? A fatal personality flaw? Too tough to get along with? A secret desire to fail? Shooting too high with his affections?

When he was tired of kicking sand in his own face, he began the phase of hating and blaming Linda. Her screwed-up family; misplaced priorities;

inability to get off the shoals upon which her emotional life had been impaled. Whatever happened to that charming and witty woman with whom he had begun? Why couldn't he have seen how messed up she was right off jump street? How could he not have put it together? Why? How? Sleep was a godsend. Waking up sucked. Shit, the alarm was ringing and he was having to face another day.

Dan completely threw himself into the hot dog-eating segment. Being in the right mood to exact revenge on anything, including his own body, Dan made sure he'd be in peak form, eating lunch the day before the taping and nothing further. He showed up at the studio Sunday morning lean and hungry.

"A lot of people don't consider what you do a sport," Dan said to Joe Cutter, the hot dog-eating king, during the taping. "What is your answer, other than throwing up all over them?"

Cutter was a good sport, answering each question like he hadn't heard them a couple hundred times before.

"What is your diet away from the eating contests?"

"I like salads."

"For the novelty?"

"Absolutely."

"Now, we have a little challenge set up here. Are you afraid an amateur eater…is that right, I mean, I eat all the time, so I'm really kind of a professional eater, don't you think?

"You're a non-competitive eater."

"Right. Are you afraid a non-competitive eater like me is going to out-mouth you?"

"You may out-mouth me, but you're not likely to out-eat me, no."

"Not afraid at all?"

"No."

"How about Marv over there? He's a big man. Figure he could give you a tussle?"

"Let me answer that," Marv Wallace interrupted. "I won't give him a tussle because I'm not insane enough to stuff all them hot dogs down my throat."

"Let me correct you," Dan sniped. "You're definitely insane enough, you're just chicken."

"Chicken, hot dogs, whatever. I'm not doing it."

The segment was going well, and Dan played it for all it was worth. "Earl, what about you?"

"I'd love to, but I had a big breakfast."

"Sure you did. Carp?"

"What?"

"What do you mean, 'what?' Haven't you been paying attention?"

"No."

"I'm asking if…"

"No."

"You guys are great. All right, Cutter, looks like it's just me and you. We've got it all set up over here."

Dan and Cutter walked to a counter, placed in front of a cheesy background picture of an ocean.

"Look at this," said Dan. "We've got the ocean right in back of us just like at Coney Island. And we've got authentic Nathan's hot dogs."

"Sounds good."

"So the rules are we have four minutes to eat as many hot dogs as we can. Now, does that include the buns?"

"Absolutely."

"I'm not sure I get that. I mean, the hot dogs are the hot dogs. Why are the buns part of the deal?"

"You wouldn't have anything to hold on to without the buns."

"Are we still talking about hot dogs here?"

"No."

"I didn't think so."

"I'll give you some advice with the buns…"

"O.K."

"Eat them separately, and dunk them in water first. Makes them easier to get down."

"I'm more concerned with *keeping* them down."

"That I can't help you with."

"All right, so we each have a plate in front of us. Gregg, how many hot dogs are there here?" Dan said to Gregg, who stood off stage.

"Twenty apiece."

"You sure that's enough? O.K., let me get warmed up here."

Dan, milking the moment beautifully, did a little stretching and exercising, then began moving his mouth into various positions making funny faces. The studio audience was absolutely loving the piece.

"You're not warming up," Dan said to Cutter.

"I'm good."

Dan went through his final machinations, looking like Art Carney's great character Ed Norton on "The Honeymooners" before performing the simplest of chores.

"I'm ready," Dan finally intoned. "Shoot the gun, and please, go ahead and hit me with the bullet."

Dan gave a spirited account of himself, gamely jamming in hot dogs and then the buns. The four minutes seemed to stretch about a half hour to him, but he kept eating, and when the final buzzer sounded, he had polished off 10 franks. Cutter, who was toying with him, downed 16 without trying. Dan made a show of it, holding his stomach and puffing out his cheeks, wrapping a towel around his head, and waving a miniature American flag.

"Let that be a lesson to you," he said to Cutter.

"You did a nice job; you might have a pretty good future."

"I know exactly what's in my future, and it ain't pretty. We'll be back, although it might take a while."

30

D an was happy enough to have the show in which to immerse himself. While he had managed intellectually to convince himself he and Linda were never going to be right for each other, emotionally he was lagging well behind. He reminded himself of his loneliness constantly over the next couple of weeks.

"So, she was beautiful and successful and smart," Gregg said helpfully.

They were sitting at Rudy's, Gregg finally having convinced Dan to get out of his apartment for an evening.

"You've got to know a thousand downtown new wave chicks with purple hair," Gregg continued. "So they don't shave under their arms; that doesn't make them bad people."

"I'm unclear. Did you drag me out here to cheer me up or make me suicidal?"

"It's such a thin line when you think about it."

"Yeah, well, I don't want to."

Gregg was performing an age-old friend's task for Dan, and both were well aware of it. Dan appreciated the effort to pull him out of the doldrums, but that wasn't going to happen tonight.

"How 'bout that one?" Gregg said, referring to a brunette at the bar.

"In the red? I couldn't afford her make-up bill. Gregg, you don't have to scout for me. I don't need to fill this order tonight."

"Well, it wouldn't hurt. You've been moping around for two weeks."

"And I'm gonna keep moping till I get really good at it. More people should try moping. You can find out a lot about yourself."

"Ah, here comes the rest of the party."

Dan turned toward the door to see who comprised Gregg's party list.

"I can't believe you made this a public event," he said unhappily.

"So, the broad got tired of your three-inch killer? That was a 4-to-5 shot."

Dan was not overly enthused as Sonny and Vic Murray took seats at the table. But he knew he had no recourse but to rise to the occasion and return fire.

"Have you ever even been out on a second date with a woman?"

"Why would anybody do that when there's new talent everywhere?"

"I told you I'd cheer you up tonight," Gregg said while Vic flagged down a waitress.

"I could actually be home working on my coin collection," said Dan.

"C'mon, numb nuts, live a little bit. You're free," said Sonny. "Did you think you were gonna marry that girl?"

"It was a possibility."

"She was a little aloof, don't you think?"

"No."

"I've seen Eskimos less frigid."

"You're an idiot."

"Let me tell you something my second wife taught me," chimed in Vic. "Do not spend time worrying about the hole you just crawled out of. Concentrate on the next one."

"Your wife taught you that, huh?" said Dan. "Hard to believe you could leave anyone that wise."

"We had other issues."

"Hey, I really appreciate the guys' night out. I just feel more like suffering in private for now."

Dan pushed back his chair.

"Whoa, whoa there, big guy," said Vic, before turning to Gregg. "Didn't you tell him?"

"Never got the chance."

"Tell me what?"

"You've never met Rudy, have you?" said Vic. "Not many have."

"Rudy, as in Rudy's?" asked Dan.

"One and the same," said Vic. "When you get to know Rudy, you get to know your way around here a little bit, you do each other a favor now and again, you get a few perks, know what I mean?"

"I haven't a clue."

"There are some rooms in the back."

"Sounds great. I still have no idea what you're talking about."

"We lined you up to get a hummer from a hostess," Sonny said, fast-forwarding to the meat of the matter. "You man enough?"

"I'm man enough to say 'no.' "

"That's not an option."

"We had to pull strings for this, buddy boy," said Vic, who Dan was coming to like less and less with each passing meeting.

"Maybe someone should have consulted me."

"Didn't want to ruin the surprise," Vic said.

"We thought it would help…" Gregg said.

"I can't believe you were in on this," said Dan.

"Just marginally. These two were the masterminds."

"Such as it is," Dan said.

"She's a real pro," Sonny chimed in. "Your choice, spit or swallow."

"What is the matter with you?"

"Hey, look, this isn't a conference on world peace," Sonny said. "Go get your oil changed."

A couple of drinks later, Dan found himself in the back of Rudy's in a room decked out like a hotel suite. His date, Donna, was nice enough, but not overly so. Dan sat on the couch.

"Can I get you a drink?" she asked.

"I'm good," Dan noted, and began to unlace a shoe.

"What are you doing?" she asked sharply, causing Dan to look up. "I mean, this is just a blowjob, right?"

"Yeah, yeah, that's all it is," Dan said, quitting his shoe and sliding down his zipper.

31

The wrap party is a nice tradition on TV shows, kind of a year-end prom when all the workers are entitled to get loaded up on food and drink and, with all immodest aggrandizement, look back on their monumental contributions.

By all measures, "Sports Talk's" second season was a big hit. For the network, it was a green gusher of cash. The ratings continued to far outpace all competition and the content, headed by its unorthodox host, remained consistently solid and informative. Even after the defection of Lawrence Sandler, Dan had been able to cobble together enough sources to deliver insights and inside information to hold his reputation. Team employees had actually started calling him with tips, making it that much easier to stay a step ahead of the newspapermen looking for the same scoops.

Dan, who knew his way around a dance floor, was working on a solid half-hour getting out his pent-up energy on the boards partnered with Nancy Woods, the station's weekend weatherperson. She was, superficially, the type of woman Dan would be instantly intimidated by—classically pretty with gorgeous, long blond hair. But inhibitions had no place at a soiree like this, particularly when Nancy had approached him to tell him she loved the show. She had moved to New York from Pittsburgh nine months earlier to pursue a career in modeling. Things were going OK, with a gig modeling swimsuits and jeans in Sears catalogs. She was 'discovered' while doing temp secretarial work at the station, and before she knew it she was reading copy off the Teleprompter about marine layers and offshore flows, informing millions about whether their weekend plans would be wet or dry.

Given the choice of sitting at the adults' table talking shop with Romano and Gregg or writhing his body in very close proximity to Nancy's, Dan was hoping the music would never stop. When it did, he made sure he kept her in eye contact as he answered Gregg's request to come over for a word. Dan had hit the tequila hard enough to be feeling no pain, so Gregg ushered him a safe distance from Romano to set up a lunch meeting for the following day. A sober Dan would have questioned the odd timing of such a get-together, but tonight's version placed it on the back-burner.

He carried his drink, and one for Nancy, to where she was being cornered by first-string weatherman Jack Dakota, a middle-aged, thrice-married, well-known letch around the station. Nancy accepted the drink from Dan and brightened up at the intrusion.

"Jack, Jerry Romano wants to see you," said Dan. "And he's in a very good mood."

"Really? Probably about the raise I've demanded. Would you excuse me?"

"Let's take a walk," Dan said to Nancy. "When he finds out I was lying about Romano, I don't want to be in sight."

"You're bad," she said, not disapprovingly.

"Of course, if you two were hitting it off…"

"We can run if you don't want to walk."

"That's my girl."

When he propositioned her about coming home with him, she hadn't hesitated. Dan liked his odds for a happy ending to the evening.

Those were only enhanced when Nancy asked for something more comfortable to slip into back at his place. Given complete access to his closet, she emerged wearing a pale blue button-down shirt and nothing else. A woman could dress in the finest European fashions head to toe and not improve on the sexiness of wearing only a man's shirt.

Dan woke up the next morning with a smile on his face. Nancy's arm laid across his chest, her face buried between his shoulder and neck. Dan looked at this beautiful woman and realized the pain accrued from his frustrations with Linda had drained out of him.

Katz' Delicatessen in Lower Manhattan is quintessential New York. It's been around since the invention of meat and generations of Jews and others have gotten their fill of fine cured beef and cholesterol there in sandwiches piled six inches high. Their sign, raised during WWII to "Send a salami to your boy in the Army" didn't exactly rhyme, but made the place even more famous. The Stage Deli and the Carnegie, both started up in midtown in the theater district, might as well put up signs that they were for tourists only. Katz', and less-famous delis in Brooklyn and the Bronx were the real deal.

Gregg hadn't been so enthusiastic about travelling that far downtown for his pastrami, but Dan had insisted. He was going to spend the first day of his sabbatical over at Mitch's office catching up on a bunch of new music videos that streamed into the place for review. Then he and Mitch were heading uptown for the Yankee game that night. Memorial Day weekend was coming, and summer stretched out before them.

Dan was hitting the sauerkraut and pickle bucket on the table when Gregg strode in.

"How was the weather report?" Gregg asked, taking a chair.

Dan didn't get the question.

"Nancy…," Gregg prodded him.

"It got humid. Moist. Some precipitation," Dan said. "Pleasant."

"You are one lucky son of a bitch. And you owe it all to me."

"That's why I'm buying," Dan said, standing to retrieve the orders that were ready.

They tore into the rye bread smothered in spicy mustard and pastrami making small talk about the wrap party and the various drunken behavior that had ensued as the night grew later. The taxi cabs had been kept busy shuttling revelers home to points near and far throughout the city.

A pregnant pause hung over the conversation that edged Dan toward his fleeting thought from the night before.

"Odd time for a meeting," he said, opening the business portion of the discussion.

Gregg put his sandwich down, wiped some grease and mustard off his face. "There are some changes coming."

Gregg had tried to keep his tone matter-of-fact, but that couldn't hide the ominous sound of the words he was speaking. Dan looked at him but wasn't going to help him along. He waited for the specifics.

"The boys at network love the job Romano's done. They gave him the big bump to head of ABC Sports. National. And he wants to take me with him, producing live events. NBA, U.S. Open, Indy 500…"

"That's great, man. When did this all go down?"

"Been in the works the last month or so. Romano let me in on it last week. It's an unbelievable shot. Really big."

"Congratulations."

"Yeah, thanks. The guy they're bringing in to replace Romano locally is some analyst from a consulting firm. I'm not sure what he knows about TV, but seems like he's got some definite ideas and plans."

Dan suddenly sensed his cholesterol and agitation levels rising from deep within his stomach.

"They want you to keep running the show, but they don't want you on-air," Gregg said evenly, finally getting to the reason for the lunch.

"What? The ratings have never been better."

"I know. I know. Dan, I made all the arguments. They don't want to hear it."

"*You* made the arguments? What am I, a mute? No one talks to me?"

"It wouldn't have done any good."

"Why not?"

"I told you, he's got his own ideas. And Romano didn't exactly go to the mat on your behalf. All those one-liners you blasted him with, turns out they didn't go over his head. He's not a fan."

"No, why should he be? I'm the jerk that pumped his revenue up and made his balance sheet look good."

"That's not how he sees it."

"What's the name of this consulting firm?"

"The guy's name is Stevens. From, uh, Sandler and Lambert, I think it is."

"Oh Christ."

"What? You know the guy?"

Dan buried his head deep in both hands, shaking it in disbelief.

"I don't know the stooge, no. I know his master. Sandler is Linda's father, the guy I tuned up in the middle of his own club."

"Eight million people and it's still a small town. Look, Dan, they still want to keep you on."

"Yeah, sounds like a great situation."

"It's the same paycheck, and it's still your show."

"We both know it's not my fuckin' show anymore."

"Will you at least think about it? You've got six weeks. They want you in the middle of July to begin working on the new season. If you haven't come up with anything better, you've got it to fall back on."

"All the shit you have to eat, Gregg, does it ever get to you?"

"It's not my network, and unless I hit the lottery, I'm probably not going to own one in the near future."

Dan had lost his appetite, and the comically large sandwich sat 3/4s untouched in front of him. When the hell was he going to be able to finish a deli sandwich? His friend across the table was moving up in the world, and yet Dan felt badly for him in a way that had nothing to do with status or money or accomplishment. What had Mitch said? 'No gain, no pain.' Dan put aside his own anger, and any judgment of his friend.

"Listen, I'm sorry. I should be thanking you for everything."

"Why change now?"

"Eat me."

Late that night Dan weighed over his conversation with Gregg, his situation if he decided to go forward with "Sports Talk," and his other options, none of which were presently known to him. He thought back to Peter Tosh and about integrity and taking the road whose path one had to clear as he went. He was up the entire night, the parade of thoughts never slowing down enough to let him slip off to sleep.

Dan got to the office early the next morning and packed up his rolodex and any papers of value. He was paging through his files when a friendly sort approached with outstretched hand.

"I'm Jeff Stevens, the new affiliate manager. I recognize you from TV."

"Very perceptive," Dan said, giving Jeff a wet-fish handshake that would make a mobster proud.

"Doing some housecleaning," offered Jeff, making conversation.

"So I hear."

"No, I mean you, you're housecleaning."

"It seems like a good time."

"We really love your work on "Sports Talk.""

"Then why are you taking me off the air?"

"Well, we have some new concepts we think can improve the show. Give it greater recognition with a top-flight popular personality. And we think you're the man behind the scenes that can help make it happen."

"Have you checked the ratings lately?"

"Most impressive."

"And so you're changing it."

"People want fresh, they want shiny and new."

"You work with Lawrence Sandler?"

"Yes, and he is as excited about this as I am. We just love what you've been able to bring."

Of course Lawrence would keep this empty suit in the dark, operating on a need-to-know basis that was his calling card, Dan thought. He wouldn't have a clue of their little history. Or of Lawrence's real thoughts, ever.

"I'd love to get together soon and toss a few ideas around," Stevens said, the smile still splashed across his fresh features.

Behind Stevens, Dan saw Nancy Woods studying some pages near the wire machine. "Yes, I felt like tossing the instant I saw you," Dan said, brushing past Stevens. Unfortunately for him, word travels faster than his feet.

"Hey, Nancy, how ya doin'?"

"Oh, Dan. Hi." The greeting was perfunctory, lacking any conviction or emotion.

"Getting an early jump on the weekend forecast?"

"Jack Dakota got in some trouble with the cops the night of the wrap party. He's sitting out a week."

"Listen, I thought we might go out, catch some music one night."

"Oh, I'm kind of busy right now." She made no effort to throw out an alternate timetable or plan, then got called by the news manager.

"I guess I've got to go."

Dan slid back to his desk, feeling the full brunt of life as an ex-TV personality. The place felt like one large chunk of depression to him, and he began tossing items in a box as quickly as he could. The phone rang as he was about to exit.

"This is Dan."

"Dan, it's Mike Apple from *New York* magazine. How ya doin'?"

"Moving out for the season."

"Glad I caught you. I was having drinks with Sonny Catapano last night..."

"And you're up this early? Impressive."

"Yeah, I know. Dedication, what can I say? Listen, he told me you're pretty good with the ponies. We love your print work, and I was hoping you'd do a piece on the Belmont Stakes for us."

32

Dan was happy to get the assignment, enabling him to change the channel of his thoughts from being busted down at the network and blown off by Nancy and generally wondering what he was going to do with the next weeks and/or the rest of his life—whichever came first—to something he actually enjoyed.

Fly By Day would be making a run for Triple Crown immortality in the Belmont Stakes. The horse had easily taken the Kentucky Derby and just inched his way to victory in the Preakness two weeks ago. Dan had caught both of the races on TV. His trip to the Breeders' Cup had reawakened an innate affection he had for the horses–their magnificent bearing and sheer size, and for the challenge of applying some formula, however faulty, to try and pick winners.

There was something refreshingly different about this game, and Dan knew what it was. The athletes weren't pompous fools; best, they couldn't speak. And the collection of cowboys and gruff handlers that served as their trainers were cut from a different cloth than anyone else in sports. These weren't golfers or tennis players who grew up in the dining room of a country club, or jocks who'd had people telling them how great they were from age 8 on. They were guys who smelled of manure and got to work at 3 or 4 in the morning every day to figure out the puzzle that awaited them in each stall.

Every morning for the 10 days leading up to the Belmont, Dan piloted the rental car provided him by the magazine through the Midtown Tunnel and across Queens to Belmont Park, on the Nassau County line, a beast of a facility built for the days 80 years ago when 50,000 patrons or more swarmed the racetrack daily. Here was, in many ways, the land that time forgot. Now, the sport revisited that sort of popularity only when a horse had won the Derby and the Preakness and tried for the third jewel of the Triple Crown right here in old New York. Only 11 horses in history had managed the triple.

It was still pitch black when Dan pulled a hard left off Hempstead Turnpike into the backstretch area of Belmont. He flashed his credential to the guard in the tiny booth and proceeded on through the oak- and sycamore-lined narrow roads intersecting the horse paths that connected the dozens of barns to the racetrack. Each morning, every horse in decent health would be walked to the track with an exercise rider on its back to go through the paces of training. Some, preparing for races, were asked for explosive workouts to get conditioning for the rigors ahead. Others went at a more leisurely pace, perhaps just having come off a race or an injury. You can't rush racehorses; they tell you when they're ready, or so said all the wise men who worked around them.

One of the up-and-coming trainers was Gary "Whitey" Winslett, a cowboy who'd grown up on a scrub ranch near the Washington-Canada border racing slow, modest stock in weekend races at county fairs. Winslett found his way to California, egged on by his major client and childhood friend, Pete Harland, who'd made a fortune constructing highway off- and on-ramps throughout the West. Now, after just a few years in the Golden State, Winslett and Fly By Day sat on the precipice of history.

Dan peered through the pre-dawn murkiness, trying to make some sense of the barn numbers posted high up on the sides of the old frame buildings. They seemed to Dan to lack a numeric order, so he parked, got directions from a guard, and hoofed it toward Barn 7, a choice location situated closest to the chute that led onto Belmont's huge main track. It was shortly before 6 a.m.

There was no mistaking how Winslett had acquired his nickname—his shock of white hair nearly lit up the pre-dawn outside the barn. He leaned up against a rail-post fence seemingly without a care in the world. Dan mentally nixed the 'pressure' angle from his story. He and Winslett had a mutual acquaintance, Mike Sapporo, the coach of the New York Jets, who loved the ponies and had a few under the care of the trainer. Dan had called Sapporo, about whom he had written a positive profile in *New York* magazine, and asked him to call Winslett on his behalf, but had no idea whether Sapporo had followed through on it.

Dan recognized the only other guy around Winslett's barn, Neil Hawkins, from his photo in the *Racing Form*. Hawkins was a real pro, knowledgeable in the game and a stylish writer. Boxing and the horses attracted their fair share of writers, Dan thought, feeling the romance of the sport out here in the dark.

He came upon Hawkins and Winslett's conversation, running to various training regimens and how to best prepare a 3-year-old for the mile and a half rigors of the Belmont Stakes. It was the longest distance most North American horses would be asked to run, and coming on the heels of the Derby and Preakness, it was a challenge both for the young horses and their trainers. Plenty could go wrong along the way, and usually did.

Fly By Day had been vanned up from Baltimore the day before, and would be getting just a light jog around the Belmont oval in an hour or so, a regimen that would be continued until a workout three days hence. Hawkins and Winslett were hashing over how long a workout would be optimum. During a brief pause in the rumination, Dan introduced himself to Winslett. Thankfully, there was a hint of familiarity.

"Sapp's guy? You must be a helluva writer if you found enough good things about him to fill an article."

"It wasn't easy," Dan replied, hoping to become part of the easy conversation. "He probably knows more about the horses than football."

"I wouldn't count on that," Winslett countered. "He called me the other day wanting me to run his horse next week because the team owner—what's his name, Morse--is going to be in town, and he wants to impress him. I told him, 'the horse just ran last week, remember?' He says, 'I really want to show this guy a good time.' I told him to get a coupla hookers. New York's full of 'em, last I heard."

"I'm not sure Morse would go for that," Dan said. "He's so straight he doesn't allow his players to grow sideburns."

"That's exactly the kind you have to watch out for," Winslett said, interrupted by a groom who wanted his opinion on a horse's well-being inside the barn. As Winslett retreated into the sanctuary of his barn, Dan turned his attention to Hawkins, who was fiddling with a cassette recorder, making sure he'd gotten his interview on tape.

"I enjoy your writing," Dan said sincerely. "Your love of the game really comes through."

"Thanks," said Hawkins. "You're the guy from 'Sports Talk.' You freelancing?"

"Yeah. For *New York* mag."

"You got an angle yet?"

"No."

"Well, don't worry, between Winslett and Harland, you'll have your choice."

"I'm amazed there isn't more press here."

"They'll all be here for the workout, and they'll all be getting the same quotes. This is where you find the stuff you can really use, that no one else has."

"Well, don't worry about me."

"Hey, listen, there's plenty of meat to go around."

Winslett returned to them in a few minutes on an entirely different wavelength. He was like a kid with wandering attention.

"Hey, we're setting up this deal later for Boudreaux," Winslett said conspiratorially, referring to Fly By Day's jockey, Clete Boudreaux. "He's getting in to jog the horse today, it's his first time in New York, and he's deathly afraid of heights."

This plot could go anywhere, Dan thought, but he was impressed by how expertly it had evolved in Winslett's prankster mind.

"Harland's booked a helicopter. After the races today we have to take the chopper to Yankee Stadium so we can get there in time for Boudreaux to throw out the first pitch. Except we're going to put down on top of the Pan Am Building in midtown with engine trouble, and tell him we can't get down off the roof. He's gonna freak."

Dan was right on the case. "How about if I meet you up there, playing a guy who came up for a smoke, and I'll have a photographer buddy with me—we can get pictures of the whole thing."

"This guy's good," Winslett said to no one in particular, approving of Dan's suggestion.

"Will Boudreaux recover in time for the Belmont?" Dan asked.

"Ten days? Should be close," Winslett said. "If not, we'll find another rider."

Dan felt a little badly for the Cajun jockey, but not enough to betray Winslett and his newfound access to the stars of the show. Just as rural Pennsylvania was the spawning ground of great quarterbacks like John Unitas, Joe Namath, Joe Montana, and Dan Marino, so the area around Lafayette, Louisiana, was for jockeys. Dozens of top riders came from there, given to the culture in which they were raised. Their fathers would match races against one another on weekends. It was racing in its purest incarnation—"my horse is faster than your horse," with plenty of money changing hands on each match.

A strip lined by two rows of parked cars would be established in a field, and the straightaway was used for racing. As it's always an advantage to have as little weight on the horse's back as possible, the male children were recruited at tender ages to ride the horses. Dan remembered a story he read about Eddie Delahoussaye, a future Hall of Fame jockey who began riding match races for his father. It seems his dad wanted him to go sit in a sauna with a rubber suit on to pull a couple of pounds off before riding. "I don't have nothin' to pull," Delahoussaye told his father. "I'm 8 years old."

Winslett's scheme went off beautifully. After flashing their press cards around, and tossing a couple of 20s to a security officer, Dan and Skip Roark, a photographer he knew, gained access to the roof minutes before they heard the first strains of the chopper's propellers and then saw the craft hovering and landing on the Pan Am building's heliport. They waited a distance away as the blades came to rest and the pilot descended, walking around his craft and making a good show of checking around the engine before declaring irreparable damage.

Winslett and Harland hopped off the chopper jauntily, putting on an act for Boudreaux, who already had taken on a green hue when he made his way down the steps to the roof.

"Nice job. I thought you said this was the best company in the field," Winslett said to Harland.

"No, I said it was the best I could afford," Harland answered, taking a swig from a can of light beer like he hadn't a care in the world.

Dan and Skip entered the scene.

"Engine trouble?" Dan asked innocently as possible.

"Yeah, this baby isn't going anywhere anytime soon," the pilot intoned.

Skip was taking pictures as inconspicuously as possible, focusing in on the stricken jockey, who was currently spilling his guts to the four directions, ignoring as much as possible the million-dollar view of New York that stretched out in front of him.

"You come up here for a smoke, and you never know what you'll find," Dan said.

"You guys, you guys work here?" Boudreaux managed, a glimmer of hope in his voice.

"Yep."

"Great, then we saved. We can get down from here." Boudreaux was already moving for the roof door as he said it, relief pouring off him until he tried the unmoving handle. Then jimmied it more and more aggressively.

"It's locked. How do you get back inside?"

"What do you mean, it's locked?" Dan asked as Skip continued clicking away. Dan moved to the door to try his luck, which he knew would be no better than Boudreaux'.

"Skip, you locked the door behind us," Dan admonished.

"Sorry," Skip said from behind his camera, not missing a shot.

"I'll radio for help," said the pilot. "But it'll be hours before they can reach us."

"Can't we call somebody in the building?" Boudreaux pleaded before having to hunch over and launch once more. He was a pitiful sight.

"Looks like you won't have any trouble making weight this week Clete," Winslett said, breaking up the group.

"Fuck you, Whitey," Boudreaux spit out.

After another round of beers, the pilot miraculously fixed the engine problem, and Winslett and Harland collected their rider following another viscous deposit.

"I know you bastards put him up to this," Boudreaux began, but once again had to pause to purge, surrounded by the great skyscrapers of Manhattan. Dan had the pilot put in a call to the security officer, who opened the door to the roof, and he and Skip disappeared.

Winslett and Harland made a big show of ushering their jockey back onto the craft, howling with joy. Boudreaux promised revenge, although he seemed to be speaking in tongues, and the only word the trainer and owner could make out was "voodoo."

33

Fly By Day led briefly in the stretch of the Belmont Stakes, but was overtaken in the last 100 yards by a horse that neither he nor Boudreaux saw coming on the far outside. It was a disappointing result for most of the 100,000 in attendance, and certainly for Dan, as it removed much of the gravitas from his story. But after 10 days of hanging out with Fly By Day and his connections, he wrote a fun-filled account of Winslett, Harland, and a new breed of movers in racing, possibly heralding a major rejuvenation of the dormant sport.

Dan was pleased with the way the article turned out. Skip's photography expertly augmented his words, and the magazine staff had created an eye-catching layout that made the piece jump off the page. Dan picked up a copy at a neighborhood newsstand, and stood on a midtown street corner, next to a

Saberett's hot dog dealer who was just beginning to set up his umbrella, and read the article from beginning to end. The humor was right where it should have been; the picture he painted of the Thoroughbred's majesty shone through, as did the unpredictability of the result even though every single box has been checked and Fly By Day prepared expertly for potentially the biggest race of his life.

Dan found himself smiling as he rolled up the magazine and bounced toward the ABC studios and offices 10 blocks away, knowing full well he was only as good as his last piece of work. Dan breezed into the studios, heading through the double doors and down the hallway to the executive offices. He noticed Stevens' name already adorning the plaque on Romano's old door, and was relieved that Joan was still handling the traffic outside it.

"How's the transition going?" Dan asked her breezily.

"This one eats less," she replied, not missing a beat.

"Hell, a starving gorilla at a free buffet would eat less."

"The gorilla asked for me. I'm heading upstairs next week."

"Sorry."

Dan opened Stevens' door with no trace of hesitation and moved inside. Stevens was "yes sirring" somebody on the other end of the phone repeatedly until the call came to a merciful end.

Spying Dan, he flipped through a calendar on his desk.

"Dan, did we have an appointment…?"

"I just made one," Dan said. "Wanted to let you know I'm quitting."

"But I thought you liked it here."

"I did."

"Well, then, I don't understand…"

"I wouldn't expect you to."

"Are you 1,000% sure on this?"

"Closer to 100. I'd say 100%."

"Is there anything we can do? Maybe sweeten the pot a little."

"Listen, it's been just incredible working with you," said Dan. "Hopefully you'll kiss enough ass to go far in this business."

Dan spun and exited a stunned young executive.

"Joanie, I'll see ya. Don't change a thing," he said as he strode out of the suite.

"Wouldn't think of it."

Dan stopped momentarily in the lobby, where he put in the mail slot 20 letters to major media outlets in the city announcing that he'd quit "Sports Talk." He then stopped at the receptionist and asked that she forward any calls for him to attorney Sonny Catapano. He left the number with her and departed the ABC complex.

34

D an didn't want this meeting with his attorney to take place in a bar with the requisite distractions and prying ears. He didn't want to be seen, and he didn't want to answer questions about his future from people who didn't care except for what his next potential job could mean for them. He made the pilgrimage up to Sonny's Times Square lair.

"Let's just say the phone hasn't been ringing off the hook," Sonny said. "Channel 9 wants to do a knock-off of 'Sports Talk,' but with a very limited budget, and by that I mean you'd have to build the set yourself."

"Could I borrow some of the chairs from your waiting room?"

"Stay with me here. They've got no money, and I'm not sure they have a clue, either."

"What makes you say that?"

"Because they're interested in hiring you. Look, it's a step backward, and frankly you're gonna have trouble competing against whatever ABC ends up doing."

"What else?"

"WINS called. The news radio station. They're looking for a sports guy. Sports reports in-house; reporting live from games. Not a bad gig. Not sure what I can bludgeon out of them as far as salary, but you won't starve."

"Anything with writing?"

"Not really. Oh, yeah, wait." Sonny shuffled papers around on his desk searching for a message slip. "Some guy called late yesterday. Complete hillbilly accent. I got about every third word. Here it is. Lexington *Herald*. In Kentucky. Guy thought your horse racing piece in the magazine was swell. I'm not sure you'd fit in, having most of your teeth and all."

Sonny tossed the slip across his desk carelessly. Dan watched its flight, got up from his seat and retrieved it. "Ed Benson," Dan read out loud. "Hmmm."

"'Hmmm'? May I remind you that's in Kentucky?"

"What's your point?"

"It's a thousand miles from civilization."

"You're right. Probably not far enough."

Dan had shifted quickly into daydreaming mode. Horses were running through the picture, and vast open expanses of fields lush with tall grass.

"I've seen that look before," Sonny said, ending the reverie. "You're about to do something stupid."

"I'm going to call the guy, if that's what you mean."

"Do not make a move without talking to me. C'mon, let's go down and get a thrill and some lunch."

35

Dan's eyes were glued on the landscape out the jet's window as it made its descent into the Lexington area. The green pastures swept by for miles, uninterrupted by anything other than the farmhouses that dotted the fields, and the run-in sheds where horses could wait out unfavorable weather. As the jet dropped further Dan could make out the plank fencing that bordered the horse paddocks, ponds that provided habitat for all manner of creatures; silos and country lanes. He was transfixed on the pastoral sweep.

Flying into New York City the great buildings looked to him like tombstones in an old, gothic cemetery, warning all what they could be stepping into.

Dan could make out the grandstand and oval racing surface of Keeneland Racecourse as they passed over it just across Versailles Road from the runway at Bluegrass Field airport. Keeneland was a cathedral of racing though its meetings were brief and sparse: three weeks in the spring and another three in the fall. Had Dan been across the aisle in the jet, he would have seen the famous red and white barns of powerful Calumet Farm, which sent out Triple Crown winner after Triple Crown winner in the 1930s and 1940s, and whose runners could van over to Keeneland in a matter of less than five minutes.

Although the racing wasn't in session at Keeneland, its summer sale of yearlings was about to begin, and business at tiny Bluegrass Field was bustling. Many of the travelers carried sale catalogs brimming with notations about the horses listed therein. Reading glasses and pens hung from strings tied around necks.

"Didya bring yur checkbook with ya?" questioned a man with an Irish lilt to an arriving passenger. Commerce was about to commence here, judging by the action on the terminal floor. Serious commerce, if the arrivees were as well-heeled as their appearance made them out to be.

Dan waited several minutes in the rental car line before being directed to a Chrysler Sebring in the parking lot just off the terminal. He hadn't asked for a convertible, but the rental company had burned through the sedans and was now mixing and matching. Dan's appointment with Ed Benson wasn't until the following day, and he had made arrangements to visit Claiborne Farm upon his arrival.

Navigating a circular parkway that ringed Lexington, he headed east out of town past a string of elaborate entrances to the great farms of the day. The tall iron gates were inscribed with the initials of the business magnates that owned the land, and they hung from great stone pillars that often had sculptures of eagles or other impressive animals sitting atop them. He passed Bwamazon, Walmac, Gainesway, Domino, Elmendorf. The lush green fields bumped one against the other along the Paris Pike, with a few mares grazing in each, their foals mimicking them nearby, dropping their heads to graze the bluegrass, or nudging one another until they set off in a great game of equine tag, showing off the spindly legs and God-given nature that made them want to run and run some more.

In 30 minutes Dan arrived in the small town of Paris, a sleepy backwater that had been settled about 80 years before by members of the Hancock and Clay families, historic Virginia clans responsible for much of the political and horse history of the area. Turning south from the middle of the tiny town, Dan was at the gates of Claiborne in a matter of minutes, and drove toward the office alongside a picturesque running brook. The farm office reminded him of a country version of Sonny's digs, furnished from a bygone era only done up in rich wood with the smell of history to it.

Claiborne was visitor-friendly and very popular with tourists, as it was home to the mighty Secretariat, the 1973 Triple Crown winner who had electrified the racing world and the universe beyond with his dominance of the three Triple Crown races, topped by an unheard-of 31-length trouncing of the Belmont Stakes field. He had simultaneously graced the covers of *Time*, *Newsweek*, and *Sports Illustrated*, a feat unmatched by human or animal. Big Red, as he was known, was the most popular Thoroughbred of the last half of the 20th century. During breeding season the stallion was busy impregnating 50 mares each year, breeders hoping against hope that the great horse could somehow reproduce himself.

But Secretariat, unlike those who had anteed up six figures for the right to breed a mare to him, appeared unconcerned with how his adventures in the breeding shed were turning out as Dan approached his paddock. A groom at the farm, Buck, had been assigned to guide Dan through his tour, and while the local 20-something gave forth his talk about the farm's history, Dan was antsy to see the great horse. Now, as they arrived at his paddock, Dan readied his single reflex Pentax and began to snap away.

Secretariat had found a tree branch somewhere and was playing catch with himself, grabbing it in his mouth and tossing it up in the air, although he made no effort to catch it. Dan clicked away giddily while Buck broke into action, trying to reach through the fence to grab the branch away before the horse injured himself with it. But Secretariat snatched it before Buck could, and moved it further into his paddock beyond the groom's reach.

"Secretariat, you no-good...bring that stick over here," Buck implored, but it was clear who was boss. The chestnut legend paid him no attention, yet appeared interested in continuing to pose for Dan and his camera, lifting his head to gaze beyond him onto the horizon. He was as big a ham as he was fast on the racetrack, and Dan breathlessly squeezed off his entire roll of 36 images before he knew it. Each time Buck attempted to climb the fence to get into the paddock, Secretariat would move back toward the stick, knowing exactly how to win that game, too.

Dan spent a half-hour pressed up against the great horse's fence staring in awe before a large group came up alongside on their tour. When their guide mentioned Secretariat's name, one of the men said, "I've heard of him." And Dan took his cue to move on, ending this visit with greatness. His mind floated the entire way back to town. There was something magical about this place, and he knew for certain he wasn't in New York anymore.

36

"I'll be honest with ya," Ed Benson was telling Dan across the dinner table at a horrifically bad steakhouse, "there's about a dozen guys'd give their left nut for this job. Trouble is, they can't write a letter home to their mommas. When I read your article on the Belmont, I said, 'This sumbitch can write. Let's see if we can get him out the city.' So, can we?"

"I don't know, Ed. If most of the restaurants are like this, I'm likely to starve here."

"Don't worry none 'bout that. Whatcha gotta do is find yourself a sweet little woman gonna cook for ya and take care of all those things."

"Job doesn't supply that?"

"Well, now, we got some fringe benefits—health plan, travel—but far as the fillies go, that's too risky for the paper to be involved with."

Ed had laid out the job over the $10 steak: Covering the six weeks of the Keeneland race meets; the three months that Churchill Downs ran an hour west in Louisville, including of course the Kentucky Derby; the horse sales; feature stories; travel to big races out of town; filling in on University of Kentucky sports in a pinch.

The salary would have made Sonny puke, the thought of which brought a smile to Dan. But the cost of living here was a fraction of what it was in New York, and the money wasn't an issue for Dan, who rejected the waitress' overture toward dessert.

"I don't know, Ed. It's a big move. A big decision."

"I understand. Move to clean air, no traffic, peace and quiet, people bein' respectful and polite, pretty big adjustments. Not for ever'body."

"Let me be blunt."

"By all means."

"My background is freelancing. My own ideas, my own words. Now, I don't mind deadlines; I thrive on them. But I'm used to writing what I want to write."

"Based on what I've read, I don't think editors are gonna need to get all inside your copy. Hell, you'll probably be teachin' them a thing or three."

"That's style. What about substance?"

"Well, now, we on the sports side; we ain't gonna be figurin' out solutions to the world's problems."

"I don't want my hands tied."

"We talkin' 'bout horses runnin' around in circles. Not that much controversy to it."

"I'm gonna need time to think."

"Take all the time ya want. How 'bout end of the day tomorrow? Speakin' of which, since you're here on my dime, I've taken the liberty of hookin' you up with a real estate lady tomorrow—go around and take a look, see how it all grabs ya."

"That's very considerate and self-serving."

"Thanks."

From dinner, Ed ushered Dan to the Keeneland sale pavilion to view the yearling sale, held at night to emphasize the select nature of this particular auction. In the pavilion proper sat well-heeled men dressed in suits with their women draped in cocktail attire. Splashy jewelry flashed everywhere, finery that made Dan laugh, at least inside, as he and Ed took seats and Dan was struck by the overwhelming whiff of horse manure, souvenirs from the stars of the show, who were paraded one-by-one to the half-oval stage at the front of the auditorium and shown off to each side of the room while the bidding proceeded. If the pace flagged, an announcer, perched on a raised dais over the horse, read off pertinent information concerning the animal's family history in a tone that told prospective buyers they were hopeless rubes if they didn't raise their arms with a stronger commitment post haste.

The oldest of these yearlings for sale had been out of the womb for a year and a half. The few days they had spent on the sale grounds being inspected represented the first time they had been off the farms where they were born and raised, and where they spent months after being weaned from their mothers frolicking in huge fields with their classmates, carefree and full of themselves.

Now, however, they had been segregated in individual stalls, and their only exercise was being led out of the barn to be walked and stood for inspection from terribly serious potential buyers who looked the hair off them, searching for flaws in the hoof, knees, hocks, and along the powerful hindquarters and shoulders. If the horse passed all these tests, his walk was also analyzed from the front, back, and side, and notations were made by the lookers in their catalogs, a page therein devoted to each yearling. Then veterinarians arrived with ominous-looking long tubes that they stuck up the nose to look inside and make sure the throat and breathing passages were wide and functioning. X-rays were taken.

The sales experience for these young horses was less than pleasurable. None of them looked happy to be there, and why would they? On the stage many complained, nickering for a return to the fields and their friends, which were gone now for them. Most grudgingly followed the lead of their handlers, but had to be constantly pulled at and cajoled to pose properly for best viewing during the auction. And finally, as a sign of their disdain, a regular dropping of equine excretion on the rubber-matted stage floor took its toll on the air quality in the pavilion. No matter how many well-dressed swells were in attendance, or how much rich wood lined the walls, it smelled like a barn.

But that wasn't stopping the bidding, the volume of which was stunningly impressive. The big board had room for eight digits, and while it was rare that $10 million was bid on a horse, it had happened. The six- and seven-figure prices that were currently lighting up the bulbs were strong enough. Dan was in awe as people regularly purchased a yearling for more money than he expected to make in his lifetime. These were, after all, completely unproven commodities, recommended only by their appearance and their pedigrees. No one has yet established a test to measure the motivation, mental capacity, or the heart needed to compete and thrive. Nobody could foresee whether the animal they just spent $1 million on had even the slightest will to win. It was a jaw-dropping spectacle, which, of course, is why Ed had brought Dan to witness it.

They walked out of the main pavilion and through a hallway toward the back walking ring, where serious last-minute inspections were going on. Dan was happy for the fresh air. Ed seemed to know most everyone on the grounds, and introduced Dan to various people of import. Dan was facile when it came to forgetting names as soon as they were announced to him, and here he was able to ply that skill by the dozens.

As the auction announcer welcomed a particularly well-bred yearling into the ring, Ed nudged Dan and nodded his jaw toward a tight-knit group of gentlemen gathered along the rail under a bid board in the back area. The leader had longish white hair flowing out from under a white hat.

"The Irish," explained Ed. "They're one of the big international operations, and they love the family of this horse. Over there," he gestured to another corner of the back ring, "the A-rabs. They like anything they can prevent the Irish from gettin', and they have the oil money to say 'F you' whenever they want. This should be fun."

There was a bid-spotter in the back to relay bids inside the pavilion. Action was slow at first, as the two groups let the rubes inside push the early bidding for the horse. When those only moderately fantastically wealthy entities slowed down near the $1-million mark, the action moved to the back, where the Irish lit up the board with the first seven-figure offer. That was quickly answered from the Arab side of the rail. The auctioneer was no longer nickel-and-diming this proceeding; after each bid he moved the asking price up $500,000. And on it went, past $3 million, up to $5 million. There, the Arabs slowed down and took a deep breath. The pause went on, but when it seemed the battle had ended, they jumped the price up a full million to six.

The buzz, and it actually was an audible wave of excitement from everyone not involved in the back-and-forth, filled the sales grounds, and rose in volume with each arrow shot. The Irish quickly went to $6.5, but now the Arabs came back at $7.5, and the steam seemed to leave the starched shirts in the rival enclave. Spirited discussion in the huddle ended with the white-haired gentleman coming out of the scrum and moving with purpose out of the arena, and the yearling was hammered down to the Arabs for $7.5 million.

"Them people got more money than Carter's got pills," Ed said. "Feel like a nightcap?"

37

"This must be it," Brenda Cox said, turning onto a gravel driveway at three bruised mailboxes in front of an old tobacco barn. The previous properties she had shown Dan were distressed. Home repairs not being his specialty, Dan had stared back at the real estate agent each time she asked, on the way back to her car, "Whattaya think?"

Was there ever in history a property so rundown, so impossibly unsellable, that a real estate agent wouldn't at least give you the chance to say "yes" to it?

They bumped along the gravel drive past a nice brick home that overlooked a large manmade pond, past some rough horse fencing that kept in a ragtag bunch of equine boarders, about ½ mile until the road dead-ended in front of a stark, vinyl-facade place with a spire going up that mimicked Churchill Downs' famous calling card. The place felt like it had been dropped out of the sky; not a tree around it.

"The property's 25 acres, so you got that field back there and then some woods going down to a creek at the rear border," Brenda said, reading from the listing sheet. "Let's look at the house first."

The place was three floors, including a basement that ran the length of the floors above it. It was way too much space for one person, and not very tastefully done. The family that built the house still lived in it, but obviously had run out of money during construction. The floors were unfinished; raw wood with no covering. The walls would have been better off that way; unfortunately, they had been painted hideous hues of pink and bright blue, or wallpapered with images of unicorns. Walls intruded on what could be nice-sized rooms. There was a lack of windows or glass doors that would allow the nature outside in.

The detached garage had no doors, and looked like it was being used for a pigeon coup, with large cages hanging from the rafters and white splotches of bird doo everywhere.

"I'm gonna go walk the property down to the creek if that's all right," said Dan.

"Fine with me. I got a book to read."

Dan took off along a path between the weed field and the horse fence that marked the border with the closest neighbor. Some horses grazed beside him, paying no attention when he tried to converse. The land rose slightly, then dipped dramatically halfway back before rising again and then gently dropping off as the field met the woods a few hundred yards away from the house. Dan tracked a path into the woods that took him sharply downhill again. Halfway down he could hear the sound of water, and as the land flattened out he came out of the trees onto a 100-foot-wide creek that flowed slowly before contracting and falling over rocks, the water picking up steam and running hard from there. Large trees, some with massive roots exposed, lined the waterside. Dan stared straight down through the water and could see every detail of the creek bottom, not knowing he was looking into Clear Creek. He sat on a rock, took a deep breath, and listened to the water and the birds, and precious little else.

A rope hung from a tree branch that stretched over the water, and Dan could see in his mind kids swinging from it and then releasing to drop into the drink. His mind wandered back to Manhattan and the sounds of the ambulances screaming through the streets and the hordes of people rushing along the avenues and the smoke puffing out from vehicles as they accelerated away from traffic lights.

An ingot squawked and flapped its way straight up through the trees and off high above the water, its peace disturbed by Dan's presence. Dan would have stayed there a long time if not for thinking about Brenda and what her patience level might be before leaving him in the middle of wherever he was. So he began the climb back to the field. He walked the other property border going back, and saw the small seasonal creek that ran along the property line on that side, pocked every 20 yards by small rock drop-offs that would become mini-waterfalls in wet weather. It took 15 minutes to get back to the car.

"It's nice back there," he said, opening the passenger side door. Brenda was, in fact, still reading.

"Good," she said. "So, whattaya think?"

38

"You are a complete idiot." Sonny was desperately trying to school Dan while they waited for their first round of drinks at a corner table at Rudy's. Dan looked at him bemusedly. There was no need to play defense now. He smiled as the abuse tumbled out.

"Every time I try and teach you something you sit there like a mook. I let my guard down for two minutes and you're off thinking you're gonna all of a sudden become a farmer. 'Hey, look at me; I've got overalls.' You've got half a brain; you will never fit in."

"It's over, Sonny. Done."

A waitress came over with way too many drinks on her tray for two people. Sonny was clearly front-loading this late afternoon.

"Sweetheart, would you please tell my friend here it's a mistake for him to move to Kentucky?"

"Is that the place out past the Hamptons? My boyfriend took me there once for seafood."

"I'm sure you *were* the seafood," Sonny said.

"Look at this," Dan said motioning with his chin as agent Brian Brown entered the bar with Jeff Stevens and a couple of men in tow, taking a booth in the back. "Is Brown stepping out these days?"

"You must have been out of town," said Sonny. "Vic got into a little trouble."

"You gonna make me beg?"

"It concerns a 16-year-old girl and her 17-year-old cousin."

"How did you miss out on that one?"

"He didn't call, the prick. Anyway, he's away for a while, in some rehab joint for guys can't keep their dicks to themselves."

"Who's with him?"

"I told you I wasn't there."

"I mean with Brown."

"Guy in the middle is some half-ass manager, used to handle comics up in the Catskills back when that was a market. The other guy is The Noz."

"The radio guy? He's terrible. Could you imagine me writing for him?"

"Look, the almost-future father-in-law would have replaced you with a talking Chihuahua if he had to."

"Instead they went for a giant set of nostrils."

"I could still get you on a competing show…"

"You think I want to live my life reacting to these jerk-offs?"

"You're such a big man it's making me puke."

"Lookit here, it's Beauty and the Beast," said Gregg Gold, taking a seat with Dan and Sonny.

"Well, New York's highest-paid gopher," Sonny said. "You finish delivering Morono's dinner already?"

"How are you, Dan?" Gregg said, ignoring Sonny.

"I thought I was OK, until I saw my successor walk in."

"Yeah, The Noz, huh? He might be OK."

"He looks like a fuckin' Toucan." This was Sonny.

"What are you, Tom Selleck?" said Gregg.

"I'm not on TV, ass munch."

The waitress thankfully stopped by. "You guys need anything?"

"Yeah, separate tables," said Dan. "But for now, six shots of tequila. The good shit from the back."

The waitress retreated. "She doesn't know where Kentucky is," said Dan.

"Neither do I," replied Gregg. "So you're really doing this, huh?"

"Sure he's doing it," said Sonny, "after you and Morono ran him out of a job."

"Sonny, leave Gregg alone, he had nothing to do with that."

"Yeah, he really went to bat for you."

"Sonny," said Gregg, "you don't know what you're talking about, and while I realize that's never stopped you before…"

"Alright, boys, let's not fight over poor little me. Believe it or not, I'm happy it played out this way."

"Have I told you lately you're an imbecile?"

"Yes."

"Good, don't forget it."

"I'll have it tattooed."

The drinks arrived, and Dan distributed them.

"To good friends. What more can a man ask?"

39

The first weeks in Kentucky Dan got busy coloring in the outlines of his new life. There were appliances to buy, satellite TV to hook up, walls to paint, carpet to lay, and a dozen other projects. None was more important to Dan than his trip to the Woodford Humane Society, where he interviewed a couple dozen prospective roommates before choosing a black hound mix he named Yogi and a female companion for him, a sheepdog covered with spots who became Babe.

He had wanted dogs since he was old enough to speak, but circumstances had always conspired against it. First it was his mother, who was afraid of them or afraid he wouldn't take care of them, or a mixture of the two. Dan remembered his father coming home one night talking about a friend who had German Shepherd pups that needed a home, and it seemed for that one evening that they were going to get one. Dan and his sister spent hours throwing names back and forth while, in another room, his mother was throwing a fit at his father. Magically, by the next morning, all talk of the incoming animal had disappeared like dog shit left out in the rain.

New York City, of course, was its own conspiracy against having one. What good was having a dog, reasoned Dan, unless you had a big one, and what good was that if you had nowhere where they could run around chasing things.

Dan fenced in an acre around his house and Yogi and Babe transitioned to their new home beautifully. Dan spoiled them in every way. Cushy pillows, a dog door so they could come and go freely, table scraps with their dinner, and, of course, his bed was their bed.

They never had a bad day or a worry, and Dan learned all he could from them. He loved getting out of the office and driving the 25 minutes home along the rural roads and then catching sight of them, already having heard his car approaching, running the fence line along the driveway, ready to go as soon as he changed clothes. There was nothing that brightened Dan more than taking them for long walks late in the afternoon through the woods and down along the creek, watching as they flushed out wild turkeys or treed squirrels or went for a cooling swim paddling about the creek and chasing tennis balls he tossed from the rocks.

This was his refuge, from the rigors of the day and those of the accumulated 25 years, his release from everything that never quite added up. Here, he could change the channel and tune it all out, the static replaced by the Canadian geese honking overhead and the donkeys in the next field blurting and the young horses running the fields in their never-ending chase games.

As Dan walked the woods his mind would sometimes drift back to the city. He imagined what Sonny would be doing at that very moment—aggravating someone into a deal, shaded by those horrible Venetian blinds. And what nonsense would be going on back in the ABC studios, the drama surrounding some inconsequential thread of a story with careers hanging in the balance. And then he'd clear a branch off the trail and smell a pine tree and hear the distant rumble of a storm still an hour away. There were no pangs, no hint anywhere inside him that he'd made the wrong move. It was no decision. A knockout. His reward was everywhere around him.

A couple of the newspaper's younger reporters took Dan under their wings and squired him a few blocks from the office through Lexington's rather modest downtown to a watering hole called McCarthy's. It was a real Irish drinking bar, the kind where the door had to be kept open from early in the morning to cut the previous night's aroma with fresh air. The essence of the ale was ingrained into the dark wood, the lighting was about nonexistent, and the waiters carried a dozen mugs at a time and spoke in Brogues.

Kate and Maryanne ran him through the minefield of office politics and characters and provided a guide to restaurants and hangouts and activities. They were quite breezy and relaxed with the stranger in their midst, and Dan found his New York defenses receding as he embraced the novelty that surrounded him.

Dan's favorite thing about the newspaper beat actually wasn't a direct part of the job. He began going to Keeneland early in the mornings to watch horses train and introduce himself to the players—the trainers on the Kentucky circuit. Even when the track wasn't hosting races, trainers stabled and trained horses there. The atmosphere was congenial and relaxed, and the horsemen were basically good old boys born and raised in big, open areas of the Midwest where farming was the family business and messing with horses was the way to get out of running heavy machinery over fields hoping to carve out a living from the dirt.

Dan took an earful about where his predecessor had run afoul of racetrack etiquette, having taken confidential information and repurposed it as his own. Trainers have an uneasy relationship with Turf writers; they understand the sport needs publicity to keep the wheels greased and the gamblers coming back. However, theirs is a business filled with remedies and medicines and techniques that they'd just as soon keep under their cowboy hats. So while reporters on the scene are accepted as part of racing's insular world, there is some distance maintained and words chosen carefully.

Dan felt well-received enough. He was happy to listen to whatever storyteller had the floor, and his wit was quick enough to be a contributing voice. He made a fast impression on Bert Clarke, a grizzled veteran who had worked the circuit for 20 years since retiring as a New Orleans firefighter. Clarke was well familiar with the Cajuns that raced around the New Orleans area, and he about exploded when Dan told the tale of Clete Boudreaux up on the Pan Am building in midtown Manhattan blowing his guts to the wind. Clarke must have had Dan repeat the story five times.

The September sale of yearlings was approaching and most of Dan's published work centered around that. It was the largest sale of its kind in the world, and Dan shaped at least a half-dozen angles into feature stories for the *Herald* in the week leading up to it. This was pretty meat-and-potatoes stuff for him. There were sales officials to be quoted; the consignors that sold the horses touting everything in their barn; international and celebrity buyers to be interviewed; hot, new sires to be gauged.

But on the eve of the sale, none of those angles concerned Dan when he approached Ed Benson about a story he wanted to write. Paul Westbrook, one of the trainers Bert Clarke had introduced him to, was down from Canada for his third year training around these parts. In other words, he was still a rank outsider. Westbrook, with a stable of about 20 horses, had seen four of them come up lame after training at Keeneland for just two weeks. He believed there was a soft spot on the racing surface that was precipitating the injuries, and he received back-up from other trainers who were also having problems. That back-up disappeared, however, when Westbrook made his way to the track president to voice his concerns.

After getting a hearty "thanks for coming in, you can go now" attitude, Westbrook threatened to go public with his situation. The following morning he was asked--make that told--to remove his horses from the grounds within 24 hours and, by the way, he would not be getting a refund for the two-month rental that he had paid in advance for the stalls. Dan got the story at length from the aggrieved party, and thought it made for a good article.

Ed Benson began fidgeting about 20 seconds into Dan's rehashing of the details. He was polite enough to let Dan finish, but his eyes were blank and his thoughts elsewhere.

"So, I think there's a piece here, right?" Dan said after summing up.

"Lemme tell ya somethin', Dan," Benson began softly. "This sale comin' up Monday, it's how people feed their families. The horses they've bred and raised and fed and brushed on and cared for and brought over here, they rely on the money they get for those animals to make a livin'. The time just ain't right to be printin' stories like the one you got there."

"So, you think after the sale?" Dan pursued.

Benson was afraid his ace reporter would sniff out the hole he'd left in his explanation and throw it back at him, and it didn't surprise him his explanation would have to be expanded. He sighed.

"Dan, you like me any?"

"You're O.K."

"High praise, and I thank you. If you'd like me to continue in my job, we're gonna have to agree about what makes news here and what doesn't. Now, I ain't no fortunate son; I come from the middle of nothin', and I got sympathy for a man losin' his horses on the racetrack. But a man thinks he's gonna fight Keeneland and be the last one standin' ain't nothin' but a fool. That goes for your trainer friend, for me, and for this newspaper."

"Well, that didn't take long, did it?"

"Son, just 'cause we country and laid back don't mean there ain't politics here."

"So nobody can question anything they do?"

"It's gotta be a real big question. The people on the board over there's the same people who breed and own horses. They the same people that pick the politicians in this city and they the same people that build the houses and run the banks and control the businesses and advertise in the newspaper. That's the whole nutshell right there."

Dan's walk that afternoon failed to soothe him. Instead of concentrating on the cardinals darting through the trees, he was replaying the voices in his head—Westbrook's, Benson's. Dan wanted a second chance to inject this point or that observation, thinking he could better advance his case. He didn't want to wrap his brain around what he already knew—he'd hit a dead-end street.

More than 3,000 yearlings were catalogued to the September sale, and the days immediately preceding it brought hordes of prospective buyers to the Keeneland grounds. The back of the sale pavilion rose over dozens of barns, large rectangular structures each with 40 stalls that were filled by the sale horses. Buyers ambled from barn to barn, or took golf carts to the furthest ones, which were a good half-mile away and up steep inclines. Keeneland was happy to provide the vehicles for all, as the last thing it wanted was to discourage any buyer from going to look at any horse.

Trainers theoretically were looking to fill orders from owners back home, and came shopping for the animals they would hopefully put in training at their bases. They examined the physical build, or conformation, of the horse, taking into account that stout, wide specimens usually made good sprinters while rangier, thinner horses were more adept at going a longer distance of ground. Knee and ankle alignment were crucial, and the feet were picked over as well, their size determining whether a horse would be better suited to running on dirt or over the grass. Then there was the pedigree to consider—the bloodlines that conveyed inherited traits and talent and would go a long way in determining how high the bidding would go for each individual.

There was plenty of information to digest and the bigger outfits hired agents to walk the grounds and look at hundreds of potential purchases before narrowing the field down to the ones they might actually bid on. X-rays of each horse were kept in an onsite repository and vets were hired to go over the pictures of potential targets.

Horse trading had become quite a science in part to try and combat the raw deals that gave the term such a bad connotation over centuries. Nowadays the hustles were more intricate, with dollars surreptitiously changing hands as favors to agents who recommended certain horses from certain consignments to their clients. Prices might even be agreed upon ahead of time, with the involved agent driving up the bidding against a plant from the seller's operation until the required price was hit and then some, and the unsuspecting buyer asked to pay the inflated amount, the surplus to be split up by the seller and the agent.

It was no business for men in short pants, and even titans of business who got involved in the racing game, men of tremendous success and savvy, often times found their pockets fleeced before they knew what hit them.

But that wasn't a story Dan would be writing anytime soon. As he patrolled the sales grounds Dan could feel the kinetic dance of human and equine with the sweet aroma of money wafting just below the surface. As Ed Benson explained, this was the bread and butter of the horse economy, where the mega-operations would continue churning livestock for big bucks and where the small guy could get lucky and bring the right horse to sale at the right time and cash in on a home run price that would send the kids to college and make his breeding operation viable for years.

As Dan cruised the barns, one of the first familiar characters he ran into was the tanned Whitey Winslett, fresh off a summer spent in California. Winslett hid his eyes and his enthusiasm for a horse behind dark sunglasses though the sun hadn't threatened an appearance for days. Winslett was looking over several horses from Tandy Farms, one of the major outfits in Central Kentucky. He didn't go much for writing down his impressions; he knew in his head what interested him but also didn't make any final decisions until he got another chance to see each horse just before they stepped into the sales ring.

Dan waited for Winslett to say his goodbyes to his Tandy host and saunter off to the next barn.

"Got your next Derby winner?" Dan said, falling into step with him.

"Hey, I liked the piece you wrote," Winslett said, recognizing Dan if not remembering his name. "Sorry we couldn't have won the Belmont for you."

"Yeah, I wanted to talk to you about that."

"Well, two out of three ain't bad, especially when one of 'em is the Derby."

"So, you finding anything here?"

"It's a pretty good group."

Dan recognized that, like the locals who chatted him up to a certain point and never beyond, Winslett was not about to tip his hand, however innocently, on anything specific he was interested in. The trainer changed the subject.

"So what's up in New York?"

"I don't know; I moved here, working for the local paper."

"No kidding."

"Making an honest man out of me."

"You better work on your accent."

Winslett, having won racing's biggest prize earlier in the year, was welcomed big-time wherever he showed up. His arrival at the Spendthrift Farm barn was no exception, and like a wealthy woman who'd just entered a clothing store in Beverly Hills, the help jumped to attention.

"Mr. Winslett, what can we show you?" said a manager.

"How about the good ones?" cracked the trainer, who immersed himself in the horse flesh moving around him.

The auction got off to a brisk beginning, with the 10th lot hammered down at the magical mark of $1 million to a member of the British racing aristocracy. The Arab and Irish contingents were in full attendance, vying for the best-bred entries, and the hum of chatter from the auctioneer was relentless.

Winslett was juggling to try and satisfy the needs of several clients at once. There was Lou Tanney, the so-called Soda King of California who controlled all the Coca-Cola distributorships in the vast southern half of the state; John Combs, who ran the biggest horse breeding farm on the West Coast; Pete Harland, Winslett's longtime friend who won the Kentucky Derby and Preakness earlier in the year; and a new client, Sam Dobbs, who owned the largest General Motors dealership West of the Mississippi, selling all five lines of GM cars off a huge lot in Orange County between Los Angeles and San Diego. He was one of those guys who did his own cheesy TV commercials that somehow lured people into his showrooms despite their almost comedic bad production.

Dobbs was sucking down a footlong hot dog in the dining room just off the sales pavilion when Dan approached and introduced himself, smelling a possible feature story. Dobbs, a Texas native and good ol' boy who made his way West seeking an escape from his family's dusty ranch outside El Paso, was just the personable sort you'd expect of someone who made his bones chatting up strangers about power drives, white wall tires, and dual carburetor exhausts. After some pleasantries, Dan began the inquiry.

"This your first stab with horses?"

"Nah, we raced some cheap ones back in Texas—my daddy messed with 'em—and I've raced a few that couldn't outrun me."

"And now you've got Whitey buying for you?"

"Yeah, I figured if ya gonna do something, do it right, so when that boy went and won the Derby this year, it kinda got my attention some."

"You looking for anything in particular?"

"Yeah, the next champion, just like all these other folks here on a dream."

"C'mon, Dobber, you can give him your life story after we win something." This was Winslett, who burst into the dining room with purpose, that being to grab Dobbs and go bid on a horse.

Dan followed them across the hallway into the pavilion, staying in the back of the room whose seats were all reserved for people making bids. His eyes remained on Winslett, who ushered Dobbs to a centrally located section and made brief eye contact with the bid-spotter, who prowled the aisle relaying bids up to the auction platform. Experienced buyers would tell the spotter which horses they were interested in ahead of time, and also how they would make a bid, so that other potential buyers would have difficulty seeing who they were up against.

Crossing a leg, touching a pen, moving an arm, the signal to bid could be anything, and the signs between bidder and spotter were just another element in this whole cloak-and-dagger undertaking.

A few horses came and went before Dan observed Dobbs turning to Winslett and the trainer giving the smallest of nods back as a son of the great Triple Crown winner Affirmed entered the ring. He was a chestnut beauty with a white blaze down his face and a sturdy body. The bidding bounced along at a tepid pace, increasing by increments of $10,000 until stalling at the $100,000 level, when the announcer came in and scolded the folks who weren't in on the horse, reciting the horse's pedigree and reminding folks of the greatness of Affirmed.

After that pitch the bidding resumed, again modestly. At $125,000, Winslett came in for the first time, adjusting his sunglasses just before the bid-spotter on his aisle called out "Yeah," indicating a bid of $130,000. There was some more back and forth, with Winslett adjusting his eyewear once again at $145,000, and moments later the yearling was hammered down to him and

Dobbs for $150,000. As the horse was led back to the barns, a sale employee carrying a clipboard with paperwork got Winslett's signature on the bill of sale, completing the process. There would be no rush of photographers and reporters converging on the principals this time; those scenes were reserved for the seven-figure transactions. This was just another horse being sold, a process that would be repeated thousands of times over the next week. Winslett and Dobbs stood and strode past Dan out of the pavilion, blue skies and dreams ahead of them. Everyone can have the Derby winner—until they start running.

40

Dan sought out a farmer down the road who agreed to seed and cut Dan's field, using the alfalfa to feed his livestock. Frank Leonard had made his living off the land his entire life, and knew every inch of soil and every piece of machinery needed to cultivate it. Five minutes after Dan introduced himself, Frank, while running down the litany of what made farm life the best life, asked him, "You drop your trousers and pee off your porch yet?" They became fast friends.

Frank planted in Dan's head the idea of a vegetable garden the following spring, and brought over a season's worth of firewood for Dan to chop down to fit the wood stove he had urged Dan to buy. Minus a generator, when the power failed, as it did at some point nearly every winter due to ice storms and fallen tree limbs, you either needed an energy source or you needed to leave home.

Although the autumn was no match for New England's, the yellow Midwest light mixed against the blue sky and green fields held its own. The leaves gave a brief show of color before being shed, and they lined Dan's walking path through the backwoods. The quality of the air was a welcome change from the city, and for the first time in years, it seemed, Dan consciously took deep, long breaths to change the air in his lungs. While the dogs hunted for amphibious creatures, Dan selected a favorite creekside rock from where he watched and listened as the water swept past him on its way to the Kentucky River a few miles of meanders downstream. Here, nothing could reach him and nobody could bother him. This was his bonus room.

Early October marked the beginning of Keeneland's autumn race meeting.

The three-week-long stand brought in most of the best horsemen from around the country vying for the enhanced purse money. Trainers looked to get their 2-year-olds up and going before the end of the year so those that showed promise would have some foundation under them when they started on the Kentucky Derby trail. It was a big event on the Lexington social scene, the human participants dressed to show off their promise as well. Dan was about to leave the office late one morning to soak up the racetrack scene when the phone rang.

"Hey, you find any barefoot pussy yet?"

Sonny had given him six weeks to settle in.

"I need some more time to miss you. Can you call back next year?"

"You getting used to shitting in the cold?"

"We have indoor plumbing now."

"No kidding?"

"How are you, Sonny?"

"Just like a pound of granulated sugar."

"Sweet?"

"Fine. Just wanted to make sure you haven't been raped by a banjo."

"As always, your concern is troubling."

"I thought you should know, The Noz got canned already. They're offering you $150,000 to come back."

Dan determined to remain silent.

"So, is that a yes?"

"No. It isn't."

"Are you nuts?"

"Are you for real?"

"No, you got me, but I needed to take your temperature. Obviously, you must somehow be liking it there."

"Sure I like it. I'm a thousand miles from you."

"I love you too. Listen, I heard ABC Sports, run by your man Morono, is gonna lock up the rights for the Kentucky Derby."

"That could actually be useful information, which would be a first for you. Is it real?"

"Of course it's real, you hump. You think I'd waste my valuable time chit-chatting with you for no reason?"

"Let's go back to the 'valuable time' part of that."

"While you're shucking cornstalks there, I got a lunch date with a woman who's a contortionist. Positions you can't even imagine. I think she can pleasure herself orally."

"So you're kind of a fifth wheel?"

"Nothing the matter with watching that."

"Sonny, thanks for the scoop. Just knowing you're out there somewhere is a true source of discomfort."

"Go screw yourself."

"You talking to me or your date?"

Two hours before the first race, cars were already streaming into the Keeneland lots. Fans used the tree-shaded grounds in the parking areas for tailgate parties, and Dan couldn't help but notice the atmosphere was more like a country fair than a racetrack, not unlike those summer days up at Saratoga when he was a kid. College kids from the nearby University of Kentucky made the scene. The local breeders and farm owners turned out to see the products of their plans and hard work, studying each animal and making mental notes about what a certain stallion or broodmare produced.

Dan had introduced himself to most of the racetrack executives during his breakfasts at the track kitchen, and in the paddock where the horses were prepared and then saddled for the races, he observed a group of them monitoring the festivities like anxious party hosts waiting for a mixer to take off. The track was 50 years old but not a blade of grass was out of place. Funded from the profits of the horse sales it hosted, Keeneland always had its best face on. It had its own nursery from which trees were selected to augment the grounds. The stonework in the walls of the grandstand and those surrounding the paddock was perfect. No corners were cut shoring up the grand old lady for its biannual unveiling.

"Isn't this a great day?"

Dan turned to the voice, which belonged to the track's president, Camden Ball.

"You've got the weather on your side."

"This is one of my favorite times of the year." Ball displayed an almost childlike enthusiasm for his plant, disarming even the most cynical attendee. "If there's anything we can do to help you along, just let us know."

And with that Ball drifted around to spread his cheer. Dan watched him cheerfully work the paddock. He didn't seem like a guy who would throw a trainer off the grounds for complaining. The illusion that masks the reality. The Mickey Mouse who greets kids at Disneyland is, under the rodent head, a minimum-wage employee. Ball carried on his joyous rounds a velvet axe.

Dan remained around the paddock all day, remembering something Neil Hawkins had told him that first morning back at Belmont Park when they were outside Winslett's barn. Hawkins stated that it was impossible to cover racing from the press box. The stories were found in the barn area and the paddock and down on the racetrack and in the grandstand.

He was engaged in constant conversation, his byline making him highly recognizable. People asked, mistakenly, for his advice and selections in the races. Dan circulated among the horse owners who played at the top of the game; the farm owners who bred and sold the stock he'd be writing about; the trainers who closed down the bars before beating the sun up to the barns the following morning; the jockeys, pound for pound the strongest bunch of them all, who seemed to party far too hard and leave with far too many women much too tall far too often; the gamblers, a murky group some of whom wagered incredible sums day in and day out. This horse racing universe was its own world, the people inhabiting it refugees seeking asylum from either the disappointments or normalcy of their lives outside it. Dan pretty much felt at home.

41

Lexington wasn't famous for its diversity. It was an insular town given some to inbreeding, and some to the next closest thing—mergers between like-minded and –powered families. The society scenes were populated by guys named Preston and Morgan who clearly had never worked a day in their lives outside their families' banking or law practices; the local women were blonds, at least in the areas open to the public, with names like Misty and Anna Belle, and their features were just a little off the mark, due perhaps to a cousin somewhere upstream in the chromosome stew. It was a pretty inside game, not that Dan strove to cut in much anyway.

After a few months, though, there were needs to be met, and typically at such times, mistakes to be made. After a longish evening at McCarthy's just days before Christmas, Dan heard himself asking his reporting colleague Kate whether she'd like to come back out to the farm with him. He had been thinking about popping the question for weeks but was certain it wasn't a good idea to bed someone from the same newsroom. This, however, was a moment of holiday cheer.

Kate had been at the *Herald* more than a year now, right out of journalism classes at a small college in the eastern part of the state, which was to say she could write at least at a high school level. She wasn't going to be accepting any literature awards in the near term, but familiarity with her beat in the government offices downtown had helped her acquire sources and confidence, and she had room to grow on the job.

Kate wasn't tough to look at. Her round face was quick to break into smile, and all the body parts were set in the right places with the right dimensions. What Dan liked was she was easy to talk to, and they had similar tastes in music and TV shows. She even knew some baseball, if only for crushes she had on some players.

His heart fluttered pleasantly when she answered in the affirmative. Kate's body was welcome against his, and they raged on a good while until climax and sleep overcame them. Kate would be driving home to spend the holidays with her family the following day, the perfect antidote to the uncomfortable decisions of how much time to spend with or apart.

Breeding farms are a beehive of activity come January, as mares begin foaling—usually in the dead of night, causing maximum inconvenience and minimal sleep for their human caretakers—and the babies, impossibly shaky on their spindly legs, take their first steps, never leaving their mother's flank first in their stall, and then once turned out in the field when the baby is ready to take exercise. As the mothers eat to replenish themselves after the rigors of birth-giving, the babies nap nearby on the hard winter ground. Upon awakening, they search out and then quickly rejoin their mothers. Thus, during that first year, the mare is said to have either a colt or filly "at her side." Soon enough the babies will begin romping with their classmates further and further away. Six or eight months after birth, the weanlings will be separated from and moved to a field far enough away from their mothers so that neither are prompted to do something drastic given each other's cries of protest. The babies grow, the mothers again give birth, and the process repeats.

Mind you, these aren't eight-pound babies popping out; they're 150-pound horses, and birth-giving can often be difficult. Even with the best possible medical care and attentive staff, a sizable percentage of these births will end up being problematic, or fatal, to the baby and/or mare. This foaling season, however, was unusually bad. By late January it was evident in the foaling barns and the equine hospitals that something far worse was going on.

Dozens, and then hundreds, of foals were being delivered tragically weakened or stillborn. The hospitals were filled up over a 50-mile radius in all directions out from Lexington. Panic does not take long to set in when the product you are producing cannot be utilized. People invested millions of dollars in acquiring a stud horse to serve mares, the payback coming when the mare foals and the mare owner pays the stud fee to the stallion owner. When the foal is born dead, that fee doesn't come back to the stallion owner. The mare owner cannot subsequently take the baby to sale and recoup his costs in acquiring and keeping and feeding the mare so, in effect, nobody gets paid. Not enough horses end up at the training farms or at the racetrack or chewing through feed or running in fenced paddocks or being shoed. A large ring of pain radiates out from the dead or unable-to-perform foal and affects all the ancillary service-providers and businesses. In short, panic.

Dan got his first sniff of the story one cold February morning at Keeneland, where the trainers were gnawing at their sausage and biscuits & gravy complaining they couldn't get a veterinarian to come to the racetrack to give any medicine or services; they were all too busy at the equine hospitals working on some sort of epidemic of sick babies. Back at the office Dan began making calls to the equine clinics, and took a couple of brisk 'no comments' before finding a doctor who was also a horse breeder who detailed at length the problems he was seeing. It had to do with a disruption in the stomach linings of the mares, causing an imbalance of nutrients getting to the foals in utero. Dan broke the story in the newspaper the next day, getting the crisis out of whisper mode, as no breeder wanted it well known that something was horribly wrong with his mares, and no stallion owner wanted it publicized that his stud horse wasn't successfully making babies. Out in the open, at least the industry could come together and work in unison to find a cause and a cure. The affliction was grouped under the name Mare Reproductive Loss Syndrome, but that name wasn't nearly as important as the words "insolvency" and "bankruptcy", which is where a lot of small breeders were heading with their dead foals.

Dan filed stories daily on the effects of what was going on. Some days they were medical-oriented, some days he told the stories of the people teetering on the edge, about to lose all they had invested in their farms. He could have filled the entire news section daily with all the stories, and the paper moved several other reporters, including Kate, over to help him cover them.

The inevitable discomfort with Kate came sooner rather than later. It's all fine and good to live in the moment, to share intimacy if just to feel for a little while like you're not alone in the world; we all need love, but those needs are so rarely equally distributed between two people. And when one wants more than the other, well, then you get real life. Dan and Kate slept together a half-dozen times, but since the MRLS story broke Dan was absorbed with work. In the morning staff meetings he could feel Kate's eyes trained on him, and he knew she wanted more from him, of him.

The thing he'd loved about Linda was her independence, her not needing him to make decisions and be the grand poobah of everything. And, of course, that ended with her not needing him at all. But he hated the feeling of being the professor, the mentor. He needed an equal.

After Dan assigned several reporters one morning to the MRLS angles they'd be covering, Kate approached and offered to cook dinner, which Dan begged off on, citing work. She then got loud on the rejection at a moment when no one else was speaking.

"Ya can't live without 'em," was Ed Benson's take on it as Dan brushed past him heading out of the office a few minutes later.

"Remind me to try," Dan replied without looking at his boss.

The first tangible effect of MRLS was on the winter sale of broodmares held at Keeneland. It was the first auction of the calendar year and could set the tone as to the health of the overall industry. However, with broodmares aborting their foals all over the region, the market for people to purchase more broodmares dried up like a summer puddle and gross sales fell nearly half from the year before. There was no way for Dan to dress up this sow. The people he quoted in his articles laid out the severity of the downturn. He just filled in the numbers.

The pages of the *Herald* were filled with bad news, it seemed, throughout the winter. Real estate sales in the region slowed to a drip, and values plunged. Bankruptcies and unemployment were up. And it wasn't just Lexington. The stock market was taking a crap, gas prices were moving higher, and banks were getting hammered by bad loans that weren't getting paid back. Credit was drying up and interest rates were sky high.

The *Herald* was no longer under local control, either. Like so many things, it had been swallowed up by a corporation that thought the way to go was to buy daily papers in small cities with upside potential. Lexington, a major college town but still fairly small-time, fit the bill. So Rigorson Media actually signed the checks, and Dan knew a corporation was built on shedding whatever was least profitable. If the horse industry continued to tank and other Lexington business indicators followed, he figured many workers at the *Herald* could be more rigor mortis than Rigorson.

Dan watched as his dogs romped through the snow, burying their noses deep into it burrowing for rodents and coming up with white faces. An inch of snow dressed each tree limb, with the light from the setting sun bathing the top half of the trees in beautiful amber. Dan could feel the strains of trouble spiraling around his new universe, but tried to hit the moving target of staying in the moment.

42

The one time each year when America sets aside all else and concentrates on horse racing is Kentucky Derby day, the first Saturday in May. Because of the fever pitch that fast Thoroughbreds can produce, the Derby is often called "the most exciting two minutes in sports."

The Kentucky Derby makes a living for its host, Churchill Downs in Louisville, about an hour's drive west of Lexington along I-64. Louisville is a far more cosmopolitan town than its neighbor to the east, boasting a greater variety of restaurants, entertainment, and worldliness. It is the hometown of The Greatest, Muhammad Ali.

Churchill Downs has been running the Kentucky Derby for more than a century. The Derby didn't start out as the institution it is today, but as a far more modest event bankrolled by local entrepreneurs. Over time, and with the backing of the state's burgeoning breeding and sales businesses, the race grew into its place on the calendar of Americana alongside the Fourth of July, the Masters golf tournament, the World Series, and the new kid on the block, the Super Bowl.

The famed racetrack in Louisville sits in the middle of a forlorn neighborhood comprised of postage-stamp-sized two-story dwellings punctuated by a tavern every few blocks. The residents don't seem too inclined to travel in the proximity of anyone licensed to perform dental work, and they make a good portion of their income squeezing patrons' cars onto every square inch of their driveways, front lawns, and curb space in front of their homes at champagne rates on Derby day.

Inside the facility, while the swells have their wood-paneled, noise-swallowing grand rooms in which to swill bourbon, smoke cigars, and wager on their own horses or those of their friends, the $2 bettors downstairs read their weathered *Racing Forms* and tip sheets in cavernous, dank breezeways that have all the charm of a subway station. They are open to whatever elements Mother Nature has in store, from searing heat to treacherous thunderstorms, packed in so tightly one has to struggle to lift his arms to ingest the overpriced, over-sweetened Mint Juleps that are the official drink of the Derby. And from no vantage point where they are allowed can they actually see the racetrack. Yet they come year after year, 100,000-plus strong, to be part of Kentucky's signature event, proud that the state is on the world's radar for one day a year.

There were no such crowds on this early February morning when Dan strode through the gates, looking for the Louisville Room where a press conference was scheduled to start in 30 minutes. The big announcement was a five-year deal that ABC and Churchill Downs had signed giving the network rights to televise the Derby, a story Dan had broken two weeks earlier from Sonny's tip, but without on-the-record confirmation from either of the involved parties. ABC had paid a premium price to land the race, which was traditionally among the highest-rated sporting events and would, the network hoped, provide a strong lead-in to its coverage of the NBA's playoff games that would follow.

Finding the proper elevator, Dan lurched upward toward the 4th floor, where bigshots and journalists alike were being fed in first-class fashion before the festivities commenced. There was nothing complicated to the way reporters operated—if you threw them some food and drink you were more likely to get into print adjectives denoting enthusiasm. Dan entered the large dining room, which had circular tables set up in front of a dais. Buffets piled high with breakfast pastries, tubs of runny eggs, potatoes, bacon and sausage, and fruit platters buffered both sides of the room.

Every local politician with a title and every businessman with more than 15 employees seemed to already be throwing back the free grub. The tables closest to the dais were packed tight and the food stations were seeing brisk business as attendees juggled the plates and silverware and napkins to gather as much foodstuffs as possible without necessitating a return trip. Dan scanned the scene, finding the open chair he was looking for at a prime table dead center.

"Y'all need any help with the horses, I'm your guy," Dan said, slapping Gregg Gold on the shoulder with one hand and giving an extra shove to Jerry Romano with the other. "Jerry, I see you've found the buffet," Dan continued, eyeing the two plates in front of Romano heaped with food.

After Gregg got up and hugged Dan, Romano made a show of introducing Dan around the table of ABC executives. "We made a star outta this guy in New York, and he runs off to Kentucky on us," Romano said before diving back into his eggs.

"I thought it was *me* who made *you* a star," Dan countered. "Welcome to Kentucky, gentlemen, where ignorance meets bliss."

"Dan is the horse racing writer for the Lexington newspaper," Gregg explained around the table. "One of the best writers in the game."

"Dan, I've got a question," said one of the suits. "We just bought the Kentucky Derby, and now I'm told the best horses can't run in it?"

"Only 3 year olds are eligible for the Derby," Dan explained. "The older, more established horses have their own series of races. Right, Jerry?"

Romano was caught, of course, with a mouthful of biscuits and gravy and waved off the referral. "Anyway," continued Dan, "horses don't begin running until they're 2, so the Derby horses are still relatively young ones."

"We bought a goddamn rookie game?" the executive said, causing Romano to choke on a piece of bacon. Dan was happy to come to the rescue by pounding him on the back. Romano kept coughing through the sip of coffee he was attempting to swallow.

"Yes, but it's a very important rookie game," Dan said in mock assurance.

"We take another ratings bath, there's gonna be plenty people around here shoveling horse shit."

"The Derby always does well," Romano managed while still trying to regain his voice. "Right Dan?"

"Having a big-name horse sure helps," Dan said, continuing to subtly stir the pot. "You need to hook your promotion to a solid story line."

"What we got this year?" asked the executive.

"Too soon to tell. The prep races are just about to get started," Dan explained.

"Sounds like a pig in a poke," said the man.

"It's a horse; it's definitely a horse in a poke," said Dan.

Gregg bulled his way in. "Let's take a walk, show me the layout," he said to Dan, almost pulling his friend up and away from the table.

"Pleasure meeting you gentlemen," Dan said, dripping fake friendliness. "Anything I can do…"

"You're gonna give Romano a heart attack," Gregg said when they were out of ear shot.

"Not as quickly as those eggs and biscuits with the coagulating gravy," Dan replied. "Besides, it was the suit pushing the issue, not me."

"They don't understand the sport," Gregg said.

"Nobody understands this sport, but the Derby's the Derby," said Dan.

"Romano laid a lot on the line to sign this deal, especially with the economy tanking. The others are edgy about it."

"You guys should make out alright. It usually gets good numbers. Unless you fuck it up."

"You look good," Gregg said, changing the subject.

"I *am* good. Southern living agrees with me."

"And a real job?"

"Well, nothing's perfect, but it's easier than I thought. People are nice and they like my sentences OK. How's corporate?"

"About as much fun as I didn't think it would be. I mean, it's alright, but there's pressure. That stuff back there at the table is typical. Everything gets filtered through a pack of guys who may or may not know what you're trying to do or what they're doing, but they all get their say and you gotta jump. But that's the network game."

"That's the game, period."

The two stood on a terrace outside the dining room, looking out on the expanse of racetrack below them encircling a huge grass infield and the small pavilion where the owner of the Derby winner accepts the coveted trophy every year and speaks to the world over network television. Now, it was still, frost melting off the ground, a single maintenance worker clear across the infield unloading some piping from a pick-up. The colors were vivid in the winter sunshine, and the grand lady looked magnificent.

"Long way from home," Dan said, enjoying the moment with his friend.

"Yeah, we've done alright for two kids sweating our balls off working the rock quarries every summer," Gregg said.

"You remember the day Johnny Alt smacked Mark Gilli on the hand with the sledgehammer?" Dan asked, and both of them broke out laughing. "That son of a bitch's middle finger went out in five directions."

"Yeah," said Gregg, "but the crazy grip gave him that curveball nobody could hit. That sledgehammer got him a full ride to Miami."

"And he said he could pleasure women like nobody else," said Dan. "With that face, that was big for him."

Their laughter was interrupted by the screech of a bad P.A. system announcing the beginning of the official B.S. session inside.

Romano was seated now on the dais looking out of place sandwiched among a coterie of Kentucky WASPs. Nervous smiles played all around, the locals tolerating Romano--who still had pieces of scrambled egg at the corners of his mouth--because he came carrying satchels of cash.

Tom Harvey, the CEO of Churchill Downs, said all the right things in heralding the network's new pact that paid the racetrack $2 million a year, but he had to look down at his written remarks to make sure he got the letters right when he said 'ABC.'

Romano got up and read a few remarks prepared by his research department about the Derby. Dan looked over at the table of ABC suits. Romano didn't appear to be convincing any of them that this was a slam-dunk moneymaker. They were pushing away their coffee cups and folding their napkins aimlessly by the time Romano wrapped it up by saying how delighted ABC was to be joining forces with the bored hosts on either side of him. One of the Churchill honchos stood up, shook Romano's hand for the photographers, and then made the mistake of opening the floor for questions.

After a few innocuous inquiries that the Churchill suits swatted away, Dan asked Romano by name what ABC would be doing differently from NBC's recent coverage of the Derby, knowing full well Romano wouldn't know. Instead of turning to Gregg, who actually could have put an answer together, Romano slogged through: "We have the best crews in the business and we will put our own stamp on the coverage of this wonderful event."

"What exactly will you change?" Dan countered.

"The ink is still on the paper," Romano flubbed. "We are just beginning to take a look at this."

At the ABC table, the executives were now sticking forks into their napkins, checking their watches, and wondering if they could catch earlier flights out of town. Dan was satisfied he'd done his job well.

43

Dan's hiring at the *Herald* coincided with a round of layoffs, because the editors felt they had to have a racing writer. The second round of job cuts had ripped through the building just after New Year's, and one by one people balefully pushed carts of their belongings across the parking lot to their cars, where they loaded what had moments before been their work lives.

The newspaper had shrunk in size by a third in just the past half year, and pointed letters to the editor let the executives know that had not gone unnoticed. The readers went into full revolt when a dozen comic strips were discontinued. Nothing angers newspaper customers more than canceling comic strips. All else was expendable but that. After dozens of angry phone calls, an editor took the remainder of the unpublished comics and pasted them in the front office window so people could come see their favorites to the conclusion of their arcs.

The survivors of the first two rounds of job cuts went about their office business quietly, not daring to bitch about the extra work they were taking on until after-hours drinking sessions. They were miserable yet happy to have a job, the common paradox among workers in bad times. Although the travel budget was among the first casualties, Dan thought he might be getting sent to

Florida to cover an important Derby prep race when Ed Benson asked him to his office a few days after the Derby press conference.

He was being asked to go, alright, but not to Florida.

"I'm sorry, Dan, but we gotta cut your position. I wish there was some other way."

"You kidding?"

"The owners say we have to cut 30% across the board. I tried for you. It's a lousy situation."

Twenty minutes later Dan was taking the walk of shame, loading his office books and some framed photos and a plant into his van. Although his firing had nothing to do with performance, he was embarrassed. Six months was embarrassing. He let his mind dwell on a few things he'd wanted to tell Ed Benson, for example, about what he thought of editors who had their tongues up the ass of everyone above them. But he knew what Benson was: a backslapper who would push anybody off the cliff to save his job.

Dan much preferred the cigar-chomping newspapermen of the ink stain days. Guys who didn't speak at the Rotarian Club, guys willing to tackle the demigods and expose the manipulators. They were gone now, that breed. Today, the bigger the story, the more likely it is to get stiffed, Dan thought while climbing into the car. Today seemed far away from the greatest newspaperman of them all, H.L. Mencken, who wrote the purpose of a newspaper was to comfort the afflicted and afflict the comfortable.

Dan busied himself for days doing all the requisite things the newly unemployed busy themselves with. Making sure his health insurance got extended three months, going down to the courthouse and signing up for unemployment, working on a resume although for whom he hadn't a clue. Mostly he slept a bit later each morning and took walks, it seemed, all day long. Being in motion cut down on rumination time. The dogs were happy to have him around, and delighted to jaunt through the snow and around the woods at all hours of the day.

Dan took a chainsaw and spent a couple of hours each day cutting downed trees on his property, then borrowed Frank's pick-up to cart the wood back to the house, where he built a stack of wood good for a couple of winters. He spent more time volunteering at Frank's to learn about farming. Although the dead of winter was Frank's quiet time, there were always things to do. Vehicles to work on, fencing to fix, greenhouses to clean up in preparation for growing season, seeds to order, and cows to feed. Dan enjoyed his time with Frank, a good man aware of the world from what he got from the people around him and the evening newscast. Frank was able to take each man as he came, and liked everyone until they proved otherwise. Which often came soon enough. Although quick with a laugh, he was a hard-nosed businessman who knew exactly what his cattle and tobacco and hay were worth, and when someone was trying to pay him less.

Dan kept an eye on the horse world after his days helping Frank. Whitey Winslett had just run a wickedly good 3-year-old owned by Sam Dobbs named Sunshine Daydream. With Dobbs' money, Winslett had bought him after the horse had run well in his first race in Florida. The horse cost Dobbs about as much as he would make back if the horse actually won the Kentucky Derby. Nobody said it was a rational business.

Dan bought an armful of travel books and at night visualized himself in towns and cities across the country. When he got sleepy it was like coming out of a trance, like he'd been transported to the place he was reading about and surprised to find himself on the living room sofa.

He decided he'd travel when the season warmed--an open-ended road trip with the dogs. A job might come in handy in the meanwhile to defer the expenses involved. Dan picked up the Help Wanted section of the Sunday newspaper like he'd used it to pick up dog crap, fearful of finding something.

Writing jobs weren't exactly growing on trees around town. Dan hoofed it to the obvious suspects such as Keeneland and the city magazine *Bluegrass*, and came up empty. Unhappily, he broadened his search back into retail, trying a couple of record stores near the university without success. He widened his options from there.

44

"What is it that attracts you to Macy's as a job destination?" asked the middle manager in charge of hiring. Dan was studying the variety of stains on his navy blue slacks, an accrual of wet weather, dog slobber, and miscellaneous foodstuffs. The dark color was a false savior from the cost of dry cleaning. His eyes slipped down to his black sneakers, showing their age despite the layer of shoe polish he'd lathered on them. Like old men, they were growing white through time.

"It's the champagne of retail outlets," Dan managed, trying to tilt literary without getting overly enthused. "Everybody knows that."

Outside the 2nd floor window sat a lifeless, frigid Kentucky February morning. Nothing left for the trees. The air said 'cold' before you even felt it. Midwest hell.

"What do you feel you can bring to Macy's?"

Dan wondered if all these guys got their questions from the same pop psyche consultant, some guy who couldn't get a real job. He wondered why they weren't more concerned with whether or not you could move merchandise off the floor. Whether you could steer customers to the check-out counter producing the plastic.

"A positive attitude," Dan noted with the straightest of faces.

Relieved to be back outside and confident he'd done enough not to get offered time in retail purgatory, the frigidness fit Dan's mood. He tossed the Macy's propaganda/study book into the first trash can he passed.

Idling at a red light, Dan studied his cold, whitening, rough hands on the wheel. Was that a kidney spot starting to form between two veins beneath his forefinger? At his age? In the mood for gratification, he pulled a right off Harrodsburg Road toward a Mexican dive for a couple of tacos. There wasn't a dime's worth of ethnicity in Lexington other than the Latinos who'd arrived the past couple years to work the farms and racetrack barns, the jobs that previously were manned by the country boys who'd grown tired of the impossible hours and dirty work, and moved on to who knows what. Assistant managers at the fast-food joints? Butchers at the Krogers market? Heating and air conditioning service in the subdivisions?

Dan was glad enough for something authentic, and the tacos at La Favorita were damn good. You walked through a store catering to Latino immigrants, who lined up inside the door to Western Union part of their paychecks back home. There were shelves full of Jesus and Mary in multiple mediums—ceramic, plastic, glass, rubber. And in the back there was a grill with six stools and a narrow shelf bolted to the wall, Spanish-language TV blaring bad soap operas with a hot Latina wailing in distress way too loudly. Enjoying each bite, Dan could forget momentarily where he was.

The cold shot of air a step outside the door brought it all crashing back to him. He thought of heading out to the farm, but there was nothing he wanted to do there.

He walked down the strip mall from La Favorita, past dollar stores and overstock discount clothing junkyards, past the Baskin-Robbins that was considered gourmet in this neighborhood, and finally past the worst excuse for an Italian restaurant he'd ever stepped foot in. He knew now where he was headed, although the 'why' would have escaped him.

Self-loathing would have been closest to an explanation. Dan had a healthy dislike for strip clubs. He'd hated the bachelor party or two that forced him into one, and saw only sadness, not sensuality, when ruminating on the stars of the stage show. Then there were the cretins ringside that supported the sloppy cycle of bad dancing and cellulite-surrounded thongs. Why would lonely guys pay money for the privilege to be teased and not laid, Dan wondered.

His eyes took a minute to adjust to the darkness inside the tiny entrance vestibule of Pure Platinum. Just doing research into the maladies of the human soul, Dan told himself. He passed the free lunch buffet, the chemical stink of the Sternos making him nauseous. There truly were no free lunches, he thought.

Dan's eyes had acclimated, and he focused in on the cheap bottles of booze that lined the shelves behind the bar, backlit by strings of Christmas lighting that remained up year-round. A real festive tone to the joint, Dan thought. Wanting no part of ringside, he took a stool at the rail on the landing raised over the pit of tables nearest the dancers. It took two minutes for a waitress to find him.

"What can I get for you today?"

"Beer. Anything in a bottle," he ordered.

"We have a free lunch buffet against the wall," she boasted.

"Yes, I've smelled it."

"The Swedish meatballs are really pretty good."

She must be new, thought Dan, spending her time pushing the only free fare in the place. He turned to the stage show, puzzling to himself whether the quality of the matinee talent was inferior to the nighttime, and figured not necessarily, the businessman crowd perhaps being more lucrative than whatever flotsam drifted in after dark.

Onstage, a bust-enhanced blonde was trying to catch up to the beat of the Stones' "Start Me Up." Dan took up the mental study of why there were so many more blondes by percentage in the Midwest than there were on the East Coast. Was it ethnicity? Hadn't the French and other European types found this area kind for raising horses hundreds of years ago? No great Scandinavian influx he knew of. Had to be the greatest ad campaign of all time, that thing about blondes having more fun.

The beer arrived with a come-on back. "Can I get you something else?"

Dan surveyed the lonely bottle. "Perhaps a piece of glass?"

The waitress giggled in retreat, and Dan went back to the stage. Mick was singing, "Never stop, never stop, never stop," but the blonde, a bit light on conditioning, looked as though she was ready to quit well before the tune did. She moved to the edge of the stage to take on a few bills in her bikini bottom, caught her breath, and went to the pole for the big finish.

Where do they come from, Dan wondered, then thought about where *he* came from. How he got to this moment. And right then he realized people got to this place, these places, as easily as they got to the vegetable department at the grocery.

A good-looking woman, covered in a silky robe that the dancers wore once they've come offstage, walked confidently in heels past the bar. The lower strands of her long brunette wig dropped to the side of his bottle.

"Dan?"

The face was familiar, but Dan couldn't find his bearings in it, studying quick and hard to figure out from where. In a few long moments, his failure was complete. She bailed him out.

"Cindy. Cindy Brandt. From advertising."

"Cindy. Of course. I'm sorry. The lighting."

"The wig," she helped him out.

"That too," he replied, quickly accepting the aid. Cindy Brandt sold ads at the *Herald*, but was let go shortly before his own dismissal. He'd thought she was cute—short, dark hair tastefully framing beautiful skin. Slim body, always tastefully dressed—until now.

"What are you doing here?" Her tone was halfway between admonishment and surprise. "I mean, you know…"

"Damn, I was hoping to ask you first."

"Sorry. Beat you."

"I heard the Swedish meatballs were the best in town."

"You should kill whoever told you that."

"I'm out job hunting. Pretty depressing, and before I knew it…"

"Yeah, I heard you got the axe, too. Listen, I'm not supposed to talk too long unless it leads to a private room. Want to have dinner later?"

45

It seemed like a good idea at the time, Dan thought to himself as he piloted his car toward the Americana restaurant Cindy and he had decided on. Now, hours later, the first-date doubts and terror were creeping in. Relax, his other voice told him. Was this even a date? Two ex-employees of a newspaper just getting together.

Of course it's a date, Dan overruled himself, coming to his senses. The tingle up his spine earlier as they agreed to get together, Cindy leaning in close, and the excitement spreading to crucial body parts. My God, the way that robe lay tentatively at the top of her breasts, and rode down ending mid-thigh, with nothing but smooth skin between it and the six-inch, open-toe high heels.

What are the warning signals, he said to himself, switching gears and taking mental pencil to paper to list why this was a bad idea. Dan couldn't tame the Virgo in him, the need to analyze until every angle had been wrung dry. She's working in a strip joint, for Christ sake, he began, lifting that nugget to number one on the Top 10.

He tried to remember her boyfriend from the office Christmas party a couple months ago. He recalled being underwhelmed by the personality, but wasn't he a cop or a mailman or something? Either was bad. A cop would have guns, and mailmen seemed to have easy access, and didn't mind using them. Dan didn't feel like being on the wrong end of a 'going postal' joke. That was number two with a bullet, alright.

His better voice told him to take it easy. It wasn't like he had anything better to do.

What if the cop was following her to the restaurant, thinking she was meeting a john? Just stop it, Dan finally told himself.

He got to the joint first. Punctuality was a habit he just couldn't shake, drilled into him by his mother. Occasionally it worked, leading someone into a good first impression. Oftentimes it was just self-annoying, resulting in a lot of staring at his surroundings. From the one hard bench seat inside the door, he recognized a horse trainer at a far table, thought about going over to say hello, but didn't want to linger over people with food in front of them, especially toting with him his newly unemployed status.

"Hey," said Cindy, arriving in a pleasant rush of fresh air. She was wearing a double-breasted Pea coat and tight-fitting jeans that flared out over heeled boots. Dan immediately noticed how much better she looked without the wig, but kept it to himself.

After the opening small talk and menu perusal, they sent the waitress away with their dinner orders—pot roast for her, catfish for him. Dan and Cindy then hoisted up their beer mugs and clicked them together. "To life after newspapers," she said, and they both swallowed like they meant it.

"All right, I gotta ask," Dan began.

"I know, I know. How did I end up at Pure Platinum?" Cindy said, so he didn't have to. "It's good money, but the truth is, that's not why I'm doing it. Partly, I'm challenging myself; it's a dare, almost. And there's some thrill to it, like chasing down a good story."

"Yeah, but I'm dressed when I'm doing that," Dan said, glad that she laughed. "How about…what's his name? What does he think?"

"Ron?" she helped him out again. "We're not together anymore."

"You're kidding?" he managed, feeling that tingle again. "You were with him a long time, weren't you?"

"Five years. I caught him screwing around. A divorcee on his mail route. Nothing even original. Just a cliché."

Dan was amazed, first, how a mutt like Ron got somebody like Cindy, and then wasn't satisfied. Something about her, maybe. Number three on the list?

"So, you dancing is maybe a reaction to that, like, proving yourself all over again? Or hating men?"

Dan immediately regretted he'd gone that far.

"Sorry," he quickly added. "I don't mean to play psychiatrist on you."

"No, there's some truth there," Cindy said, nearing the bottom of the first beer. "I think part of it is proving that I can do whatever I put my mind to. I don't hate men, though. I certainly don't hate you."

"That's the nicest thing a woman's ever said to me," Dan replied, Cindy again riding the punch line with her winning laugh before he ordered another round of beers.

"So how about you?" she said, and as Dan prepared an answer of what he'd been up to since getting fired, she refined the question. "You seeing anybody?"

Dan marveled at her easy sensuality. He could never ask a question of a woman like that, so casually and smoothly. Maybe there was something beneficial to being around a place where sex was the center of the universe. Or at least the promise of it; or at least the tease of it.

"Me, no, I'm not seeing anyone but my dogs. They're the only ones who love me, and they may be jiving, too."

"B.B. King," she said, getting the reference.

"Wow, yes," Dan noted, as they launched into the next round. He was mentally tearing the Top 10 list into a million pieces and tossing them away, overtaken by pure love that only a first date can bring.

"We saw him at his club in Memphis last year, me and a couple of girlfriends. It was terrific."

"Great town," Dan said. "A bunch of us went from college. I did about three hours in the Stax Records museum, right across the street from Memphis Slim's house."

Stax Records was not on many people's must-see list of Memphis. There was Beale Street, rib joints, and Graceland, and that was about it. Which made Cindy's comeback all the more impressive to him.

"Oh, I know, that re-created Southern gospel church they had in there, and the original recording studio from the '60s."

The catfish, pot roast, a mess of side dishes, and another round of beers arrived, and the couple tore into their dinners, having worked up powerful appetites trying to impress one another. Each took turns dropping the utensils in order to carry on the conversation.

As they were both exhaling from cleaning up the last morsels, the horse trainer Dan had spied earlier approached.

"Dan, what's up? Good to see ya."

Dan rose from his seat to shake hands. "Kenny, you doin' alright? Nice winner you had the other day."

"Yeah, she can run a little bit. Hell, even a blind dog gets a biscuit once in awhile." The trainer's eye wandered to Cindy.

"Cindy Brandt, Kenny Adams," said Dan by way of introduction. "I wrote a story on Kenny a while back, and, despite that, he still talks to me."

After Kenny tipped his cowboy hat to Cindy he returned to Dan. "Hell, you're the best damn writer they ever had at that paper. I can't believe they let you go."

"Tough times'll make a monkey eat hot peppers," Dan tried, attempting to be folksy to deflect the seriousness.

"Well, there's nothing to read in the damn thing anymore," Adams said. "Center of the horse racing world, and they don't bother covering it. Don't seem right. Well, pleasure meeting you, ma'am. Dan, you stay out of trouble."

"Not likely," Dan said. Then, after Adams left. "He's not a bad guy. Cheats much less than the average."

"High praise," Cindy retorted, hitting the right level of sarcasm.

Geez, she is sharp, Dan thought to himself, trying to figure out how not to screw up the final minutes of the evening as he motioned for the check.

"Anyway," Cindy said, "he's right. You were the face of the sports department. "There's nothing left there."

"Never make the mistake of thinking you're indispensible," he preached. "Nobody is."

Dan was comfortable the evening was coming in for a soft landing. He was finishing explaining how he lived 20 minutes from the eatery on a small farm outside Versailles as he helped Cindy on with her coat and they made for the parking lot, pausing for toothpicks at the front counter.

He mustered up as much cool as he could as they strolled the parking lot, though it was hardly enough.

"May I see you again?" he asked, as she remotely unlocked a clean, late-model Japanese sedan.

"Yes," she said, "in about 20 minutes-- I'll follow you home."

46

C indy moved Dan's pointer back into positive territory. He finally had someone to talk to about demons and bemusement of his world, thoughts he'd spoken for so long only in his internal voice. Even better, he enjoyed listening to Cindy's more artistic view of reality.

Dan began going to the club for the last hour of her shift to support her, make sure no one got aggressive with her, and because it turned him on to see her dance. Now known as her boyfriend, the girls didn't bother him, and he'd sit over a beer and watch her--beautiful and sexy and smart and funny. They'd go grab a meal after she got off, or go back to the farm where he'd build a fire and they'd lay entangled warm and happy.

"Why don't you move in with me?" Dan heard himself asking her one night in front of the fire.

"I don't know," Cindy said. "It's awful scary out here in the middle of nowhere. You could be one of those wacky freaks."

"I am. I want to dress you in sexy lingerie, tie you up, and tickle you with goose feathers until you plead for mercy."

"Really? Can we do that tonight?"

"Is that a 'yes' on the moving in?"

Living with Cindy made Dan forget about his job search. He decided not to waste time looking for something torturous. And he didn't have to. Dan wasn't even surprised when the phone rang with a writing offer. A former University of Kentucky basketball player had been busted selling bogus tickets to games, and a brave editor Dan interviewed with at *Bluegrass* magazine assigned him to write a story on the school's ex-jocks and what happened to them once the cheering stopped and they went from heroes to memories.

Dan knew that story had meat on its bones. Lexington, Kentucky, became a population center because of its proximity to the limestone-rich land that nourished champion horses, and also because slaves were auctioned off at its square downtown. The vestiges of the latter were still being felt. Legendary UK basketball coach Adolph Rupp may not have been more of a racist than the norm for white people in his day, but that doesn't mean he wasn't one. He'd had more success than any coach in the country, and built the university's basketball program into the most famous one in the nation until John Wooden and UCLA usurped that position in the '60s. Rupp had no intention of integrating his teams, not until Kentucky famously got the stuffing beat out of it for the national championship in 1966 by the all-black University of Texas-El Paso squad.

The world around the basketball dynasty was changing in so many ways in the '60s, much faster than it could be embraced in the South. So Kentucky's program fell on mediocre times, and was even surpassed by the University of Louisville, whom Kentucky did not even deign to put on its schedule until 1983. Louisville, a much more racially diverse city, was a good deal more prompt including blacks on its team.

So Kentucky became, through the years, just another basketball program among dozens and dozens of others. It lost its competitive advantage as scores of black athletes enrolled in places much quicker to welcome them. Yet the population's fascination with the sport and the program never let up. Graduates of the university come from all over the state to home games in the arena named after Rupp, whitened in hair and wrinkled in skin, but dressed in the blue paraphernalia with the big K screaming back to a grander day. Most activity stops for games, which are televised throughout the state. Players became instant celebrities, and former players used the cache to launch political careers and successful businesses. At least the white ones.

To call Lexington a segregated town was to bestow upon it too much credit. Blacks hit the glass ceiling after janitorial work or the mail room. Keeneland, for instance, fascinated Dan, who was uncertain how it managed to avoid civil-rights discrimination lawsuits since the only blacks he ever saw there were men's room attendants.

Dan threw himself into the assignment. Who knows, maybe he'd help get someone out of the bathroom.

He'd drive Cindy into work in the late morning and then was off to the university to research the whereabouts of its athletes over the past decade. Dan visited the state insurance commissioner in the Capitol at Frankfort, a hot-shooting point guard in his day. He was probably an election cycle or two away from running for governor.

There was the vice president at Central Bank, a guy who had been a bench-warmer for most of his college career; the pastor over at Southside Christian Church who was recruited out of a tiny town in eastern Kentucky for his rebounding skills and who had a calling to pay back the Lord for his ups; the color commentator on the university basketball broadcasts who used to sit on the bench and announce the games to his teammates; and the former center who owned mines in Eastern Kentucky and ran overweight coal trucks to the power plants, occasionally causing fatal accidents on the two-lane twisting highways. These were the white former players.

In Lexington it wasn't hard to find the leaders of the black community. They were encamped on the north side of town, the area somehow forgotten when it came to city money flowing in for things like new roads, parks, and business grants. The slave trade had been halted, but lousy paychecks were about all that was achieved in the last 120 years. Few minorities circumvented the minefield of poor education, broken families, substance abuse, and systemized discrimination.

Dan found Earl Thompson squatting in the Scott County Jail. The high-flying hoop star from six years ago was the guy who got caught in the scam selling UK basketball tickets that he didn't actually possess, a Ponzi scheme that grew bigger and bigger until the cops got complaints and Earl got four years. Dan asked him what had happened.

"When we was playin', they'd give us six tickets each to sell and make some scratch," Earl explained. "I figured doing good and all, I'd still get my tix afterward, but it dried up. So I come up with this deal."

"Did you think of trying to get a real job?"

"Basketball been the only job I got. Nothin' else I *can* do."

Dan found John Morton in the ground floor maintenance room in the downtown high rise where he worked. Morton last played college ball at UK 10 years ago, and now he had a wife and five children. Dan spent a morning with Morton as he spread salt on the icy sidewalk outside the building; hauled a ladder around as he changed out light tubes in various offices; restocked paper towels and cleaned the toilets in the bathrooms. Morton was one of those impossibly upbeat guys no matter the circumstance. He wouldn't trade those days playing basketball in front of packed arenas for anything. People still recognized him at the grocery store, the liquor store, on the street, and stopped and shared a moment. He loves that. Has five daughters and tries to give them most of what they want. To that end, he takes off work at the high rise at 4 every afternoon and heads over to the Northside Baptist Church, where he does odds and ends for three hours before going to his third job, picking up the day's trash and vacuuming the carpets at yet another skyscraper. He grabs a few hours' sleep before beginning the cycle again.

"What'd you study in school?"

"Not much of anything," Morton said with a laugh. "They wanted you workin' on basketball most of the day. The classes we took was just ones where we could get a grade and go on. A grab bag of this 'n' that."

"No regrets you didn't take school seriously?"

"Ah, man, no, what good is any of that do? I got a roof and a family and it's good, you know what I mean. Plenty worse off 'n' me."

Dan couldn't help thinking about the other side of the coin, that there were plenty better off too. Yet you couldn't argue with Morton's attitude. Work schedule aside, he was one of the lucky.

Sam Cross was harder to find. A neighborhood pastor told Dan he was living on the streets, the poster boy for talent gone unrealized. Cross was a local kid whose family broke up before it had ever come together—an absent father and a drug addict mother. He was raised in various foster homes, where he learned early that he had nothing to lose. His escapes were basketball and wildness, and he was proficient at both. UK recruited him out of a juvenile detention facility where he was found to have completed a GED although nobody remembered seeing him in any classes. He had a Ph.D. in jump shooting, however, and was good enough to be considered pro material.

Based on talent Cross was one of the top 10 prospects in the NBA draft. But he slipped to the middle of the second round before Washington selected him. There were alleged concerns with his "mindset" and "adaptability to the pro game." Cross averaged 21 points per game for UK, yet it took Washington a matter of one training camp to admit they'd made a mistake with their second pick. He was let go before playing in a real game, and his $30,000 bonus money was shortly thereafter on the street, where Cross remained after it was gone.

It was on Dan's third trip to the free lunch at a local church that he first caught sight of him. There was no longer anything athletic in Cross' bearing; just hollow eyes staring eerily out from under a wool cap, slumped shoulders, halting gait. Dan tried to explain the story during Cross' uninterested progress through an egg salad sandwich, but it was strictly a one-way street. After 10 minutes Dan stood to leave. Cross spoke for the first time.

"I'll talk for some scratch."

"That's not how this goes."

"Guess it ain't goin'."

"I'd give you money in a second if there was any chance it didn't get shot into your arm."

"There's other places."

"Yeah, crack wise. But here you are. Right back where it started and no smarter."

"How 'bout a couple dollars for home sweet home."

Dan was getting physically ill and only partially because of the egg salad. But he cut a deal with Cross. They'd talk, then go to the market together and buy food. Dan drove home that day angry at the system, angry at the victims, angry at a society that uses humans for entertainment and then discards them like packing material.

With his field interviews completed, Dan began the bureaucratic dance of talking with the university, which initially declined to offer up anybody. That's when Dan sent a pointed letter to the university president laying out the premise of his article and exactly what conclusions he was drawing. The day that missive was read, Dan received an invite to come talk to athletic director Larry Gatewood.

"We give all our student-athletes the same educational opportunities," Gatewood was telling Dan, a tape recorder set up between them on the AD's desk. The walls were covered with photos detailing the university's national successes, small versions of championship banners, and pictures from the White House where various Presidents had greeted UK's national championship teams. "Our graduation rate is about 70% for our student-athletes, in the top 50 percentile for the conference."

"What is the graduation rate for black student-athletes?" Dan asked pointedly.

"I don't believe we break it down along those lines."

"Perhaps you should. Unofficially, I calculate it at about 8%."

"I cannot comment on those numbers."

"Go ahead and figure it out for yourself. It's not that hard. I'll wait."

Gatewood checked his watch, hoping it was time to do something, anything, else.

"Would you say you as a university have failed people like Sam Cross, Earl Thompson, and a hundred or so others who left here as unprepared to enter the workforce as they were when they entered college?"

"It's up to each individual to take advantage of the educational and career opportunities available to them."

"Mickey Mouse courses like the ones each of your athletes uses to stay eligible seem to work a lot better for the middle-class kids with something waiting for them after college, wouldn't you say?"

"I wouldn't characterize anything in our curriculum that way."

"How would you characterize "Health & Hygiene," "Personal Finances," and "Physical Fitness?""

"Those are accredited courses approved by the state."

"Well, bully for the state. No wonder it's ranked 49th in education in the country."

And so it went just as Dan figured. He knew who would be damned when the article appeared, and it wouldn't be the university.

47

Dan got calls from the *Herald* and Louisville *Courier* the day the piece came out, letting him know they were working on follow-ups. It would have been terrific publicity for an out-of-work writer if not for the death threats.

Around about the 10th call, Cindy began answering the phone "Clark Funeral Home." That seemed to work in short-circuiting the haters, although the ringing persisted through most of the night. UK basketball was like a religion in the state, only people donated more money and spent more time on the team than their church. To criticize it was like saying the Bible was full of baloney at a Chatauqua tent revival. To blow it up, as Dan had done in print, well, that was like coming out for mixed-race marriage at a Baptist Bible camp.

After being censored in the *Herald*, Dan wasn't in the mood to filter himself. What had playing ball gotten him other than unemployed?

The answering machine (they'd stopped picking up the phone) was full of the entire range of insults. Dan was repeatedly called a "Nigger lover."

"Guilty as charged," he said to the machine. The ones threatening violence weren't so funny, particularly with Cindy living there.

"Maybe you should stay with friends for a few days," Dan said when Cindy came home from the art gallery where she worked part-time.

"Oh, it's Gary Cooper fighting the forces of evil by himself," she retorted as he suspected she would. "As the clock ticks toward High Noon."

"This isn't fun and games, Cindy. These morons are making some pretty vile threats."

"I'm good enough with a gun. Been shootin' at rabbits since I was about 6, and I've eaten my share of stew."

"Great. Another reason I have to be nice to you."

What Dan didn't tell Cindy was he'd ridden over to the county deputy's home down the road earlier that day. Stan "Sudsy" Fannin was outside in uniform affixing a mailbox to a post in front of his modern brick ranch, which sat on a sharp bend in the road, leading to the box getting clipped on a regular basis by drivers lacking steering skill.

"Where the hell people goin' in such a hurry?" Fannin said to either himself or Dan as the latter approached. "It's a country road. If people is in a hurry, why in damnation don't they live in town so they's close to where they need to be? Third damn box I'm putting up this year and it ain't three months old."

"National problem, bad driving," Dan said before introducing himself and describing the threatening calls.

"Well, I ain't much surprised," Fannin said without a lot of empathy. "Hell, I'm a big UK man myself. Not that I think you done nothin' wrong. But I ain't surprised. Lemme talk to the sheriff, see what we can do."

Leaving Dan by the road, Fannin walked the 100 feet to his deputy's vehicle and called in on the radio. A five-minute conversation ensued before he ambled back toward the mailbox.

"Looks like you saved me a trip into town today," he told Dan. "We gonna stake out your place and see what happens."

On their way down the road the two miles to Dan's place, the convoy ran into Frank Leonard, who hailed down the deputy by his nickname.

"Sudsy, what about it?"

"We tryin' to protect your neighbor here from some riff-raff don't care much for his writin'."

"Seems more exciting than ordering seeds down at the feed store," Frank noted, and within minutes Frank, Sudsy, and Dan had aligned their vehicles so that anyone looking to pass onto Dan's driveway would have to stop and talk to the deputy first. It took less than 90 minutes of chatter about tobacco and cattle futures when they got their first customer. Frank had a shotgun laid across his lap in his pick-up, and Sudsy was carrying one when he approached the beater truck that had slowed and then stopped near Dan's mailbox. Three males were inside.

"What can I do for you boys today?" Sudsy asked as down home as you'd like.

"We lookin' for the Henry place," said the driver.

"To what end?"

"Just wanted to talk," said the driver.

"Yeah, some sense into him," said the unshaven man in the passenger seat, sporting a gapped grin.

"Well, now, nobody's around at the Henry place," said Sudsy. "But I'll be happy to pass along any message."

"We'd just as soon deliver it in person."

"Well, then, here's my message to you," Sudsy said, spitting some tobacco juice on the truck's side, punctuated by the unmistakable sound of Frank cocking his shotgun and pointing it straight into the truck's cab. "Turn your truck around and get the fuck back where you come from. If I see you anywhere near here again, you ain't gonna like it much."

"You can't arrest us for being here," said the driver, obviously a Constitutional scholar.

"I didn't say a goddamn thing about arresting you, did I?" Sudsy said. "I'm gonna shoot your dick off and say it was a huntin' accident. Now, you got any more legal arguments?"

In moments the truck was off back down the line, leaving only a patch of leaked oil on the road.

"How many these people you figure you pissed off?" Frank asked.

"Enough to keep the deputy busy for a day or two," Dan said.

"None of these sumbitches better hit my mailbox," Sudsy said, holding tight on his shotgun.

Dan made it unscathed through the aftermath of his article. The stakeout snared one other suspicious vehicle, this one manned by geniuses on their way down to the campground at the river to try and sell some prescription drugs. Sudsy got the arrest on that one, and other than a couple of pieces of threatening mail over the next week, things quieted down at Dan and Cindy's. The calendar advanced through March, some of the days warm enough to wear t-shirts outside, where the daffodils made their appearance and the grass began to turn green and clumpy. It was a local source of pride not to cut grass before April. As always the false spring retreated back to freezing temperatures and Dan got busy with his woodpile.

With neither of them tethered to steady jobs, Cindy and Dan sat in front of the wood stove nights with maps strewn around the floor, talking trips and adventure. Kentucky was beautiful country, but neither of them were natives, had ties, or were hot to bust their way into its society.

They looked at New Orleans and Austin, Tucson and Boulder, Portland and Santa Cruz, and agreed on a May departure. On April Fool's Day Dan decided to make his checklist of items to bring along. The phone interrupted him.

"Dan?"

"Who wants to know?"

"Mike Apple from *New York* magazine. Is that you?"

"Mike. How are ya?"

"Exhausted from trying to hunt you down."

"I kinda went underground."

"Underground is the Village. Underground is Queens. Kentucky is the Witness Protection Program."

"It's a little out of the way."

"I'm sure you had your reasons. Listen, your man Whitey Winslett just bought himself a Kentucky Derby contender for a bunch of money. Was wondering if you want to go cover the Derby, especially you being in Kentucky already and saving us a ton in incidentals."

"I was making plans to go out of town, actually."

"Well, think about it. It would be a nice follow-up to the Belmont piece. Still getting compliments on that."

Over the course of the afternoon Dan made calls and researched Winslett's latest moves. He tried to tamp down his enthusiasm to neutrality by the time Cindy got home.

"I got an offer today if I want to take it."

"Doing what?"

"Covering the Derby. It would mean postponing the trip though, so…"

"Well, I haven't bought our dashboard Madonna yet. Who's the assignment from?"

"*New York* magazine. I did a big piece for them last year they liked OK. Whattaya think?"

"I'm getting the vibe you want this."

"I'm sort of excited about it. Not even sure why."

"To show the bastards that fired you that you can kick their ass would be my guess."

"You know, you're smarter than I look."

"I certainly hope so. Now c'mon, since you're cheating me out of a trip, you owe me a ride. Now."

"Yes dear."

48

A series of events that when combined did resemble fate brought Lefty At Heart to Whitey Winslett. First, Sunshine Daydream, the highly touted horse he bought just months before, decided he just didn't care for racetrack life anymore. He refused to train in the mornings or load into the gate for races. Winslett tried everything, including a Horse Whisperer, but Sunshine Daydream wanted no part of racing. He was turned out in a pasture in California with the hope his attitude would improve. It did. He liked the farm life and never ran again.

Lefty At Heart had been impressive as a 2 year old, winning all three of his races by daylight margins that grew with each outing. As he turned into a 3 year old on New Year's Day, he was still an obscurity having done all his running at Sunland Park in New Mexico, a minor venue outside any national coverage.

Winslett had been tipped off to the horse by an agent and watched video of Lefty At Heart's races. He was intrigued enough to jet into New Mexico for Lefty At Heart's race at the beginning of March. Watching the colt run away from an overmatched field, Winslett could feel the warmth of Derby Fever begin coursing through him. He'd liked everything about the horse—his looks, personality, stride, and professionalism.

The horse's owner/trainer was a cowboy from Truth Or Consequences in the northeast corner of the state with an 8,000-acre cattle ranch to run. He fooled with breeding some racehorses on the side, and although the old saw is that "a good one can come from anywhere," he was pretty shocked one could come from this far afield. His breeding stock would have needed a major rally to reach modest. The cowboy, Stan Festin, didn't have the time nor inclination to fool with trailering his horse around the country for months, hoping he could run the bluebloods from back East off their feet. He had plenty of inclination, however, to make himself some cash.

After the race Winslett ambled back to Festin's barn and introduced himself, keeping his interest in the horse as low-key as possible, given both men knew exactly why he was there. Festin may have been a small fish in a small pond, but he knew all about horse trading.

"You got a runner there," Winslett said with as much detachment as he could muster.

"He'll do around these parts," Festin answered, both of them keeping an eye on Lefty At Heart as he was being walked around the stable to cool down.

"Got a little hitch to his giddy-up," noted Winslett.

"Always has, since he's a baby," said Festin. "Might have a flake coming off the knee. I don't have the money to start X-raying 'em from seven angles. Just know it don't bother him none runnin'."

"Can I cut to the chase?"

"I figured you would. Everything's for sale at the right number."

"Could that number be 200 grand?" asked Winslett.

"Could be, but it ain't."

"You got an untested colt with a chip in his knee."

"Yeah, and I got a big-time horse trainer come all the way from California to the pick-ups-and-jeans circuit to watch him do nothin' wrong. Take your best shot."

"I'll double it to 4."

"At 5 you got a deal."

"Done. Except I *am* gonna X-Ray him from seven angles before the cash hits your palm."

"Knock yourself out."

Winslett's next job was finding an owner to peel off a cool half-million for the horse. Although Winslett thought Lefty At Heart could be a freak—one so good he broke all the rules—it wasn't the easiest sell in the world. There was the lack of pedigree, the problem of being unproven against top competition, and the X-rays that showed Lefty At Heart indeed ran with a bone chip that had detached from his knee. While it was possible the chip would never bother him, such chips were removed 95% of the time as a precautionary measure. However, with the Kentucky Derby coming up quickly, there was no time for that.

A couple of Winslett's clients passed on the risk. He then went back to Sam Dobbs.

Dobbs had just watched Sunshine Daydream retire himself, and with no injury on which to collect insurance. But the fast-talking car dealer was also in the middle of a messy divorce with limited prospects for his side. As it so happened, Mrs. Dobbs found ol' Sam doing more than talking clutch plates and destination charges at the annual Automobile Dealers Association convention in Vegas. Apparently some of the bikini-clad models at the auto show got their juices flowing spinning around those moving stages for eight hours. Anyway, Sam got caught with his Malibu inside a couple of Impalas, and was looking to spend as much money as he could before the court found it. He was game to take another stab at Derby immortality.

Within days Lefty At Heart was on a van headed for the West Coast to see if his show played on the big stage. Winslett did his best to water down expectations for his new charge, but privately he was getting excited by what he saw training the colt in the mornings. The horse was handy and intelligent and went through his paces like a pro. Winslett had to tell his exercise rider to keep a very tight hold on the horse during his last workout before the San Rafael Stakes at Santa Anita. He didn't want any lightning-fast times that would awaken the press. The knee already made Winslett nervous enough without having to answer a million questions about this horse.

It worked. The wagering public, chalking it up to inferior competition, ignored Lefty At Heart's perfect record and bet five of his foes down lower in the odds in the San Rafael Stakes. His 8-1 price reflected the "show me" attitude of the bettors, and part of the money behind him was placed there by Dobbs. Without his $10,000 wager, Lefty At Heart would have been 10-1.

In less than two minutes, the time it took the horses to run the one and a sixteenth miles of the San Rafael, the secret was out. Victor Bautista, one of Winslett's regular jockeys, followed instructions to the tee in the early part of the race. He let Lefty At Heart break from the starting gate at his own pace, which was fairly quick, and then settled him down near the rail to save ground, tucking in behind two pacesetters.

With a half mile to run, Bautista steered his mount off the rail to ensure he wouldn't have to try to squeeze through traffic. As they reached the final turn, Lefty At Heart cruised up to the outside of the leaders and then blew their doors off. He had opened up two lengths' lead by the time they reached the head of the homestretch, and seemed to widen his advantage with every stride.

Winslett trained his field glasses on the horses further back in the pack, and a few were picking up the pace and making moves. But by the time he shifted his view back to the leader, Lefty At Heart had already given them the slip and was cruising for the finish line without being asked by the rider. The others were left hopelessly in arrears, with Lefty At Heart winning by six lengths over his closest pursuer, and the toteboard clock froze in a time that represented a new track record for the distance.

Hobbs commenced hootin' and hollerin' next to Winslett.

"That is one smooth riding machine right there," he exclaimed, the ticket worth around $90,000 clutched tightly in his right hand.

"Keep your peter in your pants," Winslett said to him, heading down to the winner's circle. "We still got a ways to go."

"That's one runnin' son of a gun," Cindy said after viewing the videotape of Lefty At Heart's tour de force in their living room. Dan had seen the tape now a dozen times, rewinding it incessantly since receiving it from the Santa Anita publicity director.

"He did it so easy," he said. "The jock didn't even ask him for anything and he ran away from them, and that wasn't a bad field behind him. I'm going to have to go out to California for his next race."

Dan was rewinding the tape for viewing number 13.

"Our travel plans came in handy."

"I'm really sorry, baby. I'll quit this story if you want to take the trip."

"Yeah, after you've watched the race 200 times. You need to stay on this. Anyway, I got an invite to go to New York."

Dan paused the tape. Cindy's inflection had changed over the last few words in a way that knotted his mid-section.

"Whattaya mean?"

"Remember I told you about my college roommate Rebecca, the fashion designer? Well, she just sold her line to a boutique in New York. She used some of my suggestions, and now she needs someone to help her fill the order, maybe develop more."

"So you're gonna go to New York?"

"Well, not without talking to you first. Anyway, you're going to be busy going to California and then the Derby, and this is a great opportunity."

"Those are just trips for races. How long you talking about?"

"I don't know, but it seemed like we already had one foot out of Kentucky anyway."

"But we were going to decide together where we wanted to go."

"I thought you loved New York."

"I love you. I could go either way on New York."

"Dan, this could be really good for me. Please be OK with it."

Dan was staring into space, stunned.

"I could get there and hate the whole thing."

"I gotta get some air." The dogs happily scooted about Dan's legs as he hit the outdoors, his eyes fixed on the ground, his head spinning, and his heart misfiring and jumping around his chest.

49

Cindy took all of three days to blow Kentucky; Dan wistfully watched the rear end of her Honda disappear in a puff of dust down the long driveway. Twelve hours later she was in Manhattan, and the next day she phoned him up.

"It is so exciting here."

"You'll get over that."

"There are so many incredible-looking people on the street."

"They're all potential rapists."

"Would you stop it?"

"I'm sorry, I hope you're ecstatically happy."

"That's more like it."

"I didn't mean it."

"I know. Rebecca's doing really well. It looks like she's one of the next big things. She's getting calls from department stores."

"So am I. They want me to open charge accounts."

"What's going on back there?"

"Frank's cows got loose. Blocked the road for four hours yesterday. Everyone's making a break for it here lately."

"I love you."

"Yeah."

The dogs tried to cure Dan's despair by taking him for long and frequent walks through the woods. A good thing like Cindy took no time to appreciate and no time to miss.

After exhausting his chores Dan spent afternoons working with Frank dropping seeds into potting soil in large, rectangular flats that were then floated on top of temperature-controlled water in Frank's greenhouses, where they would grow and be ready to be planted by the beginning of May.

In the last light of the day Dan wrote long letters to Cindy, riffing on whatever came into his head, trying to be clever to help her to miss him. Uncertain that was succeeding, Dan hatched a plan to hit New York before flying to California for the Santa Anita Derby. Like many spur of the moment ideas, this was well-intentioned and ill-conceived.

"You're coming here to visit the woman who just left you? Solid move."

Dan knew his attempt to explain his situation to Sonny was a bound-to-fail non-starter. But he needed a place to crash in the city, and tried to deflect the incoming.

"She didn't leave me. She moved here for a great opportunity."

"Oh, so she didn't leave you. She just left you."

"Exactly."

"Well, it's been way too long, what, nearly a year, since I've seen you get all weepy over a broad. Hey, there's a great new club I gotta take you to. Wet. There's a floor that opens up with a pool under it and the chicks strip down to bikinis. It's bring your own lotion. Like going to Miami Beach."

"Any shuffleboard?"

"Don't be a putz."

"Sonny, I'm not looking to join in your debauchery."

"How about after she blows you off?"

"You know something, you really are a true friend."

Dan managed to stick the magazine with the expense of flying to New York, something about research he needed to do at The Jockey Club before heading to L.A. As the jet began circling Manhattan, though, he began to feel the dread of a very wrong decision. There were the giant tombstones below; the city lifeless. The bus ride into Manhattan didn't put him in any better mood, nor the subway trip downtown. He found the address on Bleecker Street in the Village to which he mailed letters to Cindy, and walked the three flights up to a huge loft filled with mannequins, fabric, and bustling people scurrying around wielding scissors, pins, and tape—a huge arts and crafts operation.

Cindy popped out from behind a scantily-clad mannequin and he moved toward her with foreboding. She didn't notice until he was upon her.

"Dan!" At least she seemed excited, his name ringing loudly enough around the space, and she gave him a big hug. "What are you doing here?"

"Mannequin shopping. Shouldn't that thing have more clothes on?"

"With any luck, it will soon. So, really, what are you doing?"

"What do you mean, what am I doing? I came to see you."

"That is so sweet."

"Thanks. From your look of semi-horror, not a good time?"

"We have to get this done by tonight. I can't get away now."

"I understand."

"Do you know where you're gonna be later?"

"Not really. Give me a time and I'll call you."

Dan walked to Mitch's office but he was at a music conference. Proceeding uptown, destinations popped in and out of Dan's head. Linda Sandler? Nice thought, but no. Sam? He'd like to see Sam, but how would that go, exactly?

Dan found Gregg Gold's office upstairs from the old studio. He blew past the woman outside Gregg's door and made himself at home while Gregg was on the phone in serious conversation, his presence not registering.

It was a money talk; weren't they all. Gregg was trying for more manpower and equipment to cover the NBA playoffs; the voice on the other end was arguing budget constraints. Gregg lost, got off the call, and for the second time was surprised to run into his old friend.

"Hey buddy," he said, rounding the desk to greet Dan.

"Sounds like fun," Dan noted.

"Exciting world of television—the glamour, the fame, the glory, the finances."

"Hey, you could be unemployed in Kentucky."

"You don't look like you're suffering any. Hey, what was that I heard about some threats against you?"

"Just some locals getting a little stretched out. Didn't amount to much."

"You got balls."

"More balls than brains. So what's going on here?"

"Bean counters are running the show. The economy's killing us. Nobody gives a shit about the NBA now; baseball's losing it; golf's no good. We need a boost."

"Romano must be down to six meals a day."

"He's stressed, I'll tell you that."

"Good."

"Hey, what do you know about this big horse out in California?"

"Going out to see him run Saturday."

"Are you? We've got high hopes for the Derby with him. Gonna market the crap out of it. What's his name, Home With Lefty?"

"Lefty At Heart. He looks like he could be special."

"He'd better be, for our sake. We could ride him through all three legs of the Triple Crown, turn things around here."

"One at a time there, sport."

"So, what are you in for?"

"Chasing a girl."

"Again? You're turning into a normal, red-blooded American male."

"Watch your tongue."

Dan was nursing a beer and his ego at Rudy's. Only a year ago it was somewhere he belonged, a member in good standing of some unorganized, unspoken club. He recognized nobody in the place on this early April evening. He didn't belong here; in the bar or the city. A couple of keys landed on his table.

"If you hear any screaming from the bedroom, don't come in."

Dan looked up to find Sonny taking the seat across the table.

"If it's a woman screaming, I'll call the cops, since your pop gun couldn't be causing it."

"I hear the drug companies are coming out with a pill soon that keeps your chubby up for hours. True story."

"You sign up for the testing?"

"They ain't using my dick as a guinea pig. What if it breaks out in warts and crap?"

"Like that's never happened."

"So where's the new Mrs. Henry?"

"I told her about you. She's not coming."

"I'm sure that's a problem with all your women."

"She's busy working. I don't know what I was even doing trying to see her."

"You fooled a woman into screwing you and you're protecting the investment. It's perfectly understandable. Desperate, but understandable."

"I'm gonna go give her a call."

"If you feel like taking off your dress, Danielle, I'll be at Wet."

"Your odds will be better if you put a beach towel over your face."

Dan didn't get to see Cindy until the following morning, meeting her at a diner on the West Side in the 20s. She had pulled an all-nighter and looked tired, but still beautiful as far as Dan was concerned. They embraced in a hug he wished could go on forever before sliding into a booth.

"How'd it go?"

"It's done. For the moment. It's gonna be crazy for the next week. But I should be able to get away tonight."

"I'm flying out at noon. I just wanted to see you and tell you how much I miss you."

"I know. We love each other. Remember?"

"Still? Really? Are you sure?"

"Sure I'm sure. Are you sure?"

"I'm in New York, right? Which isn't exactly on the way to California."

"Right. So we're good."

"Are you moving here? Are *we* moving here?"

"Dan, we don't have to make decisions now. Promise me you'll stay calm."

"Oh Christ."

"You're not staying calm."

"What'll ya have?" said the waitress appearing on the scene.

"A good cry," replied Dan.

"I'll bring you a bowl," she snapped back.

50

T he buzz about Lefty At Heart was deafening in Southern California, where beautiful Santa Anita Park is located, nestled in the foothills of the San Gabriel Mountains just northeast of Los Angeles. Although eight horses would contest the Santa Anita Derby, the big West Coast prep race for the Kentucky Derby, Lefty At Heart occupied the spotlight.

Dan arrived at the track early in the morning two days before the race and mingled with the other press and the trainers and owners who congregated at Clockers Corner at the far end of the Santa Anita grandstand. As always, opinions were split—some thought Lefty At Heart was a superhorse, others felt he was a flash in the pan ready to be exposed. The conspiracy theories that morning concerned why Whitey Winslett brought the horse to the track for his morning gallop when the track opened at 6 rather than his usual 8:30.

Harboring a healthy disrespect for speculation, Dan left Clockers Corner and walked through a parking lot and then along a dirt path to the backstretch barn area. A sign hung from the eaves of Barn 22 reading "Whitey's Bar & Grill," taken, by the looks of it, from a genuine establishment. Dan passed under it and, making sure no horses were being walked around the interior of the barn area, made his way to the office.

Winslett was holed up with a racetrack clocker who was in the middle of a story denigrating a mutual acquaintance when Dan knocked and entered.

"Hey, what'cha doin'?" Winslett asked, putting on a New York accent.

"Heard there was a good horse around here somewhere."

"We're gonna find out." Winslett turned to the clocker. "So what happened?"

The clocker hesitated, looking at Dan and particularly the press credential that hung around his neck.

"Don't worry, he's one of us," assured Winslett.

Dan didn't know whether to be flattered or insulted. It was fine being in Winslett's trust, but he didn't want to feel compromised. The clocker finished his story, which concerned an owner Dan didn't know who was sleeping with his trainer's wife, not a rare occurrence in this world. Dan found his opening after Whitey sprayed an insult that covered the woman and the owner.

"The place is buzzing over your early morning," he said to Winslett.

"I couldn't sleep."

"They think you're trying to hide something, of course."

"Good. Let them think there's something wrong. We'll see who's who Saturday."

"You like him, huh?"

"I wish we could run the damn race today."

Lefty At Heart looked a tremendous specimen of a racehorse when he entered the saddling paddock 20 minutes before the Santa Anita Derby. Shined to a sparkling finish he stood out even among the best collection California could offer up for its biggest race for 3-year-olds. Looking off into the distance as if posing, he showed off a majestic head and wonderful eye.

Winslett made a sharp appearance as well. A lot of people figured they could pick a winner by seeing how the trainers were dressed. If one was in his Sunday best, they figured that he figured he'd be taking a picture in the winner's circle after the race. Winslett had on a perfect-fitting black blazer, white starched shirt, and sky blue power tie. He was a photo ready to be taken.

Dan sidled up to owner Sam Dobbs, who didn't look nearly as snappy as his trainer. Dobbs was styling in a cowboy hat, boots, and one of those awful Western-style jackets with the stitching on the outside. His posse looked like—and was--the cream of used car dealers from Orange County. Dan re-introduced himself and asked Dobbs how he was doing.

"My trainer says not to worry about a damn thing, so I'm f-ing petrified," he said, slapping Dan on the back before moving on to get closer to his horse.

Dan stood down near the winner's circle for the race, which started just up the stretch. Lefty At Heart left the gate alertly, but a couple of horses and their riders to his outside were determined to get the early lead. Clete Boudreaux, who Winslett gave the mount to because he was more seasoned than Victor Bautista, was happy to let them have it, and he took Lefty At Heart back slightly and sat in fourth place as the horses moved past the grandstand and into the first turn. Dan could see that the horse had settled into a powerful and steady rhythm, and Boudreaux subtly steered him toward the outside as soon as they left the turn and headed onto the backstretch. He knew the other riders would try and trap his horse inside against the rail, and he was taking no chances. If the horse had to travel a few extra yards by going wide, it was more than worth it.

The frontrunners tried to slow down the pace in an attempt to lull the field to sleep so they could spurt away on the turn for home. But Lefty At Heart had other ideas, and began moving before his rider gave the signal. Boudreaux knew better than to fight him, so he let up a notch on his hold on the reins, and Lefty began closing the four-length gap on the leaders. It was too early a move for most horses, but Lefty wasn't most horses. With a half-mile to run he was on even terms, and as they entered the final turn he was leaving them in his wake.

The grandstand became a rolling wave of roars as he came off the turn into the stretch with the lead, further distancing himself with each powerful gulping of ground. Race fans appreciate being witness to greatness, and they screamed their approval. Lefty At Heart was putting on an exhibition. He was six lengths clear with an eighth of a mile to run, and made it 10 lengths at the sixteenth pole. Boudreaux grabbed a tighter hold of the reins, not wanting to let the horse go faster than need be. He had bigger fish to fry in a month, and didn't need to empty the tank now. Lefty At Heart crossed the finish line 12 lengths clear of his nearest pursuer, and it could have been more.

Dan looked back into the grandstand and saw a cowboy hat and a blue tie making their way down to the winner's circle. After the photos were taken and Dobbs grabbed the trophy, Dan walked back to Whitey's Bar & Grill to watch the horse cool out and get some color on Winslett and Dobbs for his story.

"We're going to the Derby!" shouted Dobbs repeatedly.

"This guy lives in Kentucky," Winslett said, nodding toward Dan. "Maybe he can set you up."

"I happen to have connections at a sleazy strip club," Dan said.

"Yes sir," yipped Dobbs, whipping his cowboy hat around in circles and celebrating in advance his divorce.

Dan absorbed everything about Winslett and Dobbs, knowing this would be the last exclusive time he'd have with them as the frenzy over Lefty At Heart's performance would build to a deafening pitch over the next four weeks. Winslett looked to him like a man holding four aces and trying his best not to show it.

51

Dan returned home to find spring had taken hold. Green buds sprung from every branch in the woods. The grass was out of its brown hibernation and growing by the minute, like in one of those time-lapse photography deals. Ant hills appeared. Swaths of dog hair began showing up on the kitchen floor. There was actual warmth to the sun.

And try though he might to stay desperately busy, Dan hugely missed Cindy.

He kept thinking of that loft and the whirlwind of activity and the city; the rolls of fabric stretching about the room like trails from hallucinations; the mannequins springing to life as they were dressed and carried around the space. And then of the tombstone buildings and sunken eyes and the deals being done as people large and small worked their hustles grand and petty.

In the paddocks the Thoroughbred foals explored their first days running on stick legs, racing back to their mothers' side at the first sound or sight of trouble, which included Dan's dogs, who loved nothing better than running the fence line trying for a reaction. New life and beauty was everywhere Dan looked, while at the same time he missed Cindy desperately. The joy and the silence; the warmth and the emptiness. It's wondrous, this life thing, he'd remind himself in his more lucid moments.

Derby fever took hold at Churchill Downs over the next weeks. First on the scene, along with the horses and their trainers, are the media, who begin prowling the barn area up to two weeks ahead of the race to cast a watchful eye on the out-of-town shippers and how they acclimate to the Louisville racetrack. You can get a sense who among the visiting trainers is just happy to be part of Derby lore, and who thinks they have a legitimate shot in the race.

The Derby horses gallop each morning, and at six-day intervals put in a timed workout, a more strenuous practice run leading up to the big day. It is during these sessions that the press fool themselves into thinking they can tell which horses are traveling well over the racing surface and thriving, and which aren't.

Whitey Winslett and Lefty At Heart arrived 10 days before the race. In a procession befitting the Derby headliner, the horse's van received a police escort for the 10-minute drive from Louisville's airport to Churchill Downs, and there were about 100 track employees, fans, and press at Barn 43 when the ramp was put in place and Lefty At Heart stepped off the van and was led to a grassy yard between the barn and Longfield Avenue, where he commenced grazing after gathering in his new surroundings with long looks in each direction.

Winslett didn't disappoint when the media descended on him as he watched his groom graze the horse.

"I hope his trip was better than mine," Winslett was saying. "The stewardesses on my flight were butt ugly.

"Should he be the favorite? Of course, but funny things happen in this race. And I don't mean ha-ha funny.

"I don't know what to do here for 10 days. The hotel is awful. Last year there was a room service tray in the hallway outside my room for five days. I think they had to give it landmark status."

Neil Hawkins from the *Racing Form* sidled up next to Dan during the show. "He's in mid-season form."

"Hey. Yeah, he hasn't stopped since the Santa Anita Derby," Dan said.

"I really enjoyed your piece last year on the Belmont," Hawkins said. "That deal up on top of the Pan Am building was hilarious."

"Thanks. Yeah, you can't make that stuff up."

"Do you know this Dobbs guy, the owner?"

"Yeah. He's a slice. King of Cars. Shoots his own commercials. Rides onto the car lot on a camel, dumps a couple tons of sand on the concrete so the kids can play while he sandbags their folks into a new Buick. He's never met a promotion he wouldn't stoop to."

"Looks like he's bought himself a Cadillac here," Hawkins said, nodding toward Lefty At Heart as the colt busied himself tearing grass out of the ground for lunch.

"He runs anywhere near his Santa Anita race, he gets the roses."

"Roses? He looks like a shoo-in for the whole Triple Crown. First time in seven years."

Winslett motioned for his groom to bring the horse into the barn. "Milk and cookies time. We'll see you later."

The rail separating the racetrack from the barn area was lined with hundreds of photographers the Monday morning before the Derby as Lefty At Heart was led out onto the track by Winslett's assistant trainer on a pony. Camera shutters clicked incessantly as the horse stopped still for several minutes staring across the track at the famous Twin Spires atop the grandstand. He walked along the outer rail nearly a full circuit before he was turned around and then was let loose for his workout.

Dan and Hawkins were up in the grandstand on the second level, both peering through binoculars as the powerful chestnut rounded the turn and set off down the stretch at full throttle. The rider let him power past the stands and then tried to open the parachute—leaning backwards in the saddle and throwing his feet out in front of him in the stirrups. The horse was a handful to try and stop once he had a head of steam, and a clocker nearby announced what his stopwatch was telling him: :58 and 4/5 seconds for the five furlong workout, very quick particularly with a mile and a quarter race coming up in five days. The theme in the aftermath would be whether the horse worked too quickly instead of saving his energy for the race.

Dan wasn't buying into the standard thinking. "What did ya think?" he asked Hawkins as they hurried back to Hawkins' car for the drive back to the barn area.

"He's a monster."

"He seemed within himself."

"Good horses work fast."

Ten minutes later they, along with half the Western world, were camped outside Winslett's barn awaiting the trainer's comments to the press. Dan saw Gregg Gold in a prime spot up front with a camera crew, barking orders to make sure they got the right shots to include on the Derby telecast Saturday.

"It wasn't too fast," Winslett said before anyone asked, causing Dan and Hawkins to laugh while the rest of the press corps went speechless, each one of them having their main question cut out from under them. Winslett, smiling, had several reasons to diffuse the issue before it got written. First, he routinely worked his horses fast and he believed this was a perfectly fine workout for this horse. Second, if the horse somehow got beat in the Derby, he didn't need the blame put on his training methods.

"Any other questions?" he asked in the stunned silence, the reporters wondering how they were going to shade this story if, in fact, it wasn't too fast.

"So you liked the workout?" asked one reporter.

"Loved it."

"That's what you were expecting?"

"Yes."

And so it went for another couple of minutes, Winslett being comically taciturn in his replies. Dan, having no daily beast to feed, could just make note of the press conference for use in his overall piece on the Derby. He had the luxury of knowing the result before going back and lashing together the elements of his story. Reporters filed by him, shaking their heads, including Dave Hass, the basketball reporter from the Lexington *Herald* who had blown Dan off the one time he asked for UK tickets, and who had apparently inherited the Derby beat in the aftermath of Dan's firing.

"Hey, Dave, let me know if you need any help with that," Dan said.

"Oh, Dan, yeah, could I run a few things by you?"

"No."

52

D
an had arranged with Frank Leonard to look after his dogs while he stayed over in Louisville several nights leading up to the Derby. That saved him the daily commute and allowed him to be out at the track before dawn each morning to watch the Derby horses exercise, and back at the barn area in the afternoon when trainers returned to feed or graze their horses in a more relaxed atmosphere. Besides Hawkins, no reporters came back around in the afternoon; every one of them could be found up in the press box finishing off their filings for the day and then betting the races. The betting window located in the press box—and there is one in every press box across America—probably handled more business per capita than any other window at the track, invariably leading to the constant cacophony of whining and griping that permeated every such facility. If the inhabitants weren't complaining about the free food spread of the day, they were bemoaning the terrible antics of jockey or trainer in their most recent losing endeavor.

But you can't cover a race from the press box.

Dan followed Hawkins' lead, talking to the grooms and the exercise riders and the blacksmiths and the assistant trainers and the breeders to find a couple of gems unique to each horse. He made it around to each barn in the morning, engaging the owners if they'd arrived, looking to research a real story beyond the recitation of facts and figures that passed for sports journalism among the lazy.

The Wednesday afternoon before the Derby Dan and Hawkins walked the barn area toward Winslett's headquarters, hoping to catch the trainer out grazing Lefty At Heart on the grass area in back of the barn. When they approached, however, there were no horses out back on the grass, but they could see some activity down the long row of stalls.

"Lot of cars out front for this time of day," noted Dan.

A couple of men carrying equipment hustled in and out from their cars to a stall in the barn. Hawkins and Dan got as close as they could without making their presence known, close enough to see the activity was centered around Lefty At Heart's stall.

"Something's going on," said Hawkins.

Two men who they assumed were veterinarians entered the stall while Winslett stood just outside watching intently and speaking quietly to them. A late-model Cadillac pulled up to the barn. Winslett walked over to meet the driver, who removed a sheet of plastic from a binder and held it up, pointing something out on it for Winslett, who also raised a finger tracing something on the sheet.

"X-ray," Dan whispered.

"Looks like it."

Feeling exposed, the two of them took cover behind the front end of a parked car by the barn, watching the scene play out. After a few minutes the men emerged from the horse's stall and talked briefly to Winslett. The mood appeared somber as they retreated to their vehicles. Winslett gave some orders to his assistant trainer before walking to his office to call Sam Dobbs in California.

Dan and Hawkins casually moved to a vantage point in front of the barn, where they busied themselves however they could waiting for Winslett to emerge. They were rewarded 10 minutes later when Winslett, fishing a set of keys out of his jeans' pocket, strode out of the barn toward his car.

The reporters, casually as they could, approached him as though they had just arrived on the scene.

"No grazing today?" Hawkins asked.

Winslett, surprised to see them, greeted them in a tone familiar but non-committal. "Hey, what are you two, lost?"

"Just making the rounds," said Hawkins, his question still hanging in the air.

"Nah, we just had the blacksmith here putting new shoes on him. Gonna let him relax inside today."

"What time are you going to the track tomorrow?" Hawkins asked as casually as he could muster.

"I don't know. Maybe early. I gotta get to the hotel. I'll see you guys."

Winslett pulled his rental car away from the barn.

"I counted a minimum two lies, three if he doesn't need to go to the hotel," Dan said.

"Not good," stated Hawkins.

When Dan arrived at 6 the next morning, Hawkins was already staking out Winslett's barn.

"You're late," Hawkins said to Dan, not taking his eyes off the barn.

"It doesn't feel late," Dan said. "Anything going on?"

"Nothing. I guarantee you this horse isn't going to the track today."

"How's Winslett gonna explain that away?"

"After yesterday, do you have to ask?"

"He can't just keep avoiding this for three days."

"Watch."

As usual, Hawkins had it right. Winslett tried to put on a performance for his press conference at 9:30. He talked at length while saying absolutely nothing, and when the reporter from the Louisville *Courier-Journal* asked whether Lefty At Heart had been to the track that morning, Winslett said he'd been out first thing. He spent a lot of time talking about the competition, which he would not have done or cared about if his horse was right. The spark and the one-liners were missing from his presentation. Anyone that wanted to could see he, like his horse, was off his game.

Dan and Hawkins had decided to move in for the kill after the conference. No need to put Winslett up against the wall in full public view, or to share what they had with the rest of the press corps. When they approached Winslett, however, the trainer was already being ushered over to a pair of director's chairs, where he would be doing an interview to air during ABC's coverage of the Derby. Gregg Gold was quarterbacking the scene, making sure all the technical stuff was working properly, and a make-up person was already applying something or other to Winslett's face.

Churchill Downs' publicist was leading some very out-of-place-looking media members to chairs set up against the barn. *Time, Newsweek, Sports Illustrated*, and ESPN were next for their shots with Winslett, and it was clear to Dan and Hawkins they weren't going to get a piece of the trainer anytime soon.

"Might as well look around and see who could win this race," Dan said.

The following morning barriers had been set up around the barn, preventing anyone from getting close to it. It was the day before the Derby and in the gray of dawn Dan and Hawkins saw the vets, moving quietly and ghost-like, entering and exiting the barn. Lefty At Heart emerged an hour later and walked to the racetrack, followed by a parade of media. He did little more than jog around once, and was back off the track quickly and back to the barn, where he got a bath and was inserted back in his stall.

Outside, behind the barriers, the media gathered for one last time to hear from Winslett. What they got instead was the overbearing presence of Sam Dobbs, attired in cowboy regalia with 10-gallon hat, coming out to take questions.

What Dobbs didn't know about racing could fill every reference book on the subject. He threw superstition to the wind by guaranteeing victory the next day.

"Back in Texas where I'm from, if you got it, you say you got it. And with this horse, we got it. I ain't gonna fancy-dance around with you and try to be all humble and talk up the other guy. This is the goods right here, and we gonna let it rip tomorrow and see who's best. I sell cars, and this model right here has got the engine and the body and the wheels. And he's gonna be showing his tailpipe to them other horses."

53

Derby day dawned heavy, as it often does, with rain and gray skies dominating the morning. Dan took his time at the hotel. He was in no hurry to get to the track, which was closed for training, meaning the barn area would be like a ghost town. Later on the barn workers would arrive with ice chests and barbecues and spend the afternoon hours leading up to the big race grilling chicken and ribs and having a party with their families before moving to the fence separating the barns from the racetrack, where they would see the Derby horses as they turned into the backstretch of the race.

Dan put on his best dress shirt and a rain jacket over it, collected his reporter's tools and went downstairs to check out. He would head home after the race and commence his writing the following day while the flavor was still fresh. He spent some of the magazine's money parking in the front yard of a home along Longfield Avenue for $25, and walked through the backstretch gate, casually flashing his media credential. The rain had stopped, leaving the humidity that promised another very warm running of the Derby.

Dan couldn't help but walk to Winslett's barn, where not a soul stirred. The barriers remained up, two deputies covered the entrance, and an awning was rolled down, preventing even the most fleeting of looks at the horses. Dan stood there awhile, waiting for some hint of action and, witnessing none, made his way slowly across the track and up to the press box, where he would try and kill some of the long day.

Hawkins was talking to a group of fellow reporters when Dan got there, so he busied himself grabbing a program from the small office that housed Churchill Downs' publicity department and asked if there were any changes or late scratches on the day's racing card. None of the changes were in the Derby, which still had 13 hopefuls ready to square off. Dan took his program to an empty seat and began going through it. There were some very nice stakes races before the Derby, but Dan was having trouble keeping his mind on them. His head kept going back to Lefty At Heart and his certainty that something was terribly wrong.

"No scratches," Hawkins said, coming up to Dan and reading his mind.

"I guess that would have been too much to ask," said Dan, as Hawkins sat down next to him. "Have you heard anything? Has anyone heard anything?"

"Some of these guys are a little suspicious about the lack of training this week," Hawkins said. "But most write it off to the fact that horse could be sleeping for six days and still beat these. Nobody saw what we saw."

"I went by there. Nothing was doing."

"I sat outside in the rain for two hours beginning at 5 this morning. It was like watching an oil painting."

"Why would Dobbs go through that whole dog-and-pony show yesterday?" asked Dan. "He went out of his way to put down everybody in the race like he was Muhammad Ali."

"Winslett sure didn't want to talk anymore. He must have shoved Dobbs out there to fill in. Give the natives something to write about."

"So what do you think?"

"I've never seen a horse win the Derby after having a week like this," Hawkins noted. "So either this is a superhorse..."

"Hell of a betting opportunity if you throw out the favorite."

"You could look at it that way."

Dan played around and bet a few of the 10-1 and 20-1 shots he thought had some talent, mixing and matching them in exacta bets. Two hours before the Derby he went downstairs and walked around the crowded mass of spectators. They were getting increasingly rowdy and drunk, the bright colors of the men's sport coats and the women's dresses darkened by spilled alcohol and perspiration. Despite being crowded like sardines, their spirits stayed high.

Dan crossed through the tunnel leading to the racetrack, passing the horses coming into the paddock for the 6th race. He walked along the outer rail of the track and back to the barn area. The owners of the Derby horses were beginning to congregate outside their respective stables with family and guests in tow. There was J.A. Peterson, the Texas oil magnate who'd been in horses 10 years without significant success. He had Slickster in the Derby. One barn over stood Reade Lilly, the Georgia chicken magnate who'd be rooting for his Click Clack. New York investment fund guru J. Miller Reskin cut a distinguished figure in his black suit outside the stall of his Dark Knight.

And so on down the rows of barns, as titans of industry and government mixed with cowboy trainers and grooms in front of the 1,200-pound Thoroughbreds they had purchased or seen be born at farms with hopes of landing exactly where they now stood.

Soon enough the squawky P.A. system crackled and a voice told horsemen to bring the horses for the ninth race to the track. Today, that was the Kentucky Derby. The horses circled in an area at the far corner of the racetrack, then began the walk over to the grandstand and the tunnel under it to the saddling paddock. The owners and connections walked with the horses, first along a cyclone fence where fans sat in folding chairs in order to see a few moments of the Derby action when the horses ran past them on the first turn.

But as the track bent toward the long straightaway, all of a sudden the giant grandstand and the famous Twin Spires swallowed up the sightlines, and the roars of 100,000 people swept over the parade of horses and handlers and owners, sending chills down every human spine. At once, they all understood the magnitude of this event.

Along with most of the people that were taking this pre-race walk, Dan fell in behind Lefty At Heart, his own heart pounding as he watched the horse and tried to analyze what was wrong, and if by some possibility it could have been fixed. He was no expert on equine stride and movement, but he was pretty bright on human behavior, so he thought it significant that while Sam Dobbs and about 20 of his pals whooped it up on the walk—engaging the fans and showing the effects of enough mint juleps—Whitey Winslett was not there to drink it all in, having decided to wait for his charge in the saddling paddock.

As the horses walked past the toteboard that faced the grandstand and through the tunnel, the odds on Lefty At Heart flashed at 3/5, meaning he would be one of the biggest favorites in the history of the race. Dan elected to stay out on the track, hugging the outer rail about 25 feet before the finish line, making that his vantage point for the race. The horses reappeared 20 minutes later with their saddles and riders on and walked right past Dan to begin the post parade.

The grandstand erupted as the track announcer introduced Lefty At Heart. The photographers were snapping away, their work to be displayed across the world the following day in newspapers and then in the magazines during the next weeks. Sure, most of the people had wagered money on the favorite, but they were cheering now not in hope of the modest returns should he win, but instead in the hope of seeing something they could tell their friends and kids and grandchildren about—seeing the great Lefty At Heart on Derby day.

The roar reached a crescendo as the horses were loaded into the starting gate. It washed over Dan as he stood in front of it all, and then came the ringing of the gate as the doors sprung open and the horses came running down the stretch in front of the grandstand. Dan peered through his binoculars, looking for Dobbs' red and black colors aboard Lefty At Heart. He found them down near the inside and forwardly placed in fourth or fifth position early. The runners stormed past his vantage point with Lefty At Heart keeping his spot down along the inside about three lengths behind the leaders with one lap to go.

The Derby is run at 1 ¼ miles, which is further than most of its participants really want to run at full speed. The early leaders of the race, if they are going any kind of fast tempo, are rarely around at the finish. So as the field spun around the first turn and headed up the backstretch, Dan thought Lefty At Heart was in pretty good shape. Dan checked the early fractions as they were posted on the toteboard. The pace was honest. Those horses in front of him likely wouldn't hold up, Dan thought.

As Dan followed the horses up the backstretch and into the final turn, the race unfolded as he figured. The three horses on the lead began laboring as they reached their distance limitations, and as they turned into the final stretch drive Lefty At Heart inherited the lead more than he surged to it. But he was running as well as any of his opponents, and midway down the stretch he was one of four horses lined up across the track. The crowd exploded, screaming for him to exert his superiority, but still the horses pounded as one down the stretch, their rhythmic gaits audible to those close enough.

As these Thoroughbreds devoured the final 100 yards Lefty At Heart's talent carried him a nose in front and then, in an instant, the rhythm and the gait and the majesty exploded. The red and black colors spiked high, too high, and the jockey bobbled up and down like a rodeo cowboy. The smooth stride became a choppy mess, and as three horses passed him right before the finish line, Lefty At Heart hopped across it on three legs, Boudreaux pulling him up to a stop as quickly as possible and then jumping off to relieve the pressure. You could hear a losing win ticket drop in the silence among 110,000 people.

The horse ambulance began its run down from the head of the stretch. While a Kentucky Derby winner galloped out along the clubhouse turn, all eyes were on the stricken horse standing just past the wire, being attended to by racetrack personnel. A lead was laced through his bridle and loving hands caressed the giant, who was heaving now from exhaustion and injury in sickening distress. He was hosed down to keep him cool. Dan moved toward him, pulled by an invisible force, eyes wide in horror. A blur brushed past him, and he saw the shock of white from Whitey Winslett's head running toward his horse, grabbing his long head in his hands and cradling it. Doctors quickly placed a cast around Lefty At Heart's right front leg and Winslett led him up the ramp into the ambulance, followed by a veterinarian. The doors were closed with a sickening thud, and the ambulance pulled away, its tire tracks carving out patterns over the hoofprints left minutes ago by the Derby horses. It exited into the barn area, lights flashing, and was gone from view.

Dan turned to walk back through the grandstand to the press box, and immediately passed the Derby-winning trainer and owner who were talking excitedly to the press, lauding their upset victor. Dan passed Hawkins, who would be writing their story, jotting down notes and quotes. He looked up and caught Dan's eye for an instant. Both gave an imperceptible shake of their heads.

"That's horse racing," explained one man to his disappointed family as Dan walked past. Yeah, Dan thought to himself, it sure is. Something always going on just out of view. He felt like an accessory to some sort of malfeasance. He could have gone public with what he'd seen. Of course, he would have been squashed and his story denied, but now it haunted him. "Didn't even try," he mumbled to himself as he hurried back upstairs.

As soon as Dan found out in the press box that Lucky At Heart was being transported to Lexington and the Woodford Equine Clinic for surgery, he bee-lined out of there, fighting his way through the crowd, running through and past people, to get to his car for the drive east, which he made in racecar time.

54

It was about 7 p.m. when Dan pulled up to the clinic, which he knew well from bringing his dogs to the small animal division. The place wasn't exactly set up for media reporting. A couple of camera crews from local Lexington TV stations filled the clinic's waiting room with their equipment. There wasn't another Turf writer in sight. Dan checked with the receptionist about any statements that may have already been released. Assured there hadn't been any, Dan stood near the inner walls trying to hear something.

He was desperate to do something, anything to atone for his silence the past few days. He paced the room like a convict, dried sweat caking his clothes. Helpless. In a half-hour a nurse emerged carrying a single piece of paper, which she mimeographed, handing out copies to Dan and the two TV reporters.

Displaced cannon bone. Undergoing surgery. Doing everything we can. On the bottom, a quote from Winslett: "One of those things that happen in racing."

The paper did Dan no good. He stuffed it in his back pocket and pushed through the front door out into the dusk. He took a deep breath, his first in several hours, and walked toward the grass beyond the clinic parking lot. Strains of wispy clouds were colored pink by the disappeared sun; surreal beauty for a moment. Dan heard a voice, loud enough that it led his eyes to a spot between cars in the parking lot.

Dan moved closer, now seeing the white head of Winslett as he talked on some sort of mobile phone. He heard the word "car" and sensed agitation in the voice. Then the connection seemed to tank, Winslett put the phone down, and Dan had his opening.

"Whitey..."

Fear was written across the trainer's face. He looked up and saw Dan and relaxed ever so slightly. "Hey, New York..."

"How you makin' out?"

"Nothing a bullet in the head wouldn't cure."

"How 'bout the horse?"

"It's gonna be an all-nighter here, and even if the first surgery works out OK we won't know anything for days, weeks, who knows. I got to get to California for my kid's graduation...You driving back to Louisville?"

"Sure, let's go."

"Yeah?"

"Yeah."

There was still some cobalt blue light in the sky as the pair headed back west, giving a sliver of hope to the day that had already gone dark around them. The two men sat mute past the two Frankfort exits on I-64 and were approaching Lawrenceburg. The silence was more understandable than awkward, and while Dan had empathy for Winslett's day, he wanted answers. He wasn't giving him this ride out of the goodness of his heart.

"Tough day," Dan began.

"Ya think?"

"Only sport you can go from superstar to fighting for your life--just like that."

"They're flesh and bone. You just don't know. I remember my first one—bad breakdown—back at Emerald Downs in Washington. My whole family was there. I got buddies from all over the Northwest, come to see this Quarter Horse looked like one of the ones. Race started, he hit the side of the gate with his shoulder, broke it, then flipped over forward and broke his neck. I spent the rest of the night in a stall in the bathroom, crying. You never get used to it. You try and convince yourself it's not part of the game, but it is."

Dan let a few moments pass while he silently practiced his most matter-of-fact tone.

"Some things don't need to be part of the game."

Winslett looked at him, Dan taking that as an invitation to go on.

"We saw you Wednesday—me and Hawkins, just so you know you can't bullshit him either—with Doc Holland and Doc Lewis and the X-rays at the barn. We came to see if you were grazing the horse and ran into a MASH tent."

Winslett was staring at Dan, who went on.

"I'm guessing you're not a guy who's gonna run a horse with his wheels comin' off, Whitey, not even in this race."

They sat in silence again for five minutes as Winslett ran the moves through his head. Bringing the vets into the story made it much more difficult for Winslett to stay quiet forever.

"Prick stabbed me in the back."

"Dobbs?"

"I called him right then—the day you were there--and told him we couldn't enter the horse. He gets here the next day, tells me the horse is gonna run. I thought he was kidding. But the bastard is dead serious. I told him, 'over my dead body.' He says, 'I don't need to kill you, but I'll move him to another trainer.' That son of a bitch got up to speed real quick, making that play. I couldn't move him off it. I talked to the Churchill officials. They didn't want to hear about the star attraction not appearing. They would have sent me to Mars before they let me scratch.

"At that point what am I gonna do? Let him go to another trainer that doesn't know him? The start of the fracture was there on the picture. Enough so you wouldn't want to take the chance. I had no say, and his only shot at making it is if he's ridden just right. Not pushed along, not asked for speed early. And then you pray. He had the best shot with me."

Winslett was good, Dan thought in the silence, but he didn't know if he was good enough to come up with a story that good that quick. There was the one piece that didn't make sense.

"Who got to Dobbs?"

"Million-dollar question."

They drove on in darkness.

55

The Derby winner, Tide Water, became an instant footnote in racing history. In defeat Lefty At Heart became a folk hero. In the days following the race he was the top national story, people everywhere hoping and praying he would pull through. Medical updates came out twice daily--briefings under a makeshift tent set up in the clinic parking lot. Dan kept vigil there the first two days. Hawkins came to hang with him for six hours the Monday after the Derby. Dan told him Winslett's story.

"You want to go hunting with me?" Dan asked.

"Know what? I gotta go to Baltimore this week, get ready for the Preakness. It's your baby. But call if I can help."

Dan fished through his jacket pocket for a piece of paper to take Hawkins' number. He pulled out his mutuel tickets from the Derby.

"What was the Derby exacta?"

"Six-eight. Paid $250 bucks."

"I won a grand."

There wasn't a lot new in the medical bulletins. Winslett had been right about that: even if the news was good it was going to be a long time before anything would be known with certainty. The horse was being kept comfortable, and may or may not have realized the pile of flowers and get-well cards and sculptures and pictures that were massing up outside his stall were for him. They came from young girls working in crayon and old, hardened fans whose tears sanctified their notes.

Ray Mercado aside, this time Dan did want to beat the hell out of somebody.

56

It was a beautiful May day in Southern California as Dan drove south from Los Angeles International Airport, the Pacific beckoning out the right side of his rental car as he glided along with the morning midweek traffic, some of which no doubt was heading for Disneyland and a fantasy escape.

Dan was driving in another direction. The Los Angeles *Times*, which he had tossed on the passenger seat beside him, had an update on Lefty At Heart on the bottom of its front page, with quotes from Winslett and the doctors. The horse had a tremendous will to live, was doing as well as could be expected, but wasn't near out of the woods. It was the same story that would be repeated daily, then less frequently and in less premium parts of the newspaper, as time went on or until there was some change in his condition. People still cared, though, a tribute to the horse's reputation and the size of the Kentucky Derby stage, and folks' love for animals.

Dan refused to call it an 'accident.' An accident isn't premeditated. If you take your car out on the highway knowing it has no oil in it and the engine seizes up and the car stops and you're rear-ended, it might technically be an accident, but it's not exactly a chance occurrence. It's stupidity.

Dan cut away from the coast, heading east on 57 and into the sun. California's magical beauty dimmed as he travelled inland, passing former orange fields that were now subdivision farms of identical houses repeated ad nauseam, fake stucco exteriors and cheap salmon-colored shale roofs as far as he could see. There was a bad transformation going on at continental America's last frontier. As the Midwesterners continued streaming into the state looking to escape winters of shoveling snow, the land was being gobbled up by developers who sold houses as quickly as they could throw them up. All the cops and insurance agents and shop owners needed somewhere to live, and they'd want automobiles.

Dan pulled into the Orange County Auto Mall about an hour after leaving the airport. He managed to find the narrow hallway to the men's room and then the popcorn-making machine, where he helped himself to a bag before being accosted by a salesman, a guy around Dan's age who had shaved that morning, put on a short-sleeved white shirt and tie, kissed the wife and kids goodbye, and come to work looking to move enough vehicles to pay for the stucco and shale three bedroom on which the bank held a $180,000 note. The weight of all that made him look older and heavier than Dan.

"I'm Ed Sanders."

"Of course."

"What can we put you in today?"

Dan was certain that, at 9:30 a.m., he was Ed's first potential hook of the day, and he wanted to keep the salesman's attention, so he suggested they wander over to the high-mark-up convertible sports car at the far end of the showroom. Ed was going over some of the obvious features as they circled the sea-blue beauty, and tossed out some perfunctory performance and engine-size info as Dan stared intently at the leather interior, trying to look interested even as he ignored every word Ed was sending his way.

"So, whattaya think?"

"I think we need to take this baby out on the road for a few minutes and see what she's got."

"We can do that. Let me have one brought around while you get your driving gloves on, 'cause you're gonna think you went right to the Indy 500 sitting in this rig."

Sanders left Dan inside while he scared up a car off the lot. Dan scanned the showroom. A series of glass-walled small offices lined the length of the place where the salesmen hustled their prey, punching numbers into adding machines, tallying up the monthly nut the customer would have to pass like a kidney stone for the joy of these four-wheeled slices of the American dream. There was an upstairs that Dan guessed housed the executive offices, which had a view of the other four buildings that made up the 'auto mall.'

Dan declined Ed's offer to take the car out on the freeway to see what it could do. He kept it on surface streets, making a show of fast, tight turns to see how it handled. The car seemed to him overly noisy and under-powered, not to mention obscenely overpriced.

Twenty minutes later, Ed thought he was in heaven, happily punching numbers into his adding machine and relaying them onto the worksheet in front of him, working up a grand tally for Dan. It was past 10 a.m., when even executives would be reporting in for the day.

"How does $37,225 sound?"

"Well…"

"I'll tell you what, if you purchase it right now, we can do $36,675. How about it? All we'll need is some credit information."

"I intend to pay cash."

"I could tell you were a man of means immediately."

"You know, Ed, before we do the deal, I've gotta say I am just so impressed with the way you've handled this today."

"Just doing my job," said Ed, barely controlling the glee of getting his morning off to a fast start.

"No, you know what? I want to talk to your boss, make sure you get a commendation."

"Well, that's not really necessary."

"No, it is. There is little enough pride in work today; it needs to be rewarded. Let's go upstairs."

Ed, somewhat bewildered but with the lure of a $36,000 sale dancing in his head, led Dan up the stairs to the second floor and headed for the general manager's office. Doing a quick scan, Dan figured the real action was off in the other direction, where a secretary sat outside a much bigger office. Dan peeled off.

"Mr. Henry…"

"This way, Ed. The owner."

Sanders caught up with Dan just before he got to the secretary's desk, more flustered by the moment.

"Margie, Mr. Henry here is a customer and he'd like a, a, word with the boss, if he's in."

"Just a moment." She reached for the phone.

Dan wasn't waiting. He strode to the door and let himself in, followed closely by the protesting car salesman.

"Mr. Henry, you can't…"

"Mr. Dobbs," Dan said, addressing the man seated behind a giant desk.

"Yes sir?"

"Mr. Dobbs, sir, this is Dan Henry, a customer…" tried Sanders, hurrying in behind Dan but still unsure what he was doing up here.

"A satisfied customer," said Dan, playing it up. "Just wanting to tell you how helpful your salesman Sanders here has been this morning."

"We always glad to hear our people are givin' our customers the finest service possible," Dobbs said, looking through both of them.

"He has really gone the extra mile," Dan said. "Just extraordinary."

Dobbs now looked at Dan for the first time.

"Sanders, great job. I'll send Mr., uh, Henry back down to you in a few minutes."

"Thank you, sir." Sanders backed his way out of the office, puzzled but pleased, closing the door behind him.

"I'm guessin' you're not actually buyin' a car today?" Dobbs asked.

"You never know, but it wasn't my top priority."

"You the Turf writer..."

"One and the same," Dan said, taking the chair closest to Dobbs' executive-sized desk.

"Pretty damn resourceful."

"I didn't think you'd be taking calls."

"I ain't talked to no one."

"That's why I almost bought your overpriced sports car."

"I might give you the hard-sell myself. Bid-ness stinks."

"Is that why you took the money?"

"What money you talkin' about?"

"I'm not here to waste your time, Mr. Dobbs. I know somebody got to you. I just want to know who."

Dobbs took a deep exhale and stared out the windows on the panoramic view befitting his station at the top of the pyramid. After a half-minute he swiveled to look at Dan.

"It's been four days and I'm still sick to my stomach. Can't sleep thinkin' about that poor son of a bitch. They told me how America was in love with him and how he needed to be in the race and that nothing would happen to him. He was a hero. I couldn't pull him out of there."

"Whitey told you something *could* happen to him, though."

"Look 'round here, Henry. Those salespeople downstairs, the accountants and secretaries, the grease monkeys over in service and parts—all of 'em dependin' on me for a paycheck Friday. Every single goddamn one of 'em. You think that's pressure in a shit economy?"

Dan let the question hang, filling the office. He'd stated his business and wanted Dobbs to blow off all the steam he needed to.

"Yeah, I went for the money. I wouldn't of, not if I knew *that* was gonna happen. No damn way. But when shit goes wrong, everything is coulda, woulda, shoulda."

Dobbs got up and walked to a filing cabinet at the corner of the office, which looked out over rolling green hills when the air pollution allowed the view. He opened and closed a drawer quickly, and came back, emphatically placing a check on the desk in front of Dan.

"I never cashed the goddamn thing."

Dan looked down at the piece of paper, eyes fixed first on the amount line, which read "Two million and 00/100." It was drawn on a cashier's check from Chemical Bank of New York, with no name or signature.

"Who gave this to you?"

"Some funny-lookin' guy from the TV network took me to lunch. My guess, his nuts was gonna be in a wringer if the horse didn't run. Funny thing was, he barely stopped eating during the whole deal. Like he passed out millions every day. More concerned with some tomato sauce he didn't cotton to. I figured it was worth the gamble. It wasn't."

"I'd like to make a copy of this."

"Knock yourself out."

Dan commandeered a pay phone back at LAX while waiting for his eastbound jet. The first call was to Mike Apple at *New York* magazine, letting him know the Derby story had turned into something more than a horse race.

The next call was to Sonny.

"You're at LAX? There's a great strip club near there, the Fox Hole."

"If only I had more time. Who's that private eye friend of yours with the connections?"

"Dante Moro? He doesn't come cheap."

"He's a friend of yours, isn't he? I got 500 bucks if he can get inside Chemical Bank and chase down a transaction."

"That's cake."

"I'll be in tonight. Can I crash at your place?"

"Might be tricky."

"Whattaya got?"

"Private lingerie party. Some political types might not be keen on a writer there, if you know what I mean."

"You're fuckin' unbelievable."

"Thanks."

The next call was to Frank back in Kentucky, who was taking care of Dan's dogs, and the last one was to the Woodford Clinic to check on Lefty At Heart. Although the story's legs were taking it elsewhere, Dan knew he couldn't lose sight of the horse. He was relieved when the tech told him Lefty At Heart was continuing to show amazing intelligence and recuperative powers, and was doing everything possible to aid his own recovery.

Dan talked his way into the high fliers club in the terminal and sent Sonny a fax of the copy of Dobbs' check. His last call was to Cindy, who sounded happy to hear from him and excited to be hosting him that evening, 3,000 miles away from where Dan, exhausted from his first flight that morning, had to be roused from sleep to make his afternoon journey to New York.

57

This was more like it, Dan thought as his plane circled Manhattan. New York at night, where every light was a possibility and the darkness cloaked the dirt. By coincidence or not, Cindy's roommates were both out when he got to her loft downtown, and gone too was the awkwardness of their last encounter. Dan told Cindy the story he was chasing, punctuated by several shots of tequila she produced from a cabinet that, along with a sink, served as the kitchen. Shakespeare—not the baseball player—would have been proud.

Cindy was still digging the fashion scene and New York, but already there were tears in the fabric. The friend she had come to help had let success go to her head, and her crew was commencing sowing the seeds of rebellion. Cindy and a couple of others talked about splitting off and creating their own line.

Dan was pleasantly reminded how sensational it felt laying next to her. He had tried to make himself too busy to miss her, and then circumstances so conspired. But now that they were together, she was magic to him, and all else fell away through the night.

Dan was alone in the apartment when he woke up. On a chair near the mattress was a note on top of a glass of orange juice. "Put a mirror under your nose and checked your pulse. Reasonably sure you were still alive. Good luck today. Thanks for the workout. Love, Cindy."

It was 11 a.m. when Gregg Gold walked into Gino's, the pizza joint. Dan was halfway through a Coke.

"Could you pick somewhere less convenient?" Gregg said as the two friends hugged and sat.

"Aren't you sentimental? This is our place," said Dan. "Besides, you're gonna be happy no one saw us together."

"Cloak and dagger. I love it."

"I need you to be honest with me, Gregg. Were you in on Romano's deal at the Derby?"

Dan looked hard at his friend for any facial signs of evasion.

"I'm not playing dumb, but I don't know what you mean."

"He didn't talk to you about anything?"

"Just general production stuff. Nothing out of the ordinary."

"Nothing about a payoff to an owner to run a horse?"

"Who, the car cowboy? Absolutely not. What have you got?"

"Any other prospects? Job-wise, I mean."

Gregg stared at him. "You're starting to scare me."

"Really? Only now?"

"Two weeks ago ESPN approached me, offered me a big job up in Connecticut. They're looking to expand like crazy. Audrey thinks it would be good, get out of the city, start a family, all that."

"And you?"

"Sounds alright."

"Romano's neck deep in shit I can't tell you about yet, but you'll know soon enough."

"You're serious. This isn't just some bullshit?"

"Gregg, you made a lot happen for me. This, right now, is me paying you back: Three words about that job offer—take it."

"That's two words."

"Today."

58

Dante Moro looked every bit a friend of Sonny's. His black moustache was strictly '70s porn and his mind likely followed suit. His request to meet at Tad's, a $1.99 steak house on 42nd Street, added to Moro's quirky persona. But he delivered the goods.

"Kid who paid for the check was young, about 20 years old, a little nervous, too wet behind the ears to be taking out checks for two very large," Moro told Dan. "I looked him up; Chris Connelly. He's got a job at 517 Madison, entry level, couldn't get the company name. Well-heeled and on the way up, otherwise they wouldn't have trusted him with that kind of transaction. Here's a photo of him off the closed circuit camera."

Dan took the picture but his mind wandered, fixed on that address. Where did he know it from? Moro's work was over.

"So, about the 500 bucks…"

"What…oh, yeah. *New York* Mag, 39th and 3rd, ask for Mike Apple."

"Pleasure."

"Thanks for the help."

"You don't look like a friend of Sonny's."

"Thanks again."

Moro stood and left, and with the smell of the joint's cheap beef filling his head, Dan was right behind him. He slowly walked 42nd, and was approached by a dozen hawkers in the doorways of places named Show World, The Globe, and Sin City. When Dan reached Broadway it him like a theatre poster—517 was the number above the windows at the corpse lounge where he lunched with Lawrence Sandler. It would have been the address for the skyscraper, including Sandler's business upstairs. Of course. Sandler bankrolled Romano's payoff to Dobbs. The network would have approached him to bail them out of this mess—save the ratings and the ad rates and keep it on the Q.T. Sandler's consulting arm already had its claws in the network. His involvement in this was disturbingly logical.

Jerry Romano's new office was in the same building, but several floors up from his old digs. Fortunately, Joan was still on his desk, and she greeted Dan like a triumphant hero returning from war.

"That Southern cooking looks good on you," she said, stepping back from their warm embrace.

"And you look as dangerous as ever."

"Did you hear the news?"

"What, is Romano fasting?"

"I can't be sure, but I think Gregg just quit. He was in there for awhile; raised voices."

"Good for Gregg. Listen, Joan, I need a favor."

"Sorry, I'm busy tonight."

"Damn it, you're popular. Can you look in his logbook, see if there were any meetings or calls with a Lawrence Sandler. It would have been last week."

"Don't need to," she said. "He went over to Sandler's office last Tuesday and then again Wednesday, right before he took off for the airport to go to Louisville."

"Any idea about what?"

"No. But he did seem even more agitated than usual."

"Is he in there?"

"It's lunch time, isn't it?"

Dan strode to Romano's door and entered. The napkin tucked under Romano's chin fell to the desk as he looked up suddenly.

"Jerry, how are you?" Dan asked with way too much familiarity.

"What the…what the hell are you doing here, Henry?"

"Working on a story."

"I mean, who let you in. Joan…"

"She's on a break. I'll get right to it, Jerry. You're in a bit of a nut cruncher here. Sam Dobbs says you paid him $2 million to run his lame horse in the Derby. People will even believe a car dealer sometimes, Jerry. Not lookin' good for you. Especially if the horse croaks, which is about 50-50. He's an American hero, Jerry. You know what that makes you?"

"What the hell are you talking about? Dobbs is nuts."

"No, he isn't. You two had lunch in Louisville at Picala Ristorante. Tomato sauce was runny. Ring a bell?"

"Henry, get the hell out of here."

"Sure, Jerry, no sweat. Oh, here's a photocopy of the check, by the way, proves Dobbs is telling the truth."

Romano had wiped his mouth, too upset for the moment to eat another bite. He took what he thought was a casual glance at the paper Dan floated down to his desk, but he looked long enough to taste a problem.

"Time to get out front of this, Jerry. Obviously, this wasn't your money."

"Shit, of course it's not my goddamn money."

Dan damn well knew Romano hatched this scheme. His job was teetering if the Derby tanked in the ratings; there were those good old boys sitting around that table at the press conference at Churchill Downs, almost spoiling for a reason to take Romano down, and Romano wasn't as stupid as he looked. Losing the star of the race would have been fatal to the ratings, and to him. Romano contacted Sandler, and Sandler would have gotten assurances from his pigeons from the network's advertising department that he'd be paid back in spades down the line. It was the kind of deal Sandler would have done in his sleep.

"I'm writing this story, Jerry. And right now you're the guy holding the bag."

"I didn't trust that Okie the second I laid eyes on him."

"Where did you get the money? Was it Sandler?"

"What do you know about Sandler?"

"I dated his daughter."

"Really? She's hot."

"Was it Sandler, Jerry?"

"I'm calling my lawyer."

"That's one way to go. Of course, then it's still you on the hook when the story comes out. You gonna out-maneuver Sandler one-on-one, Jerry? Think you can afford better lawyers? You talk now, we make Sandler the bad guy."

"Of course it was fuckin' Sandler."

"Thank you."

"Wait, that was off the record."

"You can't take it off the record after the fact, Jerry."

"Get the fuck out of here."

"By the way, your ice cream's melting."

59

It was just past 3:30 when Dan settled down at a window table in the coffee shop just across from 517 Madison. The place was empty, and a middle-age waitress descended on him in no time.

"What'll it be?"

"Large order of fries and a coke."

Dan skipped to the next table, making sure he had the best vantage point for the front doors of 517. A half-hour later Sonny, holding a worn and torn briefcase, arrived, making his annoyance known immediately.

"You couldn't pick somewhere that serves booze?"

"Sit down. You got the binos?"

Sonny pulled two pair of binoculars out of the briefcase. And a flask.

"Good thing I brought my own."

Dan removed a pair of binoculars from the case and trained them across the street, adjusting the lenses.

"Bausch and Lomb. The best," Sonny said.

"Your deviant behavior finally comes in handy," Dan replied.

The waitress approached.

"What'a ya have?" she demanded of Sonny.

"Just a club soda. I'm saving myself for dinner."

LONG WAY FROM HOME

"Here's the picture of the guy we're looking for," Dan said, pushing the photo across the table. "Study it. There's gonna be a ton of people coming out of the building."

The waitress returned with the club soda. As soon as she left, Sonny emptied a good deal of the flask's contents into it."

"Must you?"

"Listen, you get me here when happy hour's starting…"

"All right, the answer is 'yes.'"

The wait continued through another round of sodas. When the waitress returned with the check, both Sonny and Dan had their binoculars trained across the street.

"Hey, you guys cops?"

"Do we look like cops?" Sonny asked.

"You look like a cabbie," the waitress shot back.

"We're investigators," Dan said, defusing the situation before Sonny got them kicked out of the joint. "A guy's been cheating on his wife. She hired us to follow him."

"Same thing happened to me."

"Hard to believe," came, of course, from Sonny.

"They're all cheating bastards. I hope you catch him."

"Thank you," Dan said, successfully ending the chat.

"Remember," Dan said, "I need you to be quiet and act official, like you're a detective."

"I could lose my law license if we get caught running this."

"You kind of passed that plateau with the unstamped cigarettes."

"The lead work's on you. I've got a buzz on."

"Shocking."

At 5 o'clock a rush of humanity poured onto the street from 517 Madison and every other building in the city. Dan concentrated hard on the doors, scanning every face for a match.

"Maybe he took the day off," Sonny chimed in. "Let's find a bar."

"Up-and-comers like him don't take days off. Keep looking."

It was past 5:30 when the crowd of workers finishing their office hours thinned to a steady trickle.

"My eyes are getting tired," complained Sonny.

"Pretend you're at a peep show on 42nd."

"I can't. These people are wearing clothes."

"Beige suit! Beige suit!" Dan exclaimed. "See him?"

"What the fuck is beige?"

"Tan, you moron. That's him. Let's go."

Dan and Sonny stuffed their binoculars into Sonny's briefcase and bolted onto the avenue, criss-crossing through traffic until they were on the other side of Madison. Up at the intersection of 53rd Street, the man in the beige suit had stopped with two dozen other pedestrians, waiting for cars to pass before crossing against the traffic light.

"Stay here and look fucking official," Dan barked to Sonny, who leaned up against the building edge closest to the corner while Dan hurried to his prey.

"Chris Connelly!" he shouted at the man's back, trying to catch his breath. The man turned around. He was young and looked younger, with perfect white skin that said he was out of the best Catholic schools his folks could afford. He was better-dressed than his years would have indicated.

"Yes?"

"Henry Daniels, investigator for the Kentucky Racing Commission. You *are* Chris Connelly?"

"Yeah, but I don't have anything to do with Kentucky."

"You took out a cashier's check last week at Chemical Bank."

"I…I may have. I don't remember."

"It was for two million dollars, Mr. Connelly. You think you might remember that one, or do you walk around with that kind of cash regularly?"

"What's this about? How did you find me?"

"The clerk at the bank, sir. You signed for the cashier's check."

"O.K., let's say I did."

"That money was used to unduly influence the outcome of a horse race, Mr. Connelly. In Kentucky, we take that sort of thing rather seriously. Like up to 10 years in prison kind of seriously."

"Whoa, hold on. I didn't do anything with that money."

"Relax, we know that. I need the person who authorized the check."

Here, Connelly paused, took in the moving mass of people striding by on the street, all heading somewhere seemingly free of the apparent mess he currently found himself in.

"I have a very good job, Mr. Daniels. Big firm, lot of upside. I don't want to put that in jeopardy, and I'm thinking that being a rat isn't the way to get ahead."

"Understandable. But right now you're all we've got, Mr. Connelly; you're the smoking gun. We may or may not have enough to convict you, but the stink from your legal mess isn't the way to get ahead, either. I'm guessing they may not like that sort of attention upstairs."

Connelly was slowly approaching distress, and Dan went for the hammerlock.

"This wasn't some cheap race on a Wednesday afternoon, Mr. Connelly. Somebody tried to influence the outcome of the Kentucky Derby. Horse in question, with millions of his fans standing vigil, is currently fighting for his life. He should have never been in the race, and he wouldn't have—except for a two million dollar bribe somebody gave to the owner to run him. Not coincidentally, Mr. Connelly, it was the very check you signed for. This isn't going away.

"That man standing against the building," Dan continued, nodding toward Sonny, who was feeling his vest pocket for the flask, "is a Kentucky State policeman, and he's got a warrant in his briefcase to extradite you to Kentucky. We can be on the 8 o'clock flight out of LaGuardia, the three of us."

"I don't want to go to fuckin' Kentucky."

Dan switched into good cop mode.

"I understand. I know you're just the middleman here. But unless you give up a name, you're on that flight."

Connelly was playing his options in his head. It was like a game of chess you know you're gonna lose in a few moves.

"Does he have to know I gave him up?"

"We'll play it as straight as we can. But he's pretty paranoid, Sandler."

"How did you…?"

"Let's go write it up, and you'll be free to go."

Dan and Connelly crossed back to the opposite side of Madison, with Sonny trailing two paces behind. They entered the coffee shop. Sonny, playing the drunk and silent type, pulled a pad and pen from his case. Connelly sat at a booth and began writing. Their waitress friend appeared and hovered over the table, staring down at Connelly.

"You bastard," she said to him. "I hope they nail your ass to the wall."

Sonny and Dan caught each other's eyes and could barely contain their laughter.

60

It took Dan two full days working in the *New York* magazine office to get the story down on paper. He wrote and re-worked constantly, using the first day to spill everything out on the table, and the second day to whip up the style of the article, shaping and choosing each word for maximum effect. He told the story from the point of view of its victim--Lefty At Heart. People already felt the horse's struggle as their own, those emotions raising Dan's story from an exposé to something much more personal. Just past 4 p.m. on Friday afternoon, on a special deadline moved back for him, Dan sent the copy electronically through the newsroom to his editor.

"The Men Who Failed An American Hero" appeared on page 43 of the May 13 edition of *New York* magazine the following Monday. Although the print run was increased by 10%, it sold out nationwide as soon as it appeared on newsstands. By late Monday a second print run was added. The magazine was fielding 30 calls an hour from TV and radio stations and newspapers looking to interview Dan. He could have appeared on every news program in America had he stayed in New York and the spotlight.

But when the magazine hit the streets Dan was nowhere near New York. He had stayed till Saturday to go over every word and reference and piece of documentation with Mike Apple. He wanted to make sure the story would appear exactly the way he wrote it. Then Dan caught the last flight out of the city to Kentucky, and by Sunday morning just after dawn he was camped out at the Woodford Clinic, where Lefty At Heart's fleet legs were no longer able to prevent time from clicking off with painful slowness.

Dan and Apple had agreed Dan would write a follow-up piece for the next week's magazine on Lefty At Heart's recovery. Dan hadn't gotten to see the horse at the clinic, but that changed Monday when a staffer came in with a copy of *New York*. Doctors brought Dan back to see Lefty, visit with the horse, feed peppermints to the horse. Every procedure they had performed on him was documented to Dan along with the reason and outcome. Every time Lefty At Heart sneezed, Dan knew about it.

Dan was provided his own small office where he could write and talk on the phone. His first call was to Sonny for advice on how to set up a charitable foundation to help injured and retired racehorses.

"Why didn't you tell me before the race he was hurt?" demanded Sonny. "I lost a hundred bucks betting damaged goods."

That was the last crack from Sonny, who came up big. Within an hour of that phone call, Dan received a fax detailing the Save The Lefties Fund that Sonny had legally established, allowing Dan to plug it in every one of the many interviews he was about to give.

New York magazine, still inundated with media requests, set up mass phone call-ins with Dan in which reporters from dozens of news outlets at a time could ask him questions. At every opportunity he sought to deflect the focus onto the horse and publicize the fund, with the money being handled through the Woodford Clinic.

"Am I still your manager?" Sonny found Dan at home late one night a week later, after the second article came out and proved as popular as the original.

"Do you need to ask?"

"What the hell am I supposed to tell people? You're actually in demand, and I got no answers for them. You want to hear options?"

"Not really."

"Of course not, why should I actually make 20% on something substantial?"

"20%? How loaded are you?"

"That's what managers get. And plenty, thank you."

"I'm gonna take some time."

"Take it where? You're hot now. This is the American way—cash in when you can and then cruise on your name."

"Wait, I'm writing that down."

"By the time you get off your ass, nobody will remember and you'll end up at a weekly newspaper in Potsdam. I got *Sports Illustrated* here. CBS TV and radio. *Newsweek*. Washington *Post*. Some guy from Watervliet who says he knows you; they can't all be winners."

"Sonny, don't ever change. Like there's a chance of that."

"You can't improve on perfection, my friend."

61

The hottest writer in America spent the spring helping his farmer friend Frank sow fields of vegetables to be sold at various farmers' markets in the area. The physical labor and seclusion were just what Dan needed, and Frank even let him run the big tractor to cut hay. Late in the afternoons they'd sit in a covered swing seat that moved back and forth on rails, sipping cheap vodka from small glasses and waving at pick-up trucks rolling by on the road and talking about the weather and the land and the livestock and the crops and the equipment. The disappearance of men like Frank over the next 50 years was going to change the country's soul, and not for the better. Dan began organizing his thoughts to write a book documenting a disappearing breed and way of life, another American hero.

While Dan planned his homage to the farmer, the Lefty At Heart fallout continued. Jerry Romano was canned by the network two days after Dan's *New York* story hit the streets. He and Sandler were formally charged—by real law enforcement personnel this time—with trying to illegally influence the result of a horse race. Romano got six months at a federal farm; Sandler was acquitted on a technicality, but had to endure a lengthy trial with his name and face and company being dragged publicly through the mud. Satisfactory punishment, Dan thought, at least for this crime, for a man who for so long was dependent on operating in the shadows.

Sam Dobbs ended up keeping the money, paying half of that famous $2 million check to his wife and half to the Save The Lefties Foundation. Once his divorce was finalized, he got out of racing, no longer needing the business write-off. Winslett came out unscathed, and was back on the Derby trail with two contenders the following spring. Chris Connelly testified against Sandler and then entered law school at Columbia. There, Sonny kept him supplied with female company to make the small detail of he and Dan illegally impersonating law enforcement officers go away.

Lefty At Heart made as full a recovery as possible. He had a bigger hitch to his giddy-up now, but was sound enough to breed. In a unique arrangement, Dobbs gave him to the Kentucky Horse Park, a tourist attraction near Lexington, where he was allowed to breed 40 mares a year. Tens of thousands of fans and visitors come to see him annually, a portion of each admission going to aid injured horses and fund medical research.

62

On the day Dan turned 27 the following September, Sonny was having no success trying to reach him. The answering machine in Kentucky had a cryptic message that it would be some time before he'd take calls. Sonny cursed as he dropped the phone back into its cradle.

Gregg Gold had called Sonny an hour earlier. His career soared as an executive producer at ESPN, which was eating up the sports landscape. Gregg had work coming out his ears, and he wanted Dan aboard. Sonny admitted he didn't know where the hell Dan was.

Ten minutes after Gregg's, Sonny fielded another call, this one from Columbia University, informing him his client had just won the Pulitzer Prize for investigative journalism. This impressed even Sonny, who asked the person on the phone what the dress code for women was at the awards dinner.

Sonny poured himself a Scotch and savored it, celebrating on Dan's behalf. "I got a 20% stake in a winner, and the jerk-off goes all D.B. Cooper on me, disappears into thin air," he said to himself, draining half the Scotch after toasting his friend.

At that moment Dan was swimming under the awesome power of a 126-foot waterfall near the head of Calf Creek Canyon in southern Utah. A gorgeous pool of crystal clear, cold water lay in front of the falls, and underneath the cascade, hard against the rock, Dan felt the enormous power of the tumbling water's energy as it crashed to the pool two feet away, sucking the breath out of him. He listened to it roar, felt the backsplash against his face and chest. Next to him, looking like a goddess in cut-off shorts and a halter—and those only for the benefit of other hikers that had reached the falls—was Cindy. Those travel plans hadn't gone to waste after all.

They were in the canyon country of Utah, the sheer rock rising spectacularly in walls above the great river beds that time, wind, and water had created over millions of years. They had been out camping for two weeks and had hiked through slot canyons barely wide enough to squeeze through, under giant arches, and up steeples of red rock. They saw the carvings and wall paintings of the ancients, and stared at night from their sleeping bags into a sky too filled with stars to be dark.

Behind the water's veil, Dan took Cindy and kissed her as if it was his best moment on earth.

Made in the USA
San Bernardino, CA
13 March 2014